# BACK THROUGH
## THE
# FLAMING DOOR

## POLESTARS 7

# Liz Williams

NewCon Press
England

First edition, published in the UK April 2024
by NewCon Press
41 Wheatsheaf Road, Alconbury Weston, Cambs, PE28 4LF, UK

NCP324 (hardback)
NCP325 (softback)

10 9 8 5 6 5 4 3 2 1

ISBN: 978-1-914953-73-6 (hardback)
978-1-914953-74-3 (softback)

Our thanks to Nadia Van Der Westhuizen
for permission to use her image on the front cover.

Cover design by Ian Whates
Editing and typesetting by Ian Whates

# Contents

*For Tanith and for Storm: inspirers and friends*
*And always for Trevor*

# Introduction

*Back Through the Flaming Door* will be my fourth short story collection, and I am delighted once more to be working with Ian Whates and New Con Press. Many of these stories have featured as part of my short story bundles over the years and I'm very pleased to have had the opportunity to put these together into this new collection. Some of the stories, however, are entirely new. They are set in a variety of locations: from alien planets, to the far future matriarchal Mars of my *Winterstrike* novels, to the freeport city of Singapore Three in the Chen novels, and to the Wiltshire Downs.

More and more of my short fiction, as well as my recent novels, is now set in the British landscape, the country with which I am most familiar. It remains a significant inspiration for me, as does the folklore of Britain, and its history. I feel as though I am in a story mine, rich with the ore of the landscape in which I live. This includes London and the cities of the South West – you'll find a story set in a magical Regency Bath in this collection, and follies and grottoes, those anomalies in the British landscape, appear in it, too.

I enjoyed writing all these stories. I enjoy writing, despite its multiple frustrations: it is journeying in the landscape of the mind, for me. I hope you enjoy reading the tales in this collection, too.

*– Liz Williams*
*March 2023*

# Back Through
# The Flaming Door

*This is a post-fairyland story. Sometimes people who return from fairyland crumble into dust – they're probably the lucky ones. The experience has always struck me as being similar to addiction, but you shouldn't treat this story as a metaphor.*

There aren't so many of us now. Even we must die: sometimes at the moment of return, but sometimes many years later. Enough time for the newcomers to find us, explanations given as best we can; jealousies guarded, secrets kept. At the last, though, such tensions have to be put aside, for we are all the same. We are the ones who came back; the ones who did not stay. We are exiles from a place that could never be our home.

The latest back-comer – we have our own words, you see, our own language – did not want to talk, at least at first. She shrouded herself with secrets; they clustered about her like mist. She appeared permanently in shadow. We tried to help her, and found her a room: in Mary's house, which is at the end of the lane and very quiet. Beyond, there's nothing for miles except moor, scrubby oak, towering piles of slate. The village itself – which is a hamlet, really, for it has no chapel – is bounded by trees. I look out into beech, which is gold and bronze now in the September sunlight, and if I partly close my eyes, it reminds me of where I've been. But not entirely: we are damaged goods, past our sell-by date. If we were in Tesco's, we'd be marked half price and faintly rotting. They didn't have supermarkets when I left. For us, this world is like seeing everything through a film, as though we had cataracts. The colours are dialled down; nothing's sharp. Yet, we still need trees.

The back-comer, who could not remember her name, slept a great deal. We reassured her that this was normal. Mary took milk up to her, eggs, cream. Tea would be too strong and it was debatable whether she'd be able to eat meat again: a lot of us can't. Vegetables and fruit, just, but it's really all about the dairy. The people down the valley think we're some kind of weird commune with peculiar food rules. I suppose they're right and we are. Mary and George keep a small herd of Jerseys; I have goats. We've all got chickens. We share and share alike. I was glad when mass-produced food started coming in, though – I like the cheese section, all the different kinds of milk and butter. I can cope with neon, with brightness, because of where I was, so I mainly do the weekly shop. We have a horse and cart; a car would be too much. It adds to the general reputation for eccentricity, but we're not harming anyone. We can't claim benefits; it would mean giving our names, dates of birth, all that sort of thing and it just isn't possible. We sell the surplus fruit from a stand on the road, and I get my clothes in charity shops. Social services occasionally sniff around; it never comes to anything. I suppose we're just too odd and they've got enough on their plates up here. We're not drug addicts; we don't have loads of challenged kids. We get by.

The back-comer had barely a rag to her name; I had to lend her a sweater and skirt, but she clung to the thing she was wearing, a tatter of feathers and reeds. It wasn't even really woven – a lot of the time they don't bother. But of course, once they're back, it just falls apart.

She didn't say anything for the first few days and she didn't want a candle, either, or the curtains drawn. I went over to help Mary out and all I could see were a pair of eyes, like a cat's, from the huddle on the bed. I asked her a few questions. I shouldn't have, I suppose, but I can't resist and Mary's the same. We ask about our one, the special ones. Goodfellow. Ragged Robin. Dancer. We all had different ones and that's a mercy but sometimes I wonder if they're not actually all the same. And I had to know: had she seen *him*, the back-comer? Did she have a glimpse of *him*?

She didn't answer straight away. In fact, not for several days. It wasn't until the Friday that she whispered, when she was sure I wasn't looking at her, "I saw him once. Yours. Mine was called Campion."

"What did he look like?" I spoke with my back turned, so as not to frighten her. "Yours?"

"He had yellow hair. Like spun sunlight. And his eyes were blue as the sky."

She didn't say anything else. She didn't have to.

"Yours?" she said, in a whisper.

"Bracken." It took a while for the name to come off my tongue, as if stuck. It fell heavily into the silence, to my mind, when it should have been as light as the wind. Hair like a fox's fur, eyes of ice. He was a winter prince, I remembered; he'd come at Christmas. Not on the Lord's day, of course – the earth would have burned his feet – but just before. I'd been up on the hill: I had an armful of ivy and the fells were bitter with snow. I was pretty then, not the faded thing I am now; my hair was bright, not cobweb, my gaze was steady and clear. I had red cheeks from the cold, my face blazed and maybe it was that rosy light that drew him. He was there suddenly, out of nothing. I blinked. I thought he was human. I was wrong. He said, persuasive-like, "I can show you a wonder. Would you like to see?"

I'd not seen much. I wasn't that innocent, but something in his pale blue stare was open as the sky. I knew what he wasn't offering me. I said, "Yes. Why not? But I must be home before full dark. I have to take this to the church."

He flinched and his face grew small and ugly and old, but only for a minute. He laughed. "You know, don't you? I can't take that, don't like it." I nodded. I nearly understood.

"All right," I said.

"Take my hand," he told me, so I did. It was cold and did not feel like a hand. A little prickly, maybe, like a bundle of twigs. He drew me forwards and I saw the door: an outline of flame against the snow and the greening sky. Beyond it was summer.

I was not home before dark. That twilight was the last thing I saw, before the brightness flooded in: a brightness that did not come from the sun, for there is none in that land, and no moon either. All my days were light: lit by skin like milk and icy eyes. His name was Bracken, as you know, and he became the sun of my world. For how long, I did not even think to question.

I did not see how I was becoming cobweb thin, how my hair was changing to straw and the roses of my cheeks becoming ashen. This is what they do: on the edges of life, they leech it and you, you grow pale as the light takes your brightness, draws it in, and at last, spits you out. For they grow bored and colder, the men and women both, and their attention – more like hunger than love, I know now – wanes as the moon wanes, even over that great span of years.

He did not bother to dismiss me. I already knew. I glimpsed my face in the reed-fringed mirror of a pond and did not know it, but a flicker in the still water made me look up and there was the door, a flaming arch in air. My feet dragged me through it, tottering, I fell out upon the hillside.

11

Something terrifying roared overhead; I could see a distant city, where a village had been before. The old church still stood at its limits, like a snail.

I went to the church, down a road which plunged with machines, but I could not go in. The earth burned my bare feet and the air froze me, and I knew that I was unredeemably changed. I went away and for a long time I lived in the city, under bridges, in the bushes of the parks, finding food in bins. I lived slowly, learning. It took me a long time to understand, both the new world and what had happened to me. Every time I saw a fox, it made my heart grow closed and smaller. I called to him in the night, my one, but he never answered and I knew that it was as though I had never existed: to say that he had forgotten me was to attribute too much. I would have been wiped from his mind like dew in the sun and another girl would be dancing with him now in the ever-day.

One day I met a woman. She was tall, gaunt, black haired, rag-dressed. A witch, I thought, and I was right. She took one look at me and told me where I'd been.

"There are others," she said. "Did you think you were the only one?"

"I know I was not."

"There's a place," she said. "You'll be safe there. At least, as safe as it gets." Then she gave me the village's name.

I'd learned about begging, by then. About buses. I took one next morning, out of the city, watching the hills roll by through the dirty glass. I took another bus, then walked. It was late autumn, the trees all fire and flame, but it was as though I was still behind the muddy pane. When I saw the woman working in her garden, I knew her at once, because she looked like me.

She glanced up and became very still. I walked towards her, slowly. She knew what I was immediately. She did not speak; I later learned that this was one of the things that she had left behind her. She made me a cup of tea, which we drank in silence. Then she got up, went out of the house, and came back with a man. His name was Jacob: he, too, had been walking on a hill, and met a girl. An old and familiar story. I don't know how old he really was, but he had been one of the first and his hair was white now; he turned as the years turned, back under the spell of time. He explained to me how things are done here; how we make do. The village gave me a place and I have been here ever since.

I think about those others a lot, of course – the ones I left behind. They are more real than my father and mother, who died so long ago. I think about Bracken and the others, the women who stared at me with sidelong smiles, who touched my hair when they thought I wasn't looking. The other men, some of whom were little and wizened and old. I used to wonder if that was what Bracken would become, when he wore out at last. But I only wondered that when I came back. I'd given up any hope of seeing them again – of seeing him – in the city, and the countryside was full of flickers, but they were always only birds.

And then, one day a short while after the last back-comer came, I saw a girl. It was from the track that led to the mountain road, lined with wild roses in summer. I saw a spark against a background of firs, a fiery twitch of light. For the first time in years, I felt my heart lift. I dropped the bags I was carrying, clambered over the stone wall, and though I was no longer a girl, I ran like a hare towards the band of green and black shadow.

She was still there. I could see the cones of the firs through her body: she wavered, like heat. I didn't recognise her, but I knew that she was very young. She was the colour of milk and sunlight, and her eyes were green. There was a corona around her, shimmering.

She was looking at me over her shoulder. She was smiling and it was sweet, not like some of the women's smiles. Another clue that she was young, no time for weariness and too much knowledge to carve its way onto her face. Then the light changed and she was gone. I lingered for a long time, to see if she came back. There was a cloud over the world. I collected the shopping, walked back, told no one.

Next day I saw her again. This time she came closer, through the stony meadow. It was misty that day, and wet. She looked like a shaft of pale sun. This time I did not run to her, but let her approach me. This time, she had an animal's eyes, yellow and slit-pupilled. She circled me and abruptly vanished.

That night the back-comer came to see me. We'd learned that her name was Edith, but she still didn't say much. She stood twisting a piece of wool in her hands – it helps if we have something to fiddle with. She said, "I saw you today. I saw *her.*"

I didn't bother to lie or ask her what she meant. Part of our remaining freedom is this; that we do not have to pretend. "What do you mean?" or "There is no such thing." – these are not words we need to speak. I said, "She was in the field. Did you see her from the window? She was in the firs yesterday."

Edith stared at me with resentment. "Has she come for you?"

13

"I don't think so." Women do take women, but it's not so common. And I didn't sense that kind of interest, although it's true that ever since I'd glimpsed the girl by the firs, the wish had burned in me that I could go back.

Edith looked a little happier, relieved. "Very well, then," she said, in more conciliatory tones. "I suppose if she'd wanted to take you, she'd have done so by now."

"I don't know what she wants," I said.

Edith snorted. "She's curious. Once she's seen what she wants she'll go away again."

I thought she was right, but I lay awake that night all the same. The moon was full and its light hammered the room into silver. At last I got out of bed and went to the window. There was a frost, drawn up by the moon's cold light, and the girl was dancing in the meadow. I pulled on some clothes and hurried downstairs and through the back door. The chill hit me like a punch, knocking my breath into smoke. I expected to find her gone, but she was still there, twirling on the hard ground. I stumbled after her, feeling a twinge of the old pull, like toothache.

She danced towards the firs, a line of darkness under the moon. And as I followed her, I saw that there was someone waiting. Black and white, moonlight and shadow. When he turned his head, I knew him. The girl gave a laugh, jumped and disappeared.

He had changed. The thing I feared had overtaken him: he was bent and wrinkled, as if he had been put through a press. He saw it in my face, gave his old mocking smile.

"As you see, I am old now, too," he said.

"Did you run out of women?"

A grimace. "I came to see you."

"As you see, I am old now, too," I said.

"There's no one left," he said. "People now – they don't go out on the fells so much. Or if they do, it's all boots and backpacks and hearty laughter. And if they do, they don't see me."

"No. They have other glamours."

"I came to ask you to come back."

His eyes were the same, like river ice. I felt my heart flare up with anger and love and burn down into ash. I thought of the village, a drab leaden existence, with its trips to Tesco and worrying about the hens, but suddenly real, in a way that it had not been before. He held out his hand.

"No," I said. "Not this time." I stood there and watched as, gradually, he faded. And when he was no more than smoke upon the air, I turned my back and walked back across the frost-sparkling land.

14

# Blackfast

*I can't remember where I came across the term 'black fast' – it definitely was in some magical book somewhere and I don't think I've made it up. Perhaps I'm just thinking of Buckfast Abbey in Devon, though...*

The house was silent before the storm came in. First heralded by mist: a thick fret seeping up from the red cliffs of the coast and blanketing the winter landscape in woolen drifts. Espair stood on the parapet of the roof and stared out into whiteness. No point in speaking a word to banish the fog: it would make no difference. The fast would start tonight, whatever the weather was doing. He took a breath of salt mist and cold air. Soon, Richard would be dead.

Brothers can be too close sometimes. Richard and Anselm Espair, a year apart in age, but there had been no other children because Richard's birth had killed their mother. Espair liked to think he remembered her, but knew that he did not. She lived on in the many portraits that his father had commissioned to fill the house, all the way up the stairs and the long gallery, and then in every room. Her black eyes followed you wherever you went, whether she was twisting a strand of fair hair in her fingers, or laying her hand on the head of a hound, or gazing across the knot garden, garlanded by roses. The early portraits must have been realistic enough, especially if you looked at Richard. Espair himself took after their father, that dark-browed, blue-eyed man, but Richard was all gold and black, with silken hair that made young women jealous. Later, though, the paintings began to change. Espair never dared to say to his father that he thought memory was fading – for the old man painted them himself and the longer he grew apart from his subject, the stranger the paintings became. Lady Espair's black eyes looked more like those of an animal, by the time Anselm left home, and her face was subtly altering, with the shadow of a muzzle, too long, not human. Sometimes Anselm, waking shuddering from midnight dreams, wondered if it was

15

the other way about and if his father's recollections of his mother's face were sharpening, rather than becoming increasingly dulled.

For there had to have been someone, or something, from which Anselm had inherited his powers.

The mist would help. Espair opened the long windows and stepped inside. Wreaths of fog accompanied him, the tentacles of the weather, but soon died in the heat from the fire. Espair went to the hearth, scooped up a handful of coals in the shovel, and tipped them into a brazier. Then he took a bowl which had been sitting on a nearby table and placed it in the cradle that hung above the brazier's heart, so that the bowl would be warmed by the coals. He surveyed this for a moment, then went to the bureau. From this, he took out a bottle of ink and poured a midnight stream into the bowl. The ink began to steam, releasing a faint, dark vapour.

Espair closed his eyes and felt the vapour seep into his nose and lungs like the mist. He had a sudden impression that the house had not been blanketed by fog after all, but was disappearing: taking itself into a different place, out of the world of men. In the red-blackness behind his eyelids, there was a single spark of light.

"What is your need?" a voice said, chill and silky inside Espair's mind.

"Where is my brother, Richard, now?"

A small picture appeared, a window on the world. Espair glimpsed a ship, sails unfurled, riding the windswept waves ahead of indigo cloud.

"Do not worry," the voice said, with malice. "He will be quite safe."

Espair grunted. It was not what he wanted to hear. He said, "You know what I want. Tell me what to do."

"You know what to do," said the voice. "The black fast."

Then it was gone and when, opening his eyes, Espair looked down at the brazier, he saw that the coals were cold and old and dead.

The most important information that a grimoire contains is that which is not written down. Espair had learned this early; learned it, too, the hard way. It had resulted in his early ejection from the University and a sulphurous whiff of scandal which had followed him home. It had made marriage complicated, his father complained, but Espair had no interest in that and eventually the subject had been dropped. No interest, that is, until the Marchmonts had moved to the county and Espair had first seen Rethe Marchmont behind the wall of her fan at a local ball. Frail and pale, she had instantly appealed to him and Espair had set about luring the pink-eared little rabbit into the trap – but it had not worked. She had run away, and married Richard instead, thus adding to the litany of grievance that lay like a finely linked chain between Espair and his brother.

Espair had smiled throughout the wedding and wished them both happiness. On the night of his brother's marriage, he had sought counsel in the book that had got him thrown out of university. His memories of what followed were necessarily dimmed: it was always like this. He remembered the smoke of the brazier and the stench of the blood, then the brightness of the being who came to him, her long-clawed hands and glimmering golden gaze. She whispered in his ear and he was as helpless under her hands as he had longed for Rethe to be under his. But she had given him a key, and told him to wait a year.

That year was up tonight.

Espair sat by the remains of the fire and waited for the brazier to burn out. A year, and where was Richard now? Riding the waves, home to his bride. But Espair had the key: he had not remembered it a year before once the bright being had gone, but he remembered it now, encapsulated in two words: black fast.

The practice was not to be found in most of the grimoires that Espair had read, but he had heard of it, long ago. The old man who had taught him magic, his tutor, the man who had stepped back and not spoken when he could have saved Espair's university career: that man had once told him of the black fast.

*You must be very sure*, he had said, *that you want someone's death. You must hate with the purest hate, a hate like a black diamond, as hard and enduring.*

Espair did not think that this would be a problem.

He climbed the stairs, slowly, feeling the weight of his mother's gaze, repeated a hundred times. By the time he reached the library, the painted eyes had become opaque, whiteless and unhuman. He gave the last portrait an ironic smile, a tiny bow. Perhaps she might have smiled back, but the painted lips were the wrong shape.

The library was sealed from the outside world, except for a squint set into the wall. Through the tiny hole in the stonework, Espair could see nothing but mist. The fog still blanketed the moor. He walked to the end of the library, lighting his way with a single candle. The place seemed full of odd shadows, movement glimpsed from the corners of the eye, and

17

there was a thundery pressure from above. Espair knew what this was: someone was still interested, then.

In the shelves at the end of the library, the books were chained, some heavily. In an ordinary library, belonging to a university or a cathedral, the books would be tethered thus to prevent theft. This was not the case here, for Espair lived alone and the servants were not allowed up here. They would not have come, even if permitted. At the very end of the last bookcase, the chain was empty, attached to nothing.

Or so it appeared. Espair settled himself on the reading bench and gave the chain a gentle tug. Gradually, the book appeared, out of the air. First, the sliver of a spine, a bright line of red, and then the book itself. It was covered in a mottled hide and its pages were rimmed with gold, firebright in the shadows of the library.

"Well, hello," murmured Espair. He had been waiting for this. The manifestation of the book, tonight of all nights, suggested that he was on the right track. He reached beneath the reading bench and took out a pair of black kidskin gloves. He put them on with care, snapping the fingers to ensure that his hands were fully covered. Then he opened the book and began to read as the words glimmered into view.

A day for each year of the victim's life, times three. Richard was twenty seven now: Espair did the maths. Over two months of fasting, in the manner specified by the grimoire. But what would eighty one days be, in contrast to a lifetime of resentment? Espair laughed aloud and opened the window to let in the coils of mist. Two months of coals and dust, and water breathed in from the air: this would not be hard, thought Espair, in the dank clime of the moor. And at the black fast's end, his brother would be dead.

A month went by, taking Espair into the depths of winter, close to Christmas. He paid the servants extra, told them to feast at the inn. Dinner was a plate of earth, taken from the dark heart of the moor, consumed slowly, washed down with fog. On the eve of the new year, Espair stood alone on the parapet and clenched frosty air into his fists. He could almost feel his brother's death within his grasp, as though his hands closed over it. It crunched, like the frost. Midnight came with the ring of distant bells, sweetly chiming down the valley, and Espair felt each one like a hammer blow: the church's unwelcome touch. He stepped back and went quickly within, heading down the stairs to the hall and silence. As he did so, he felt his mother's eyes upon him, the weight of her gaze as tangible as the sound of the bells, and when he reached the hall, where the great portrait hung above the fireplace, he met her eyes. They blazed, alive with something he could not identify. Anger, perhaps, or was it a fierce pride? Perhaps she, too, had hated her youngest child, in the brief moments left to her before she died. Perhaps she hated Richard still? Espair drew this thought to him like the glow of a fire as he dined on ashes.

The year turned and the black fast wore on. Not long to go now. Espair felt that the house had become colder, though the winter was green and mild. The old people said that a green winter meant a full churchyard; it was not the cold that killed. He lit roaring fires in all the grates but the house remained chill. His joints ached, as though he had become an old man, but this was to be expected, Espair thought, given the nature of his undertaking. He still deemed it worthwhile, dreaming of Richard's putrefying corpse in the middle of the night. Perhaps he would contract some disease off the African coast, would blister and bubble before death... Meanwhile, he was finding it increasingly difficult to climb the stairs. His hands shook as he crossed off the calendar days.

One evening, shortly before the black fast was due to end, Espair sat in the great hall looking up at the portrait of his mother. In the painting, she was smiling faintly, but then she turned her head and looked at him directly. Her lips curved. In the fluttering firelight, her eyes widened into gold and Espair, marvelling, saw a flick of black wings within. Then the bird was flying out of her left eye, swooping down along the length of the table, and he felt the soft touch of its pinions.

Spring came early that year, after the gentle winter, and Richard Espair rode up from the port on a fine bay horse. After the long voyage, the air of the English countryside was very welcome, although he could still smell the sea. The daffodils were out beneath the hedges and the trees were starting to burst with green. Richard spurred the horse on towards the blue-purple sweep of the moor and cantered up the winding road to the house.

He hoped that Anselm had not found the winter too hard, all alone up here. And doubtless his brother would not be pleased to see him, yet Richard felt that, as a matter of Christian charity, he had to try. Poor man: locked in a bitterness that nothing and no one had been able to break through. He had spoken to Rethe about it, often.

"He is your brother, after all. And it must be harder for him to bear his own nature than it is for anyone else." She felt sorry for Anselm, while still untrusting. She would not come with him to the house, she had said, on Richard's first night back in the country, as they dined in the white house overlooking the sea with her fair hair gleaming in the candlelight. "But I will be with you in spirit, Richard, and I will welcome you home again. Perhaps this time it will be different."

Perhaps it would. Richard tied his horse to the balustrade and knocked at the door. But no one answered. He waited.

"He's gone away," a voice said. Richard turned to see one of Anselm's manservants, a stoat-faced man whom he had always disliked.

"Indeed? And where has he gone?"

"He left no instructions," the servant said.

"What, none at all?"

"No, and no money either. I come up here once a week to see if the old – to see if the master has returned. You're lucky you caught me."

Very perplexed, Richard gave the man a coin and went around the back of the house. The kitchen door yielded to a push and he went inside.

"Anselm?"

There was no reply. Richard wandered through the house until he came to the great hall. The place smelled musty and odd, as though it had been gutted by fire. But everything was untouched, just dusty. The grate in the hall was filled with ash and the room was dark, the long curtains drawn against the bright softness of the day. Richard twitched one of them aside to let in the light.

A book sat at the end of the table, open. Richard glanced at it and recoiled. The pages were empty except for a red line of writing: *to kill he whom you most hate*, it read. Richard reached out a gloved hand and flicked it shut. The chair at the table's end was also empty, but covered in a black, gritty stain, like greasy soot. Richard did not want to touch it. He looked up, blinking in a sudden shaft of sun, and saw the familiar paintings of his lost mother. Familiar, except for one thing: in each portrait, her eyes were tightly shut.

# Colder Than the Day

*I don't really do vampire stories. I quite like reading them but I got very tired of this seemingly endless genre and its tropes. So this isn't a vampire story, except in a sense.*

I came out of the earth in late winter, a slow clawing up through the black soil. Above ground I found a white sky, bare trees, a scattering of snow. There was a message waiting for me, written on earth, in leaves, invisible to everyone but me. It said: *go to the road, start walking*. I knew what this meant, and so I brushed the soil from my skin and stepped through the brambles until I reached the straighter track.

It did not take long before a truck slowed to a halt. In it, was a man, wide-eyed. He spoke to me, but it would be a while before understanding came and so I simply stared. Looking back, I suppose he was surprised to see a naked girl standing by the roadside, at dusk, with the cold coming down. And when I climbed into the cab and he reached for me, I do not know what he was intending to do, although I can guess. It did not matter. I leaned forwards, and stole what I needed from his breath, not sipping, but in a greedy rush and perhaps he did not even feel it. He fell forwards, a heavy dead weight across the seat, and I stripped him of his clothes: a tartan shirt and denim trousers. Too big, but that didn't matter. Then I jumped down from the cab and walked away from the truck, which stood with its engine idling. Here, the air smelled of pines and snow; I breathed in, watching what I'd stolen, but there wasn't enough. It was too slight, too meagre, like drinking watered milk, and I almost spat it out in disgust. But I could have been wrong: I'd taken from such before and it had been rich and varied. This man – no. I needed more and I wasn't sure where to find it. So I kept walking, all the way down the cold road as dusk fell, until at last I could see a light.

It was a little town, no more than a strip of houses along the road. A general store with a flag hanging limply from it, a small building that I thought might be a school, and my spirits rose at that, and at a sign on another place that said 'Library.' The store would be no use to me, most like, but the others – yes, they might have what I needed. I could have licked my lips. But not now. It was close to dark and no one would be there; I would have to wait till morning and survive as best I could throughout the night.

The clothes did not protect me from the cold; I did not need that. They were to deflect attention: I had learned not to go naked if I wanted to be unobserved. I found a hollow beneath a pine and curled into it, waiting until the lights went out one by one and I could feed on a breath of air.

Children's dreams come first. They go to bed earlier, after all, falling into the depths as the light dies and the first fears flicker out. I could see those fears like moths, grey-winged over the brambles and I sucked them in. I knew from mirrors that when I do this, there is a brief candleflame in my own eyes, a flash and flare, and that's why I stay away from people in the main – and yet, I can't, because if I do, I'll die. I need them. But they don't need me.

The dream that came was of monsters: something vast and black, smothering. A common dream for little children and it did not bring much nourishment. More followed, schoolyard tales, playing with friends, a beloved dog… One child dreamed of a man with a gun – the modern terror. None of it was interesting, none was original.

Then, later – someone else. A dream of forests, with a silver girl dancing in the branches, spun out of sunlight. I watched her turn and I took the dream and turned it into flesh: this, at last, was good. And I knew I had to find the dreamer, to keep myself alive a little longer.

In the morning, a pale dawn came up and brought snow with it. I sat beneath the pines, remembering the dancer, feeling the warmth of her silver form. I waited until the first light came back on and the dreams faded away – I always hoped that someone would stay sleeping, someone sick, but it seemed they were all too healthy in this place. The forest was filled with birds, not the rags and snatches of thought, and I rose from my place under the pines and padded towards the schoolyard. I wanted to find her.

The children came into the yard in pairs, or singly, or in small groups, bundled up against the snow. At first, I thought she wasn't there. Then I saw her, a tall girl, probably early teens, hanging back against the fence. I sidled close and she saw me. Usually, they thought I was a child like themselves, no threat, even in my too big clothes.

"Hello," I said and saw her grey eyes widen.

"Who are you?"

I shrugged. "I'm just hanging out."

"Are you a ghost?"

That surprised me. They generally can't tell that there's something wrong. "No," I said.

"What are you, then?"

I don't think there's a name for what I am. I've only met one other, and he did not know. "I don't know," I said.

"Are you dangerous?" She lowered her voice.

I thought about it. "Sometimes."

Her mouth opened but the school bell rang. "I've got to go," she said. "Will you still be here at recess?"

"Maybe." But I knew I would. Her head was full of thoughts, imaginings, things on which to feed, and if she did not run dry then I would not kill her. She nodded.

"I'll be back." Then she ran towards the school door, following her friends, if she had any. I smiled, melting back into the trees and the snow. But I could feel her imagination, the tendrils of her thoughts spiralling out across the air. She was excited, inspired, making up stories: I was ghost, vampire, demon. I was none of these, but as I fed on her imaginings I became more real, fleshed out from shadow. Not just her thoughts, either, but from other children, too – stories in, I thought, an English class, sending familiar fairy tales out into the world again. I knew these, written like grooves into my self, but I could still extract grains of nourishment from them, could still feed.

At recess she returned.

"You're still here!"

I nodded. "Where else do I have to go?"

She stared. "What about your family?"

"I don't have any."

"Are they dead?"

"They never lived." I did not say: *I am the child of stories, tales fleshed into a semblance of life, made out of words.* I didn't think she would understand and she changed tack.

"What's your name? Do you have one?"

"What would you like to call me?"

She blinked, considering. "I could call you Ash. I had a friend called Ashley, but she moved away."

"It's a good name. Like ashes. Yes, that will do. And you?"

"My name is Hayley."

"Hayley and Ash." I smiled. "Good enough."

I followed her home; she seemed to expect me to. But that night I left the place in the yard where I had set up my minimal camp and roamed the little town. I did not want to drain her too soon. There was a light snow falling and I felt myself fade and disappear into its silence, the illusion of warmth and life given to me by story leeched out by the world and the weather. We can't hold it for long, whatever we are. Or maybe it's just me – as I said, I only met one other. I drifted back to the library, but the tales contained in the pages of its books were like eating dust. Television was even worse. I was born into its age, though I'd lost track of when: all I knew was that it didn't sustain me. It was only imagination that worked and imagination was in short supply.

I knew I ought to head for the city, but it's hard for girls who live on the street. Invisible to systems, without documentation, the best I could do would be a squat and then the imagination of others is too draining, too obsessed with power and control and fear. I was Ash now, for a while, but I'd had other names, less neutral. Here, at least, the silence of the woods might make me fade, but it wouldn't rip me apart. I stood under the trees, looking up, feeling the flutter of snow on my face and waiting for dreams.

That night, she dreamed of beasts: wolves and a single great cat, running together through tightly packed pines, pursuing something that I never quite managed to see. A man or a boar, or some combination of the two, with the full moon beating down and then it was day, and I came shivering awake.

Hayley was giving me life, and I told myself that I should not feed on her alone. But no one else here was so sustaining. At recess, when the school bell rang, I was once more standing by the fence.

"I didn't see you last night."

"No. I was outside. I don't come into houses very often."

"Weren't you cold?"

"I don't feel the cold."

She frowned. "Can't I – bring you something? Food? A blanket?"

"No," I said. I licked my lips. "But you can tell me a story."

She thought for a moment. "I will. But not now." She glanced over her shoulder at the other kids, thronging around a snowman on the other side of the yard. "I don't know if they can see you and I don't want them to think I'm talking to myself."

24

I had to accept that.

"I'll see you in the lunch hour," she said. "We can talk then – I sometimes go home. I'll meet you on the back porch. My mom and dad are at work."

So this is what we did, that day, and the next and the next and the day after that. She told me stories of silver girls and golden cats, of dark men with amber eyes, and trees that spoke. And I could not help but see, reflected in the frosty windows of her home, my own rosy glowing face, in contrast to her increasingly pale one. I don't know if she knew much about addiction, but both of us were addicts: she to telling tales, retreating into her own head, her own world, and I encouraging all the while. Enabling, I think they call it. She knew what was happening. Once, on the last day, she said to me, "Was this how you began?"

"What do you mean?"

She looked down at her mittened hands. "Were you like me, once? Maybe you don't remember. Maybe you told stories to someone and at last there wasn't anything left, and you had to go out in the world and get more."

I was silent. I really didn't remember but perhaps she was right. Maybe we'd swap places and I'd become a girl again, and she'd be the wraith in the woods.

"I ought to go," I said at last. "I ought to leave you alone."

"Don't," she whispered. "You're the only one that listens. You're the only one who doesn't tell me I'm being silly."

"Is that worth so much? You'll grow up one day and you won't have to listen to them ever again." *If I leave you alone.*

"I don't know what it's worth," she said, almost inaudibly.

I did leave her alone after that, at least for the weekend, when her parents were at home. From the distance of the trees I watched her through the frosty windows, watching TV, reading a book, eating cereal. But often her gaze drifted up and out, to where I stood: she might not be able to see me, but she knew I was there. I should have left then, but I didn't.

I saw her again on Monday. She looked healthier, more alive, whereas I had grown more frail.

"Maybe we can just go to and fro," she said hopefully.

I shook my head. "It doesn't work like that."

"Are you sure?"

I thought back over years of victims. "I'm sure."

On Wednesday, Hayley asked me to meet her at the door of the library, after school. "I have a class project and my mom's at home that lunchtime – she has a hospital appointment so she's taking the day off work."

"All right," I said.

"I know you don't like to go inside places. But you won't have to."

By the time I got to the library, the snow was falling heavily. Sometimes I leave footprints, sometimes not, but today it was coming down heavily enough to mask any traces I might have left. I slipped through the snow, towards the yellow square of light coming from the open door of the library. Hayley was standing in the entrance, muffled in her parka, waiting for me.

"I've got a story for you," she said.

I was hungry. "What is it?"

So she began. "Once upon a time, there was a girl. I don't know where she was born or even if she *was* born, but she exists now. She doesn't know her name. She might be lying, but I don't think so. She's sort of a vampire and sort of a ghost, and she steals imagination. She feeds off stories and legends, especially if the tales are new, and when she feeds, she takes, so that the storyteller becomes less and less and eventually they possibly die."

I tried to speak, but the snow was falling harder now and she was disappearing behind a wall of luminous light, glowing and fading at the same time, and it was as though I was rooted to the spot, forced to listen as she told my story on.

"I don't think she wants to do what she does. I don't think she means to. It's like she can't help it and I know she just wants to survive. I do get it. But I've got stories of my own that I want to tell – I want to be a writer myself one day and I can't let her take everything I've got, not even for –" she hesitated, "– not even for love."

I tried to speak, but my voice was a whisper. I could feel myself starting to unravel, fragmenting into snowflakes, each one a word, as my own story was told back to me and I entered a spiral, falling.

"I called her 'Ash.' And she's like ash. She's like a fire that's about to go out and she needs to blow on the embers to keep herself alive, but it won't work because what she needs comes from the inside and she doesn't have an inside…" She spoke on and it was a relief, in a way, saving me from the constant hunt, the need to feed. Maybe it was time for the story to end, I thought, as the last of me span out into the snow and the last thing I heard was the slow single clap of a closing book.

# Dog Days in
# the Ghost Garden

*This story was written relatively recently in the very hot summer before Covid. I don't sleep well in the heat and spent a lot of nights watching Mars, which was very close to the Earth at that point, moving slowly across the southern sky. But I was fascinated by the news reports of parch marks emerging from the baking soil in the grounds of stately homes.*

The ghost garden cannot always be found. Only when the summers bake and burn and the heat brings phantoms out of the land, when Sirius is blue over the oak trees and the dog days slow everyone down – that's when old patterns choose to reveal themselves. And so do other things.

Whitehart Hall is a quiet place these days. When it was built, in the sixteen hundreds, it stood on top of the site of an old stone tower, now gone, and that in turn stood on the place where a Roman fortification had once overlooked the curve of the river Hartspey. When I was a child, we still found bits of broken tile, ochre and red and cream in the brick-coloured earth. My brother and I made up stories about them, spoke of ghosts, thought we might have glimpsed a centurion with a sharp spear and a cold face, marching. We were given the run of Whitehart, although it did not belong to us: our mother was the housekeeper, employed by the National Trust, and we lived in a small brick house in the grounds. But in my head we were the heirs to empty, conserved Whitehart, with its silent wood paneled chambers, its secrets and history. Now, I live in nearby Holmeleigh and I am the housekeeper now: a job I did not inherit, for which I had to obtain a degree and work in northern museums for a decade. But perhaps the memory of my mother did serve to get me the place after all. I have never wanted to work anywhere else.

I knew about the ghost garden. I would say 'of course' but in fact I had only seen it twice before, once in the summer of 1976, and again a decade later. But now they talk about climate change or climate whim, and the world warming up, and it's like holding invisible ink over the flame of a candle. The year before this one had been wet: very English, a summer drenched and green and everyone complaining about the rain. But this summer was different.

It started at the beginning of June, a warm spell broken by a storm that cracked lightning over the estate and caused water to stream in rivers down the Hall's steep dark roofs. People made jokes about British summers and that being 'it' until next year. But the next day saw the heat return: a cloudless sky, the sun roaring down into fiery darkness at the end of it, and the day after that, the same. At night, there was a red eye in the south, crossing the sky: Mars was close to Earth, the papers said, and watching the planet pass in the sleepless small hours, I thought that perhaps it was affecting the weather somehow, bringing the burn out of the land.

By the end of the month we were all complaining about heatstroke. The dog days had begun when blue Sirius joined the red planet, rising with the sun. I took to getting up at dawn and going in early to see to the cleaning and do paperwork.

Whitehart was silent then. That and the evenings were my favourite times, when I had the Hall to myself. The Hall is a person to me, you see. Being alone here is simply spending time with an old friend. When I opened the windows, the spice of the long lavender beds snaked into the house and battled with the smell of age. All old houses have a particular smell: Whitehart is sage and lavender, woodrot and dust.

The house is supposed to be haunted, of course. We play up to the old stories, from the heritage angle. Witches lived here, caught up in the local trials (they were a Catholic family, like some of the witches of nearby Pendle) but released. We have a Grey Lady, a wisp of a thing who runs across the lawn to meet her dead lover, towards a grove of trees that no longer exists. We have a Cavalier, riding with a crucial message in winter midnights. All of these ghosts are, well, normal as far as ghosts go.

But the garden is different.

The historians and archaeologists call them 'parch marks.' They are the traces of castles, forts, Roman villas, burial sites. They appear when the heat dries out the grass so much that areas which have a slightly different soil composition, like the soil beneath lost walls, and which cause the roots of plants to struggle, show paler against scorched gold. This simmering summer, an amateur archaeologist with a drone discovered an entire henge in Ireland, not far from Newgrange, for you can see such signs more easily from the air. And another thing that the heat draws forth is traces of lost gardens. In 1976, when the parch marks last appeared across the country, we had hosepipe bans, a Minister for Drought.

It was around this time that the ghost garden appeared. One afternoon, late, as my brother and I had come to the hall to wait for our mother to finish work. The hall had closed to the public, but the sun was still high. It was August and the light slanted thickly between the leaves of the oaks that surrounded Whitehart, casting barred shadows across the lawns and the black-and-white geometries of the walls. The air smelled of the box hedge, of heat. I was standing on a raised bank at the end of the garden: wide lawns of grass bordered with the lavender and box. When I looked down, the light shifted. For a moment I was dazzled and then I could see. The parch marks appeared at first, scorching out of the ground, and as I watched the old garden restored itself, rising up from the marks themselves. Low hedges delineated a knot garden and the air was filled with the scent of lemon balm and rosemary, as well as the herbs of my own day. A four pointed star, within a square. The hedges were only knee high to an adult, and low enough to see across to the hall. I looked for my brother but I could not see him – I could see someone else inside, though, a woman. She looked out from an upper window. She was no one I had seen before. In my day, some of the staff wore period Elizabethan dress, living history, but when I was a child this was not so common. This woman's hair was covered with a white cloth and her dress had a ruff of starched fabric. She withdrew from the window and out of sight and I wandered in the garden, breathing the scents of another summer, until the sun went down and a full moon that was the colour of butter sailed up over the gables. As soon as its light touched the garden, it disappeared, and I was left alone on the lawns with my mother calling me in for supper.

Later that week, my little brother asked me about the garden. He had seen it, too, and had played among the lavender.

"Where does come from, Ellie? And where does it *go*?"

"I don't know."

Matthew was still quite small, perhaps five.

"Sometimes it's there and sometimes it's not," he said.

"That's right." He nodded as though I had given him an answer and perhaps I had, for he went back to playing with his Matchbox truck and did not talk about it again.

That summer faded to its end and a rainy, windswept autumn, but I did not forget about the garden. I saw it once more after that, some years later, when I was a student and visiting the Hall in the summer holidays. My mother was still working there and I was waiting for her in one of the upstairs rooms. The tourists had all gone home, disappearing into coaches and cars, and I was enjoying the silence. I walked to the window and looked out through the diamond-leaded pane and there was the garden again. But unlike last time, this was early spring. Small white narcissi starred the lawn and above the furthermost box hedge was a cherry tree in blossom. It was so fresh and green in comparison to the baking summer that I threw the window open and breathed it in. But it was already late and I could feel the moon coming up over the shoulder of the house. It was then that I realised that the garden was tied into the moon, somehow, a tidal ebb and flow of time. I turned to look at the light flooding in through the other side of the chamber and when I looked back the garden was no longer there.

I would like to tell you that I met someone in the garden, like all the best children's stories. A friend: a young girl like myself, or a boy, from another age. That we had adventures and there was magic. But apart from the woman, I saw no one there. The garden was empty and therefore, I felt, somehow mine.

But this year, just as in 1976, I saw the garden again. And this year, too, we've had fires.

Beyond Whitehart and Holmeleigh lie the moors: mile upon mile of rolling land, covered in heather and bracken. The few trees are fire-berried rowan, with alder along the courses of the moorland streams. This summer, the streams had dried to a trickle and the fire began somewhere up on Moss Ledge, caused by a thrown cigarette end, perhaps, or someone's illicit BBQ, or arson. It swept across the moor, igniting the brittle heather and leaping the dry stream beds. The cloud of it, and the red glow at night, were visible from Holmeleigh and the Hall's desiccated lawn was, one morning, covered in a fine layer of ash, soft as silk and smelling of smoke. Fire engines from the whole area were directed up to the moor and there were some impressive photos in the national press.

It was not until the fire started coming closer down the hillside that we began to worry. There is a line of woodland between the Hall and the start of the moor, but the river snakes behind the house, on the other side. I spoke urgently to the Fire Service and they told me that the army might be called in. The national press were using terms like 'apocalyptic' and we were beginning to be seriously alarmed. There was a meeting at the Hall with a representative from the National Trust and we decided to close the Hall.

"It's not like we haven't had to do it before," Marcus told me. "Lyme Park in the Peak District – that got a bit uncomfy in 2012."

We were standing in front of the Hall. There was a haze over the cloudless sky and a smell of burning. Marcus wore tweeds even in the summer heat and was prone to upper-class understatement.

"Too close for comfort," I said.

"People come first," said Marcus. But I wasn't sure he actually meant it. His passion was for the buildings, not the visitors, although I think he would have been horrified if I'd said so. Yet he would have understood, too.

At night, the sky was lit by a red glow. There were terrifying photos in the newspapers: the firefighters' figures tiny against a wall of smoke, the flames snapping at the heels of local villages. "Dante's Inferno" was frequently cited. I spent the days with a hollow at the pit of my stomach and I could not get the smell of smoke out of my hair or clothes: I felt like a kipper.

Then the fire service issued a warning to Holmeleigh. People started talking about evacuating. We could see the fires from our back gardens and everything stank. My aunt drove from Lancaster to pick up my cat and my neighbours sent the kids to their grandparents in Bradford.

That evening, I stood in the upstairs wing of the house and looked across to the long ledge of the hill. It was crowned with flame. I opened the window and pulled down my facemask to smell fire and the dry scent of bracken burning. For a moment I fancied that the heat had touched my skin, but it was only the summer warmth, the long lack of rain. A line of fire was running down the hillside, like a train on a track. I heard sirens and the air was, quite suddenly, dense with smoke. Gasping, I slammed the window shut. I ran downstairs. I saw the flames leap into the oak grove and the dead bracken along its edges sparked, tinder dry. The fireline snaked swiftly through the trees, devouring dead leaves. But I was already ringing 999.

When they heard it was the Hall, the fire service was quick to respond. So were the Hall's garden team. We had a plan in place: the edges of the property were already stripped of any fuel, but the fire had taken hold in the peat up on the moor and was sending out more outliers into the trees. As I reached the front of the Hall, the fire engines were pulling in. They set up a beating line at the edge of the trees and told us to get out. But I hesitated.

"Go!" I screamed to the gardeners. "I'll catch you up!"

I ran back through the silent hall and onto the terrace. I held out my hands to the lawn, shimmering in the heat haze. I said, "If you are there, then come. Remember me? You've let me come before. Come now!"

Nothing happened. I shut my eyes and prayed to the garden.

When I opened them again, what seemed like a long time later, the outlines of box hedges were rising up through the haze along the parch marks. I saw roses, and the tall bowl of a fountain. I doubled back, into the garden. Here, the evening air was cool and fresh. The Hall flickered briefly, then stabilised. But beyond the peace of the garden was a wall of smoke, rolling in like fog from the sea.

I walked up to it. It seemed almost solid, like the clouds you see from a plane, but when I reached out and touched it, my hand vanished into it. There was no heat, however, only a cool prickling. The sky above me was clear, an underwater glow, bearing a single star. I walked around the edges of the garden as though I was beating the bounds, and the Hall seemed to watch me and so did the star. The Hall was shadowy and I saw no one within, only the single flame of a candle in an upstairs room. It made me shiver and I looked away, focusing on the garden and the quiet splash of the fountain.

As I walked, I prayed for rain. I could hear a distant thudding sound like the swift beating of a drum, and it was a few minutes before I realised what it was: the noise of a helicopter's rotors. The Chinook roared overhead, quivering out of sight as it flew over the Hall and the garden, then reappearing as it climbed up over the saddle of the moor. It was dropping water or foam. I turned away from it and walked on, round and round. I felt as though I was winding a coil of wire, tighter and tighter. I looked up and saw the star, bright overhead, but a second later it was swallowed by a cloud, towering and dark. I jumped as a fat drop of rain hit the back of my hand. With a sudden sense of achievement, I stopped walking and turned my face to the gathering downpour. It rained and rained. One by one, the petals fell from the roses and the leaves shivered and withered. The season of the garden was turning, unwinding what I had inadvertently wound, a clock running backwards. Soon, the raindrops turned to snow and the cold bit my bare skin. I stood until the garden was covered in a blanket of white.

Then the garden, a photographic negative against the black and white of the Hall, began to fade and so did the smoke. As the garden disappeared around me, I could hear the rain pattering once more on the roofs of Whitehart, and up on the moor the fires hissed out. A shout went up from the fire team. Before they could see that I had not gone away as instructed, I slipped into the Hall and up into the room where the candle had burned.

There was a faint smell of aftersmoke, but perhaps it was only the legacy of the fires. I thought for a moment that I heard footsteps, running down the stairs, but there was no one there. I went back down to speak to the fire crew, who thought, it seemed, that I had come back up the drive. But when they had gone and the rain finally died, I returned to the upstairs chamber and looked out.

Above the saddle of the moor, I saw a thick rind of light. At first I didn't recognise it, but then I realised. It was the full moon, rising. It rolled up over the moor; it was the colour of blood and smeared with smoke, but it grew paler as it rose. There was no sign left of the ghost garden. The moon sailed high and clear, the cloud retreating eastwards, carried on the wet wind from the sea. I stood there until the red eye of Mars travelled the sky, until it, too, vanished behind the trees and the dog days were over.

# Doveblack and Rosewhite

*A lot of my work features things which are mistaken, or which shouldn't really exist – like black doves.*

The black dove holds war in its beak.

I was fourteen years old and on the eve of my marriage when the black dove first came. I was in the chamber of my father's house, Holydore, on an evening in July. There were roses climbing around the leaded panes and the sun was going down over the oak woods, casting patterns of old golden light across the floorboards. I wore a gown of ivory and green and felt as though I was falling. Nothing after this would be the same. I was to marry the middle son of Lord Oldsmere, Jamie. I had known him all my life. I did not love him, but I did not hate him, either. I think we both had hopes, and we both accepted the marriage: it was the way things were. But I was frightened all the same and I went to the window and threw it open, to let in the air and the scent of the roses, and look down into the courtyard.

The dovecote stood to one side, tall on its pedestal so that the stable cats couldn't get at the doves, although there were occasional casualties. It was the customary small white house, and the flags beneath it were scrubbed clean every morning by one of the maids. (Doves make a mess). Fresh corn was scattered for them every morning, too. I loved the doves; their soft pale feathers, their gentle eyes and the almost-under-hearing whispering sounds they made. I found them peaceful. And, of course, they are a sign of peace, the peace of Our Lord and Saviour, yet more than this, too.

"We have them at sea," my uncle told me. Saul, a sailor in the Navy. "Like Noah. We send them out to help us navigate towards land – so old Noah used a sailor's trick, you see?"

I nodded, sitting on the hard bench in the sunlight with my uncle. I was perhaps six or so then, and it was my task to feed the doves, although I couldn't reach the dovecote. I scattered the corn on the ground instead.

35

"They are the spirits of God Almighty," my uncle said, and I imagined the doves cooing on the flagstones as scraps of light, torn gently from Heaven and fluttering down through the towering clouds to the world. It was a view that never really left me, and I have felt close to the doves ever since, generation after generation, for their lives are not long. Perhaps they, too, were swept up to Heaven on the evening wind when their flesh failed them – but I did not voice this thought aloud, for scripture and Father Andrew told us that no living thing has a soul, save man. But I could not shake the thought away, either, unlike my mother, who has a mind that is regularly whisked clean with a broom of the spirit, not countenancing anything of which she does not approve. Her mind is a tidy house, whereas mine is more akin to an attic, full of old beloved things that no one else wants to look at.

"You must be more firm with yourself, Nell," my mother would say. "Less dreamy. No man will stand a dreamy girl for long."

This was not my experience, but I had learned (from that broom of the spirit) not to contradict her.

The doves were part of my attic, I supposed. And my dreaming did not seem to sway Jamie away from me: I think he was keener than I. I would go and live in his father's house and I would take a pair of doves with me: I had already told him this.

"A dowry of doves," he said, perched on the edge of his chair as my mother sat and sewed. "How charming." He was nineteen, and a grown man. I was afraid he would think of me as a little girl, not a woman, but he was kind and did not let me see it, if so.

On the evening before our wedding, as I leaned out of the window towards the sunset, I saw to my displeasure that a crow had made its way into the courtyard and was pecking at the doves' corn. I took a pillowcase from the bed and flapped it; the birds all rose up in a spiralling rush, many light, one black. The doves descended like snow but the crow remained, settling down on the windowsill.

"What are you doing?" I asked. "Stealing my dove's corn!" But then I looked more closely and saw that it, too, was a dove. Its feathers were soot-black, soft and lightless, and its small sidelong eye was crimson. In all other ways it was a dove, however. It looked at me out of that fiery eye and then it was as though a sudden wind snatched it up and sent it sailing into the clouds: a speck of night, soon gone.

I went to my bed thinking of the black dove and when I woke it was my wedding day.

*

The breeding pair I brought to Mayfield House laid eggs, in time, and soon we had a dovecote again, for the foxes had dealt with the Mayfield doves and so this small part of my dowry was valuable after all. I settled well to married life, though always at the back of my mind was fear, for Jamie was a soldier at times, as many noblemen must be, and might one day go forth to war. And I had come to love Jamie, in time – not a girlish love, which settles on fancies, but the love of someone who knows another from day to day. I was with child, too, and that stills all manner of foolishness. Perhaps I too was in possession of a spiritual broom. I did not see the black dove again and I began to think that I had dreamed it, or been mistaken, or that it was some sport of nature. After all, a white blackbird had been seen in the village: we knew the woman who had found it in her hedgerow. Such things do exist, maybe the work of the devil, or simply a mistake. Though God does not make those, they say.

I lost the child and bore another, then three more. Two daughters, two sons. And still Jamie had not gone to war. But then the day came when the murmurs and rumours gained more and more ground.

"They say it will not be long," my uncle Saul, now an old man, said. He had come back from the sea, though many times we feared he would not, and now his place was in the sun in front of the old dovecote, at the home of my girlhood. I was sitting there with him. Down in the meadow, three of my children tumbled among the buttercups and the baby lay swaddled in my lap. Beyond, the oaks were the dark, heavy green of midsummer.

"But we have been to war with Ireland. Again, and then again."

"It could be the Spanish," my uncle said. He had fought against them, under Raleigh, whom he revered as a kind of saint. Raleigh was real to him, whereas the saints in the church were only plaster and stone, regardless of the reality beyond in the Heavenly kingdom. He looked at me sidelong, like a bird. "The Spanish are more to be feared. The Irish never fight for long."

"The last war lasted nine years."

"Ah, but that was under the old Queen. It's different now." But I did not really understand how. It was men's business, though, and I had my children to care for. We must be thankful that Jamie had then been too young to go to war.

As we were sitting there, I remembered the black dove I had seen; its image fell into my mind like a leaf to a pond. Had Saul seen such a thing, ever? But he looked at me, puzzled.

"No, maid, I've never heard of such. Was it a blackbird, maybe?"

"Maybe." But I knew it had been a dove.

That night, at Mayfield, the nurse was putting the children to sleep and I had the window open. The day's warmth lingered, and there was a full moon rising in the eastern sky, trembling just above the hills and balancing the vanished sun. I turned and the bird was sitting on the windowsill, just as it had done so many years ago. A dove, nightblack, with the moon shining in its sideways eye. This time, it carried something in its beak: it looked like a live coal. I stared at the bird and it looked at me, then fluttered into the darkness. I could trace its path by the thing it held, firefly in the night.

I knew what it meant; it was plain enough. If the white dove with its branch of olive brings peace, then the black dove brings war. I had never heard of such a thing, but that did not mean it did not exist. So I was not surprised when, next day, a rider came to the house and told Jamie to put his affairs in order.

We did not speak much. He knew what I felt. He told me to look after the children and in wide-eyed silence they watched him ride out. The house seemed quiet after he had gone, though he was a soft spoken man. He left me with the children, the servants, and his old mother (his father had died some while before) and still Mayfield felt empty. We got on with our chores and tried not to think of what might happen. The wheat would still need bringing in; the hens must still be fed. Slowly the summer passed and we sank beneath its rhythm. In early September a letter came from Jamie, saying he was well, and might be home before Christmastide and I read this out to the household, rejoicing.

A day later, the black dove came again.

September is often beautiful in this part of the country, with the hedges filled with blackberries and the hillsides bleached pale by the summer sun. This time, the dove did not come in the evening, but at noon. I looked up from laying wet clothes on the bushes and there it sat, staring. The coal flared in its beak, no whit diminished by the bright noonday. The dove was perched on the stone wall of the kitchen garden and as I watched it dropped the coal from its beak. The coal sank into the earth and when I looked up again from its brief descent, the dove was no longer there.

I did not know what this meant. I did not believe that Jamie was dead; my heart still felt whole. In twilight I went back to the place where the coal had fallen, and found a sooty shoot springing up from the soil. I said nothing to anyone about this, but next day the shoot had grown, as if seeking the last of the summer light, captured golden and slow in the September hills. I did not like the shoot. It looked like a black bone, or something that had been caught in fire, but a day later it unfurled a leaf. This was soft and feathery, as though it had fallen from a bird's soft breast, and it coiled up into the gathering light. More leaves joined it. I was afraid the old man who tended the kitchen garden would notice it, but he did not seem to see it and neither did Margaret the housekeeper, garnering the parsley and sorrel. I began to think that only I could see the shoot and this made me afraid.

Three days later, on the Sabbath, the shoot's leaves had hardened into thin black spikes, losing their softness. And I saw that the shoot had put forth a bud, fat and beetle-shining, tinged with green fire. I went to church that morning and sat in the pew and prayed that the bud would come to nothing. I had tried to cut it with a knife but it was tough as iron and would not yield. I bent my head over my hands and prayed for Jamie, for all the men at war and the women waiting. When we left the church the day was still and hot. The orchards smelled of apples and a thrush sang, sweet and far away. There might have been no such thing as war. But when we reached the house, the black bud had ripened. By evening, as the sun fell into fire, it had split.

It was a lily, like the shadow of a flower in high sunlight. Its petals curved against the stone of the garden wall and although there was a breeze, the lily was utterly still. There was a flutter of movement from the top of the wall. The black dove had come back. Its eyes glittered red in the sunset. It opened its beak and said to me, "You have to take the lily to the grave." Its voice was like a bell.

"Which grave?" The breath was hard in my chest, as if my throat was closing up. "*Whose* grave?"

"You will know when you see it," the dove said.

"Is it my husband's? Is he dead?"

"You will know," the dove said again. Darkness seemed to spread out in a tide from the flower, eclipsing the dove's red eye and the last light from the sun. I swayed. I felt the flower creep into my fingers and it felt like a strange soft hand. It felt awful but my own hand closed around it all the same. I looked up and saw the stars: Orion the Hunter striding across the sky, for the first time that autumn, with the blue star at his heels. He was a friend to me and I felt a measure of strength returning.

Holding the flower, I set out. Through the gate of the kitchen garden, then the meadow. There were paths through the grass, made by foxes and badgers, trodden down by the children as they made their summer way to the river, which ran deep and slow between its rush-fringed banks. I could see it glimmering, for now the moon was coming up, just past the full and with plenty of light by which to see. As I made my way down the meadow, the light of the moon grew but I could no longer see the moon itself: I thought it had been hidden behind the trees, yet when I stopped and stared, there were no trees any more. The land seemed to have opened out into parkland. The river had broadened and on its banks, on a small rise, stood a temple.

It was white, perhaps marble. It had columns and was open to the night air. I stopped when I saw it, because it filled me with fear. Then I thought of my husband, who had not hesitated to ride to war, and I gathered my courage, took the soft flower more firmly into my grasp and walked to the temple with the lily held before me, like a dark bride.

Inside, the temple was cool, the air watery. It was also empty, except for a marble scroll at one end. I went to look, for in the dim light I could not see the name. I knew it marked a tomb. But the words shifted when I looked at them and changed; I could not make them out. Even if it was Jamie's grave, I knew I had a task to do. I knelt down and placed the black lily on the marble step. There was a flutter from above.

"It is the grave of the war," the black dove said.

I looked down at the lily. Blackness spread out from it, melting into the stone, and when I looked at the bird again, it was dawn-grey. Moments later, a white dove sat on a white tomb, looking at me from a golden eye.

"You will not see me again," the dove said.

"You will not come back?"

"To the world, I will. To you, no. Live your life in peace," it said and flew up into the arching roof of the temple, just as the sun touched the walls. I stood alone on the bank of the river, with the trout rising to catch the early morning flies. There was no sign of the temple and only a faint dark dust on my palm, soon gone.

A week later, Jamie rode in, as we were bringing the harvest home. The war was over, he told me. I did not say that I already knew. I followed him into the quiet house, past the dovecote in the kitchen yard where the white birds pecked at the corn, as they had always done.

# Flowerface

*This started as a serious story, about the Welsh mythological figure Blodeuwedd who is transformed into a bird, and it's set around the Spring Equinox. But it wouldn't stay serious. In fact, it got very silly.*

When my sister Osta came through the door, she was choking. Her eyes bulged, her face grew scarlet and then, spluttering, she coughed up a pellet of bone and fur onto the rug.

I looked at her, coldly.

"Could you not do that outside? I've just swept."

"Sorry." But she wasn't. I could tell. She flounced up the stairs, with the long folds of her cloak swirling behind her, and I didn't see her again that night.

In the morning, I found a letter on the step.

*If you are going to compete so blatantly for resources, kindly inform the People first. This is intolerable and will not be permitted to continue.*

I showed the note to Osta, and to Mother.

"Well, it's not the first time we've had trouble with the neighbours," my mother said.

"But what are they talking about? Osta? You know, don't you?"

"I haven't a clue," she said, not looking at me.

I knew she did, though, and I thought Mother did, too. I left them muttering together in the kitchen and went out to the well. There was no sign of anyone about but then it was the middle of the morning and people don't expect you to be up then. I hauled some water up in the bucket and took it back to the house. I had a notion to make some soup.

Osta was nowhere in sight when I got back in but my mother was perched on the back of the chair, hunched and cross. Ignoring this, I started chopping up the vegetables. Mother and Osta weren't so keen

41

on carrots, but they are good for you, I understand. And they liked rabbits well enough, obviously.

"I hope your sister eats something," Mother grumbled. "She needs to keep her strength up. Especially at the moment."

"I'm aware of that. I'm trying to make stuff she likes." When had Osta ever *not* eaten? She was constantly picking at stuff. But I didn't want to annoy Mother more than she was annoyed already.

When I had made the soup, I went back outside. The sky was stormy above the trees and I could smell rain on the wind. This was a chancy season, seesawing between winter and the oncoming spring and back again. Under the land I could feel the great swell of a tide of time, gathering for the flood. We were not far off the equinox and it showed. I dusted off my hands and sparks showered to the ground; I felt myself ripple and shiver. And I knew I was being watched.

I looked around as casually as I could manage. There, behind those leaves – the blink of a golden eye. But when I looked again, it was gone. I thought I knew who the watcher might be, but I was not certain. I went over to the leaves – a low elder tree, just out from bud – and behind them a message had been scratched into the mud. A crescent moon: tonight. A waving line and a circle: a stream and a pool.

Very well, then, I thought. You have come to me. I shall come to you.

The dusk fell cold and blue. As I made my way through the wood, twisting and turning between the still-bare branches, I could see the new moon rising: a sliver of light in the shimmering sky. It was still low and the evening star hung close to it, burning like a lamp. I reached the meeting place and waited.

After some time, during which the moon climbed higher and the blue light sank into black, I heard a rustle in the brambles which ran along the stream.

"I did not know if you would come," a voice said. I looked down and saw a pair of gentle golden eyes. The air shivered. A girl stood there, gazing up at me, wrapped in a soft grey shawl.

"I thought it was time," I said. I slipped down to join her. "This has gone on long enough."

She nodded. "I'm so sick of it. My sisters, my mother…"

"Your brothers?"

"Up on the high chalk. They want no part of it. They have their own kin now."

"What is it that you wish me to do?" I asked. She started at me. Her eyes were huge in the thin light of the moon.

"I did not think you would be the one to offer," she said.

"Perhaps we're more reasonable than you think."

"We are prey," she said. "We cannot afford to trust."

Well, this made sense and I said so. And it was then that she told me; told me, too, who she wanted me to meet.

I bided my time after that and kept quietly in the house. Things did seem to have subsided. My sister spent most of her nights out, and my mother stayed huddled in the kitchen, staring into the fire and saying little. But all the while I was aware of that tide of time: growing, growing, growing under the land until I thought it must surely swell and burst even as the moon herself grew.

And then it was the eve of the equinox, when day and night are of equal length and the summertide would be upon us. The world felt crammed with meaning, ready to explode. The day dawned fair, with a hazy sunlit mist. I made breakfast and went to the well, then cleaned the house. Getting the little bones and gristle out of the rug was difficult and irritated me, but I said nothing. Both my mother and my sister thought there was too much of my father in me, still. I did not want an argument, on this day of all days. I did not want them to know what I was doing.

I think Osta felt the same. She spent the afternoon preening, painting her face, trying on different clothes. I kept glancing out of the window, waiting for the first shadow of dusk. When the trace of haze started to creep across the land, I told my mother I had a headache. She snorted. But it was not the first time and she let me go upstairs without protesting too much. I could hear her chuckling and whispering to my sister as I went.

I sat for a time by the open window, waiting for twilight to properly fall. The land smelled of the spring: a fresh green scent, daffodils and lily of the valley. And although darkness was coming on fast, there was still a light in the west. I did not wait any longer. I went through the window and out.

I met my companion in the heart of the wood. It was completely dark by now and the stars prickled amid the branches. I could sense the leaves starting to burst from the bud, in beech and oak, but they were not fully out yet and the sky was visible, along with the rising moon.

"I came as you told me," I said.

"Good. And your sister?"

"Has been tarting herself up all day."

"So has mine."

I nodded. We had expected as much.

"They will meet at the stone," my companion said. "We do not have much time."

"No, we need to get going. Do you trust me?"

I could see a trace of fear in her golden-brown eyes but she said, "Yes. Well enough."

She was quite heavy, but I am strong. She had wrapped a pad of leather around her waist to save her from my claws and we managed, just. I did not want to drop her and I was relieved when we reached the edge of the glade. The stone stood at the centre, a spire of ancient granite. It had not been put there by men: we see few enough of those in any case.

I could not see my sister but I knew she was there. And from the way my companion's head went up, I thought she had sensed her kindred, too.

"It will not be long," she said. "Do you feel him coming? He is on his way."

She was right. I could hear him moving through the undergrowth, a distant crashing, as of hooves. And there was a strong wild smell, too, like the scent of the springtime earth itself. The great equinoctial tide was rushing under the land.

Osta stepped out into the glade. She wore a brownsilver dress, which shimmered and shivered in the moonlight. On the other side of the glade, not far from us, I saw another woman walking: dressed in fawn and gold, with a circlet around her hair. The unstable tide quivered and took us and all at once Osta was owl again, and the other girl was hare. I looked at my companion. We were in human form. But only just.

"He's nearly here," my companion whispered.

"And the other?"

She smiled. "I gave them full instructions."

"I'll be glad to see an end to it."

"Oh, so will I. Perhaps we can be friends?"

"If you were a mouse – but you are not. And I have no animosity to the mouse kindred, or any. It is just – "

"It's not personal."

"No."

There was a rushing wind. Osta and the hare girl met at the standing stone. Their gazes locked.

"You!" my sister said.

"You will find that I am triumphant, tonight," the hare girl told her. She twirled and her brown dress whispered with her, like dried leaves. She was golden eyed and beautiful, but so was Osta.

Then someone else was in the glade. I saw the moon's glint from his antlers, the sheen of his skin. He turned and for a moment I wanted him for myself, as we all must. But the hare and I had a job to do.

"Come on!" Together the hare and I, still in our human dress, ran out into the glade. "Osta! I want a word with you!"

"Tellury! We need to talk!" the hare girl commanded.

Osta's mouth fell open. For a moment I glimpsed owl but then she was human again and angry.

"What the hell are you doing here?"

Behind me, the great antlered form swept by. He trod past me, past Osta and the hare girls, and then he was gone. A moment's distraction had been all that it had taken. But in the moment of his passing I saw another form rise up and take his hand and be led into the wood. Someone who had been crouching, white and dark beneath the new bracken, who stepped upwards as a girl in a checkerboard dress, a moonpale streak in her nightblack hair.

Osta stared open mouthed.

"Bloody badgers!"

45

"This," I said, "Has gone on long enough. Us and the hares, the rivalry for the Lord of the Wood. It's poisoned the neighbourhood. It's got to stop."

Osta was owl for a moment. Her feathers ruffled and shuffled, she gave a sharp angry cry. Then she sat down, human, in the grass.

"You're too like your dad. Bloody humans and all."

"She's right," the hare girl named Tellury said. She slid down the standing stone and put her arms around her knees. "Long enough – your mother not speaking to our mother, all the whispers and rumours, the lies…"

"And for what?" my companion asked. "Some male creature, Lord or God or no." She produced a small round flask. "Have some mead. We can all share it."

So we did, and we talked, and when the moon sank down behind the trees it was springtime, and we were enemies no more.

# Greene Lyon

*I've had a long term interest in alchemy, and this is an alchemical story, which might explain some of its weirder aspects. If you're intrigued, it should supply a lot of alchemical rabbit holes to go down!*

The Queen has started to decay as she lies in her bath. The fumes are unpleasant, but necessary. We have all agreed that things are going well, proceeding as planned: after all, this is not the first time it's happened.

However, the King refuses to die and that is a problem. I don't recall that ever occurring before and it strongly suggests that something has gone wrong with the process – which is unthinkable. I go up to the highest tower of the castle to contemplate it, and have a look at the land, too. Maybe from this summit, I can spot what's gone wrong.

We'd prefer to keep this from the lower servants, but of course it's impossible. I pass one of the bath attendants in the hallway. She's carrying a bowl of salt and her face is creased with worry.

"Oh, Lord Lyon – is there any news?" She grasps my sleeve.

"I'm afraid not. Not yet. But I'm sure we'll get to the bottom of it soon. Try not to be concerned."

I hope I'm being reassuring. I can smell the Queen as she rots and it's a comforting smell, acrid on the air. The maid can smell it, too.

"At least something's going right," she says. She gives me a weak smile.

"I'm sure you're doing an excellent job," I tell her.

"We're all trying our best."

Up, up, up. The stone stairs spiral into the heights of the castle but even if I stood in the lowest courtyard, I would still be high up, for the castle stands on a hill. The hill is green and speckled with flowers in the summer, and even at noon it is possible to see the stars. When I stand on the top of the tower now, I can see Mercury, low over the horizon and bright, and above, very faint in the blaze of the day, is the perpetual wheel of the fixed stars. The land rolls away in patterns of hill and field and all of it has meaning, for this is the nature of the realm in which we live.

I study the constellations above but there is nothing to tell me why the King refuses to die. I go back downstairs, and seek him out. Up till now, he has been seated upon the great throne, with its symbols and signs, but when I enter the throne room this time, it is empty. The curtains which cover the long windows float in the light breeze and I can smell the summer air, but there is no sign of the King.

We search the palace. He's nowhere to be found and everything is as usual, except for one. High in another tower, there is a small dark door, and this is ajar.

Lord Rule and I look at each other. We know what this means.

"No one's ever done this that I can remember," says old Rule.

"Nor I. But someone's going to have to go after him." And we both know who that someone will be.

I take a flask. It contains liquid mercury. I take a box, with brass filings. I don't take food or water, because I won't need them where I'm going, and I don't even know if I'm going to be able to come back. I say goodbye to Rule and to my wife: we clasp hands. She doesn't like it but she knows we have no choice; without the King, there's no point to anything and it would only be a matter of time, anyway. I also say goodbye to the Queen.

She is progressing nicely. Her legs have gone, now, as she lies in the glimmering fluid and she has no hands. She opens her eyes when I come in, and smiles at me. Since she has no tongue, she is unable to speak, but I know what she wants to say. I think she rolls her eyes, but it's difficult to tell.

"I'll find him," I say. "I promise. Whatever it takes, I'll bring him back."

Then I set out, going up the winding stair to the small dark door. There are guards at the door now, to stop anyone else getting out. Or getting in.

"Take care, Lyon," says old Rule, gruffly. "Come back safely."

It's good of him to be so concerned. But I'd be the same if our places were reversed. The door creaks open, the guards fall into position behind me with their weapons crossed, and I am through. There's a breathless, airless second and then the door slams shut behind me.

I look ahead. There's a black, featureless plain – moorland, with a few small scrubby bushes. This is the Starlit Land, which surrounds all realms, all kingdoms. Some believe that it is the world of the dead, but I have never seen anything animate here, never glimpsed a stray soul, except those who for their own purposes enter the Land. It is dangerous all the same: bogs which will suck a man down, patches of grass which hold the feet fast, or cause a hunger that can never be satisfied. Here, there are rushes which weep blood. I have to be careful and the King has a head start.

I have been here twice before. Third time, I remind myself, is the charm. I ask with frustration, though not aloud, why the King has chosen to come here in the first place. This is infuriating. We need to be getting on with the Work, not pursuing a rebellious and possibly delusional monarch over the cosmological landscape. I want to be sitting in my study with my feet up, while King and Queen rot obediently down into their component essences, not chasing about in this black land.

I set off along a downward slope. There's no way of telling where the King has gone, except that a faint odour of sulphur lies in his wake. It gets to the point where it's hard to keep track of it – if you try to smell something too much, you strain your nose. And the spongy earth doesn't take footprints. I'm not sure if I'm heading in the right direction.

I've been going for about an hour (it's hard to keep any sense of time here) when the accident happens. I tread on a bush. It's flat and spiny and it has sent branches out that are level with the earth and hard to see. The bush objects. It bursts into flames, a hard white fire which dazzles me. I stumble backwards and fall, which probably saves my eyebrows. The bush flares up, burns, and then the fire is gone as if it had never been. A thorny spine snakes across the path. This time, I take care not to tread on it. But this is the problem with the Starlit Land – nothing ever changes here, unless it is the visitor.

I plod on. The stars burn above me but they never shift position. The Land is locked into place, eternal. The sulphurous smell recedes and grows stronger, recedes and grows stronger and I follow it. Then, at last, I see the King.

He is lying on the shore of a dark lake. It is mirror-flat, unmoving, and the stars are reflected in its depths until I am no longer sure if the lake is night or the night is water. The King lies face down, in a crumple of robes. In this light, they are silver and that makes me shudder in case he's atrophied, although it's only a reflex. I know the robes are still red. I make my way over to him and try to turn him, but his body is heavy, weighed down like rusty metal.

"Your Majesty!" My voice sounds rusty, too, as if there isn't enough air for me to speak. But this is an illusion and I force myself to speak louder, calling for him to wake up.

Eventually, the King stirs.

"Who?" Words start to fail them, even before the tongue rots. He blinks his golden eyes. A beautiful face, of course, before the flesh started to corrode. The King has the sun behind his eyes.

"It is Lord Lyon, Your Majesty. Your Secretary, remember?" But he might not.

"I …don't know."

"Your Majesty, we need to bring you back to the castle. Can you remember why you came here?"

"To –"

"Yes?" I can barely hear him. His tongue is on the point of disintegration.

"To start…"

I think I know what the King might be trying to say, but it's too late now. And he's already started to rot, so why put us all through this now? I really am furious with him. Somehow, I manage to haul him to his feet. He can't stay here and neither can I. His arm, decomposing and sending red stains down my sleeve, is around my shoulder and I drag him, away from the black lake and up the dark hill, under the unchanging stars. The air tastes of sulphur until I stop noticing it.

On and on we trudge. The King becomes heavier and heavier, and at one point I drop him. I haul him up, cursing roundly. At last we are up the hill and close to the rectangle that is the castle door.

"Wait," I tell the King, although he can't go anywhere. Turning, I take the flask of mercury and the box of filings, and I pour one and tip the other out onto the black soil. It swallows them without trace, for the Land may not change but it still requires an offering. Then I take the King's arm around my shoulders once more and I rap on the door and pull him through.

It's just as well that awareness has drained out of him by now. All we have to deal with is the body. It's not the same for the Queen, although they're physically around the same stage. She keeps her awareness for longer, I think, remembering her tongueless smile. But he's safely back in his bath now and that's good enough for me.

After that it all goes to plan. Rule and I oversee the process and eventually our monarchs are where they should be: *prima materia* rotted down and the lapis shining above the baths, the spiritual essence glowing. The perfect Red King and his White Queen, sulphur and mercury, Sol et Luna. When the ceremony is due, we take the contents of both baths in two big brass pots and have them carried down to the courtyard, to the long field which slopes down to the river, where the green land begins. We mix the contents of the two pots and then we leave them, once the sacred marriage, the *conjunctio*, has taken place.

But I have a secret. I have taken some of each, in the flask in which I carried the mercury, and that night, I take it up the winding stair to the dark door and open it. The guards have been called off now and there's no one to stop me. I step through and I pour the *conjunctio* onto the black earth. I think this is what he was planning, in his addled way, but he didn't have the Queen with him and probably he was in no state to realise this. I don't know what might come of it but I think the King had a plan, and he is wiser far than I, can see all manner of things when he is in his rightful mind. Then I go back through the dark door.

Three days later, Rule and I go down to the field. It's a lovely day, with the sun shining. On the place where we poured the *conjunctio*, two little shoots are emerging from the soil: two small naked heads, the size of a human thumb. Their features are rudimentary as yet, but recognisable: two pairs of eyes, tight closed; a nose and mouth. Our new King and Queen are coming up through the soil and the land itself is renewed, we can see it glowing.

Later, I go back up to the tower and look into the Starlit Land. I can't see a King and a Queen. But on the place where I spilled the *conjunctio*, where the mercury and brass filings had been placed, something has changed. There is a small green shoot, pressing up through the soil, under the unceasing stars.

# Mow Cop

*Another of my abiding interests, as will become clear to the reader in the course of this collection, is follies and grottoes – manmade anomalies in the landscape. This one features the former.*

The whispers say I can't be buried; say the earth won't take me. That leaves Heaven or Hell, or a reliance on my own devices, and God knows I'm used to that. My birth killed my mother, and my father died when I was fifteen, leaving me the house itself. I have rarely left it. I learned early that I couldn't live anywhere else.

This admission – made rarely, for I have few friends – has earned me a great reputation for sentimentality in this, a sentimental age. Such attachment, such filial duty – so they exclaimed, particularly the mothers of young ladies who fancied me as a suitable husband for their daughters. All that's long gone now. A shame that this admiration could never be reciprocated, but when I removed my shoes at night and glimpsed the fresh scars on which I walked, I knew what I had to do. And that was to keep to the moors.

Mow Cop is an old place, clawed out of the land of the north by my ancestors, not long after the Normans came. A stone house now, replacing an earlier manor; forbidding, setting its face resolutely against London and the south, looking out over an expanse of purple and black, rolling to the sea. By the time my father inherited it, much of the place was already inhabitable, and by the time of his death, still more rooms had succumbed to the sea mists and the rain. There were, in places, more holes than roof. The damp showed through the faded flowers of the wallpaper and rats had chewed the upstairs carpets to a musty lace, leaving bare boards between.

I did not greatly mind. The part of the estate which was hired out to farming would pay my meager expenses. I dismissed all but the most devoted servants: two sisters and a brother, whose family had attended mine for over three hundred years. They knew why I kept to the house, I believe; I could see it in their faces, a knowing sadness. They lived in the remnants of the servants' quarters, while I resided in the top of the west wing, the most complete part of the house. Here, I watched the moors from behind the heavy drapes, day after day, knowing I would see nothing. I was not waiting for anyone. What I sought was already there.

On the days when I felt stronger, and the pain had begun at last to ebb, I took to walking. Here, I did not compromise: stout boots, a forked hazel staff. Hazel is the lightning rod, bridging heaven and the land. I needed that mediating power. On the first day, I could only go as far as the end of the formal garden, now badly overgrown. Midsummer, and the box hedges were unshaven, entwined with bramble and flowering rose, trimmed with rosebay willowherb and cow parsley. I remember one day when I stood in silence at the end of the garden, watching the swallows skimming over the long pond. It was very quiet. I sat on the edge of the water, on a low stone wall, and waited until the shadows grew long, then I went back into the house. Next day, I did it again.

By winter that year there was no corner of the estate that I did not know. The land was bisected by swift streams, tumbling down the narrow gorges past the feet of alder and oak. The highest point, however, was the hill named Mow Cop: an outcrop of rocks culminating in a high apron of grass. I went up here in all weathers, finding myself looking down on the sway of the land to the iron sea. The frequent rain calmed me. I felt so light that I could have stood on tiptoe and flown. The seed of what I had to do was starting to grow in me, but I did not know how I would achieve it. For that, I needed money.

I had little expectation of work, because I could not safely leave the land. I wrote to a number of acquaintances, seeking scholarly tasks. But it was a small living, not enough for the grand scheme I had in mind, and which over the years that followed was to grow into an obsession.

Then, one of my tenants came to me, twisting his cap in his hands in a gesture which I mistook for anxiety. It was not. It was excitement.

"A landslip, in the far field," he told me. "And in it the earth is all black, black as night."

"What do you mean?" I was sitting in the drawing room at the time, surrounded by peeling wallpaper, and the fire sputtered in the hearth as if giving me an answer. I saw the man's eyes flicker towards it.

"My lord, I mean coal."

I went with him to the far field, to see where the recent heavy rain had caused the land to slide away, sheer down the side of the valley. It was poor enough ground, suitable only for the sturdy Swaledale ewes, and the grass was thin. Beneath the soil, gleaming in the wet, I saw the strong seam of darkness running like an artery into the side of the hill. My tenant was quite right, it was coal, and the opportunity was not lost on either of us.

Within a few months, by the end of the winter, the seam had been opened up. I was regarded as a benefactor, for my land was providing work and pay. And it was providing me with the funds to carry out my will, too – except that it was not enough. I needed more. And soon the opportunity came that would allow me to achieve my ends. But to do that, I needed to leave the land.

When I was a child, my condition was not so marked. We did not travel far, true – mainly to the local market town of Mowick, in the governess' dogcart. As long as I remained in the cart, all was well, but shortly after my seventh birthday, I noticed a curious thing. I had left the cart and walked across the square to a market stall that sold sweets. I bought a twist of butterscotch and returned. When I reached the dogcart, I found that the soles of my feet were burning against my thin leather soles. I said nothing, having learned early on that it was best to keep my feelings to myself. But when I removed my shoes, in the relative privacy of my chamber, I saw that my soles were scarlet. As I watched, the skin began to blister, as though I held a candle over a flame.

It did not happen again for some time. I was sent away to school and ran and played like other boys. But when I turned nine, I came indoors from a game with feet that were too sore to allow me to stand. After this, it happened more frequently, but never when I was at home.

I thought, at first, that it was some fancy of mine. I disliked the school, though not enough to make me refuse to go: my father would not have allowed this, anyway. Perhaps I was imagining it, I told myself, or persuading myself into some ailment. But when I was thirteen, I went with my father to a neighbour's house and there, standing at the summit of the stairs, the pain was enough to make me faint and fall.

I was carried home and placed in my bed, where my shoes were removed. When I regained consciousness it was to find my father sitting by the bedside, his head in his hands. He said, without preamble,

"I'd hoped you'd escape this."

"I don't understand." I sat up, and winced.

"It means – I don't know what the cause is. An illness, a curse. There are many stories, few explanations. It happens every so often and it skips a generation or two. The last – my grandfather."

I knew about him. He'd been confined to his bed; a permanent sickness, apparently.

"Sometimes it's worse: you can't step on the earth at all. It burns your feet, eventually eats away the flesh. It's a hard way to –" he hesitated, "to die."

"If they don't know what causes it, then they can't know what's to be done," I said blankly.

My father sighed. "My grandfather had the best doctors – the family had more money then. They tried a number of things. None of them worked."

"Did they try – prayer?" I found this embarrassing, not to be spoken about. My voice dropped to a whisper. My father looked equally embarrassed, although both of us were church-goers.

"Yes. A faith healer, too. One of the local farmers, said to have power in his hands. The vicar prayed. It's said they tried exorcism. No matter, nothing was successful. He died after a while."

"So what will happen to me?" But he did not need to answer that.

After this, I did not return to school but was educated, such as it was, at home. I quizzed my father about the fate of my great-grandfather, and others. And I decided that the line would end with me. The world is changing, anyway. England is different now: more movement of people, new industries. The world of the landed gentry is no longer as solid as it used to be and perhaps it was time that we ended. I did not tell these thoughts to my father, fearing his disappointment. I told him I would do my best and with that we all had to be content, but when he died, it was almost a relief to me, that he was spared what I might become.

The money from the coal would build the foundations. I had drawn up the plans myself: initially I knew little of these things, but over time I had ordered books and made a study. And I intended to employ someone, a person who understood such matters and would not ask too many questions. A nobleman, whimsical, eccentric, planning a folly: this was not unusual. I would not be able to progress unless I garnered more capital, however, and as these things often do, my affairs fell into place.

An elderly cousin in London died – one of my mother's few remaining relations. He left his property to me, on condition that I myself went down to the city to view it before I disposed of it, or kept it as I might. Being from my mother's side of the family, it was unlikely that he knew of my affliction: my father had never told my mother, apparently. Perhaps Lord Chase considered me a stick-at-home, or some dilettante, or perhaps he had some other reason for insisting on my presence in the city after his death. Maybe it was punishment for never visiting him – and yet he had left everything to me. I was both guilty and grateful and, more than that, afraid.

I took a closed carriage, fearing to place my feet upon the ground. I told the coachman I was unwell. Accustomed to the foibles of the aristocracy, he merely grunted. I left the house in the care of the servants, and set off. It was a long journey and I was obliged to stop once, at an inn in Hertfordshire. The short walk from the carriage to the building was enough to set my feet aflame and by the time I reached the bedroom, they had blistered and seared. I spent an unpleasant night. I suppose I could have insisted on being carried, but I preferred pain to humiliation. I was, to all intents and purposes, a fit young man in my twenties, not some fragile fop. I could not bear the stares and whispering that would surely ensue: let it be thought I had some injury if anyone saw me wince, but one that I would endure, uncomplaining.

We reached the smoky outskirts of the city in due course. I immediately realised that it wasn't just the issue of my footsteps that would be a problem, but the very air. The soot seemed to congest into my lungs, reminding me that although I might curse my confinement to Mow Cop, it nonetheless bore privileges. It was spring then, with the young oaks flaring green against the stormy northern sky, and the pall above the capital did not appeal. We made our way to the house, trundling slowly through the filthy streets, and already I felt the soles of my feet start to tingle again.

The funeral had not yet taken place and my cousin lay in the parlour in his coffin. It was sealed, but the fume of decay was evident in the room: I suppose we should have been grateful that it was not high summer. There was murmured talk among the servants who, nonetheless, seemed grateful for my appearance. But there was much to be sorted out: the lawyer to meet and consult, and so on and so forth. Although the servants must find other work when the house was sold, it was at least a decision. By the evening I was exhausted by pain and retired early. The chamber that had been set out for me was on a higher floor and I found, to my relief, that the pain lessened the higher I climbed. This was an indication, to me, that my plan was the right one.

Next day, I tested it. The highest place in London was the great cathedral, Wren's masterpiece. When my other business was principally done, I took a carriage there and scaled the stairs, hobbling out onto the Golden Gallery into the rainy afternoon. London reeled away below in my initial moment of dizziness and I cursed: bound too closely to earth, the height snatched at me. But then it steadied and I watched as at a marvel. The tiny figures scurrying mice-like beneath, the snaking gleam of the Thames and the ships upon it, the shadow of the hills beyond. It was cold, with an east wind from the sea snapping at my hair, but the pain was a distant glow.

A tower. High enough that I would be borne away from the hating earth, a place where I could be free of its constraints and live out my years without agony.

I sought an architect once I had returned home, finding one in York. It took some weeks for me to recover, but I think my healing, temporary though it was, had been speeded by the knowledge that I need not leave the land again. I wrote to the architect and he came to see me. By this time the money from my cousin had been placed in my bank, and I was able to present myself as an eccentric young peer, longing for a folly. I had my father's study decorated and did not show the architect the rest of the mouldering house. If it decayed after my own death, so be it. In due course, his plans came back to me and we pored over them together. I'd had a fancy, so I told him, to stay in the tower at night sometimes, so that I might study the stars, for I had a great interest in astronomy. He took this without comment and I saw that he had little interest in why I wanted a tower, only in the planning and construction of it – as a craftsman, my reasons meant little to him.

Thus the tower was built, on the high ridge overlooking the sea. As soon as it was completed I moved into it; into a high chamber at the summit. It had a well not far away and the servants were instructed to bring me food twice a day. I spent my time reading, or looking out to sea. I studied the light on the water, both moon and sun, and starlight too. I became used to the wheel of the constellations above sea and land. I grew to learn the nature of the tides, and of the vessels that ploughed their way up and down the coast.

And time went by. I kept track of the years at first, but then lost that in the play of the seasons. I had not equipped the tower with a looking glass, either, although I kept my beard and hair trimmed with scissors. I rarely saw the servants, but one day the old woman who had attended me with her husband climbed the stairs to the tower to tell me that he had died.

"But you, my lord," she said, eyeing me askance, "You look little different to when you were a boy, and I a young woman, but now I am old, and you –"

I could not explain it. I told her that it was a measure of my illness and perhaps she believed me. I hoped she did not think it some form of witchcraft, but no one came to confront me. She continued to bring food, but soon after, this stopped. But by that time I had ceased to feel hunger. I expected to die, but continued to remain much as I had been, with an absence of bodily functions. Perhaps I would become ethereal, incorporeal, I wondered. Some months later, I sealed up the door of the tower with bricks.

In saving my life, I did not consider that I might not die. Yet here I remain. I have seen differences in the world: changes in the ships that plough the coastal waters, which once had sails, then did not, then gained their sails again but in much vaster form. Or the things, which I believe to be vehicles, which soared through the air for some years, then ceased. I have seen others, which again are larger, and of stranger form. I have seen people in many different costumes, coming now close to the tower (this always alarms me) and then moving away, but lately no one has come at all and no one to my knowledge has attempted access. Sometimes I wonder if the tower is even visible. The soles of my feet have long since healed. I do not care to experiment by walking once more upon the quiet earth, and so I shall remain, watching the light and the sea, and the stars, until my end, or their own.

# Nightjar

*When I first started writing, I went to a writing workshop in Brighton – I didn't think I was a workshop person, but it was very well run and out of it came a story called "Dancing Day", one of my first short stories. I sent it to Storm Constantine and it was edited by Graham Joyce – both sadly no longer with us and great losses to SFF – and published in* Visionary Tongue. *It was set in an alternative Constantinople which is divided into the mansions of various great families, and in which Christianity has never happened. Nightjar is set in this universe.*

*My family say that I am mute, but it's not true. I cannot speak the language of men, true enough, but I do speak another tongue, a secret language, which the world does not hear.*

*Shh, though. Do not tell. They must not know.*

The House of the Moon stands at the summit of the city, surrounded by sombre cypress. We pride ourselves that it was one of the first to be built here: our temple rooms lie deep within the rock of the citadel, the passages winding down like a root into the red stone. We have been here forever, forever, and we have given queens to the city, ministers, scribes, for this is a house of women. We breed carefully, selectively, with the male houses, and our bloodlines are guarded like gold.

But occasionally, those bloodlines produce people like me.

As a child, I learned to listen early. I understood what was said to me. I learned to read. But I did not speak. I did not see why I should; it seemed to me to add to the sound around me, which was already overwhelming. People's voices hissed or boomed; they battered, washing over me in blasts of noise. The sound of carts going past grated on me, the uneven clatter thundering in my ears. It seemed important to be as quiet as possible, as hushed. And so I did not speak. Sometimes, alone, I whispered a single chosen word: I had favourites, based on sibilance and syllable. I whispered them over and over, delighting in their taste on my tongue. But in public, never.

61

My mother and aunts took me to physicians, of course, all manner of quacks and even eminent people. I did not really understand what they were; I was too young. I only knew that we visited a lot of people who did a great many tests, involving both science and magic: I was assessed for possession, and found to be clear. My tongue and throat were examined, with great attention, and said to be sound. I thought all of these tests were boring, and withdrew even further into the recesses of my own head, telling stories to myself, rocking.

At last I was pronounced, by a consensus of doctors, to be either defective or merely wilful. This was a relief: I was not punished as such, but I was left to my own devices, instructed to keep to my own chamber and the gardens, and not to bother my family with my inconvenient and embarrassing presence, particularly when they had visitors. I understood this. Mute as I might be, I was nonetheless not an unappealing child: small, neat, my dark curls confined within a golden net, and I was always clean. I liked being neatly dressed. So when I was seen, I was admired, but then the admirer would discover that I could not speak and would begin invariably to offer advice. Since my family had more or less tried everything at this point, this was naturally infuriating, not least to myself, and it was, I thought, reasonable to keep me out of sight. And I was happy to be there. I liked my chamber, and the garden: it was contained, neat, controlled. I did not have to worry about it. And so I moved between chamber and garden, quite content. It did not occur to me as a child that I might be an actual burden, but later I realised the possibility and was able to disregard it, a result of overheard conversations about my elder sisters' dowries.

I had little to do with my sisters. I saw them occasionally, but they kept to their own chambers and lives which had nothing to do with me. They were not wicked, like the elder sisters I read about in my fairytale books, nor ugly, but I think it was more convenient for them to pretend that I did not exist. I used to watch them departing for the various balls and dances that filled their season, admiring from the summit of the stairs their gold, veridian, snowpale dresses and their ornately arranged hair. That glance was enough for me; I did not want to go where they were going. I wanted to stay behind.

On the night that I first talked to *her*, my sisters had gone to a ball, along with my mother as chaperone. I knew, from overhearing the servants, that this was a sun and moon ball, with costumes to match. I liked that idea. I was nine, and the idea of the two worlds, one fiery and blasting heat, the other cool and glowing, appealed to me. I pictured them revolving about one another: I had no idea of how the universe was actually arranged, that the astronomers of the city had many theories, of orbits and powers. I only knew that the spheres in the sky were beautiful, although I preferred the sun when it was a crimson ball, setting low over the limpid sea that I could glimpse from the upper reaches of the house. My sister, however, was no setting sun, but resplendent in bright golden net, while my younger sister Mennetta was the cool moon, tightly lashed in silver thread. I watched them glide across the hall to the great double doors, then they passed into the evening and, quite content, I went back inside the house.

I was not supposed to open the garden door at night. I was not supposed to know how, but I had paid careful note once I had grown tall enough to reach the handle, and was able to open it silently, hitching it up so that it did not creak. It was a door made of glass, a very faint green so that through it, in daylight, the garden took on an emerald tinge. Tonight, it was not quite dark: a crescent moon rode on its back in an aquamarine sea and a single faithful star followed. I wanted to see it without the intervention of glass and so I opened the door and stepped out into the cool evening.

The garden was scented with flowers, heat, the distant sea. I stood ankle deep in grass, tracing each one: jasmine, the velvet roses. High in the leaves, something gave a whirring cry: I knew what it was, the bird called the nightjar. After a moment, my eyes adjusted to the dusk and I could see it – a hunched shape, with its black-barred tail shadowy against the tamarisk. It whirred again, a warning call, and then it spoke.

"Who are you? I have seen you before." It had a clear voice like a bell. It looked at me sideways, out of a cold blue eye. Moonlight fell into that eye and was swallowed; I saw it drown. The eye grew brighter, a tiny lamp.

I said, "My name is Grania." But when I spoke, it didn't sound like words. I spoke in notes, whistling.

"You speak well," the nightjar said. It ruffled its feathers. "Who taught you?"

"No one."

"Then how is it that you can speak the tongue of birds?"

"I don't know."

The bird seemed affronted. "Someone must have taught you."

"I don't remember it if they did. I do not speak to people. Perhaps that has something to do with it."

"You do not speak to your own kind? Why not?"

"I don't think they'd understand me."

"Humans are fools. Most probably you are right."

"So do you think that I can speak to you because I do not speak to them?" In my mind, it made a strange kind of balance.

"Perhaps. Do you speak with other birds?"

"No. You are the first."

"How curious," the nightjar said. "I shall go now, but I think I shall come and see you again."

"I'd like that."

Without another word, the bird spread its broad wings and sailed up towards the spikes of cypress at the citadel.

In the morning, I rose with the sun. My sisters would not be up for several hours, late after the ball. The household slowly gathered itself together. I read my book in the window seat. Then, around three in the afternoon, my mother's maidservant, flustered, came to tell me that there was a visitor.

"A Madam Lilitu. We have not seen her before. We don't know who she is."

I smiled politely as she fussed with my hair, accompanied her to the hallway. I recognised Madam Lilitu at once, of course. I knew her cold blue eye, her black feathery hair, and the grey-and-night barred train of her dress. The nightjar had a disguise as a woman, or perhaps the other way around.

She turned her head when she saw me and fixed me with a moon-coloured eye. As human, it had a tiny dark dot at the centre.

"So," she said, "This is Miss Grania. I should like to talk to her."

"My daughter," my mother said, looking awkward. "She does not — does not —"

"Speak. I know. No matter."

My mother fell back under that chill blue glare as Madam Lilitu swept me into the study and closed the door. Her gown was collared with feathers, black and grey, and they shivered and trembled as she moved.

"You're the nightjar," I said, whistling.

She put a gloved finger to her lips. "Hush. Do not speak the language of birds here. Someone might notice. You would be surprised at how many eyes there are, all manner of spies."

"Spies?" I whispered.

"Oh yes. The temples. Always on the watch, for likely spirits."

I did not know what she meant and was too shy to ask. But she went on, "For instance, the priestesses of the Wife, the many-eyed. They always like to know about potential candidates."

I had heard of the Wife, of course; the temple was a powerful one, and big. I was not sure if I had understood her correctly but the idea that such an institution might be interested in me was alarming and I felt myself shrink.

"Of course," Madam Lilitu went on, "This is why I myself have come." Her collar trembled. "This is not a form I prefer. No wings, for a start."

"What do you want from me?"

"A mute child. No one will suspect. I want to present you as a candidate to the Temple of the Wife. When you are there, I want you to listen, to the Wife's birds."

"The peacocks?" I'd seen them once. They were very beautiful, but all they did was shriek.

"The many-eyed, yes. I want you to find out what you can from them."

"But they would never consider me," I protested.

"Why not? Many of their priestesses have taken a vow of silence. What better candidate could there be than one who does not talk?" She looked into the distance for a moment and I could almost hear what she was thinking: *besides, her mother would welcome the chance to be rid of her.*

"I don't want to leave my home."

"It might not be for long. It depends what you find out." She shut her fan with a decisive snap and I knew that I had no choice in the matter. "I will speak to your mother directly."

As I had suspected, my mother jumped at the idea. Three days later, a carriage appeared, bearing the insignia of the Wife. A sad-eyed, solemn girl climbed out, bowed to my mother, handed over some papers, and my mother handed over me. I was shown into the stuffy interior of the carriage and we trundled away from the House of the Moon, to the Temple of the Wife.

My first impressions were that it was huge and cavernous, built of dark red marble that reminded me of meat, and hung with heavy velvet drapes. The acolytes' dormitory was at the back: neat rows of beds, each concealed behind a curtain. No one spoke to me, although the acolytes eyed me with faint curiosity and approval: I would threaten no one. The occasional eldritch scream from the direction of the gardens suggested the presence of peacocks.

But I did not understand how I was to carry out the nightjar's mission. The acolytes, including myself, were cloistered. It was not an unpleasant existence. We had classes, in which we were instructed in methods of silent ritual. We had prayers, in which we did not participate directly, but sat with meek, bowed heads. We had tasks to perform, such as cleaning candlesticks and statues. All in all, it was not onerous and I found that I did not mind the routine: it was calm, and in the main I was left alone. The other girls were kinder than my sisters, if distant, and did not pinch me or pull my hair, or any of the other ways of bullying in which I knew some girls indulged. I spent a lot of time, however, worrying about my task. I did not know when the nightjar would be coming back: what if she found out that I had failed? I had not glimpsed so much as a peacock's tail feathers since my arrival, and their distant screams were just that: shrieks beyond the walls.

Then, a week or so after my arrival, we were given a treat. We were allowed outside.

The gardens of the Temple of the Wife were beautiful: carefully sculpted, with vistas and fountains. They were far larger than the gardens at home and I stared, amazed.

"Aren't they lovely?" one of the speaking priestesses said, smiling at me. "You have two hours. You can go where you like."

I nodded and when she turned away I ran off, across the daisy-starred lawn, to the edge of a high cypress grove. I needed to find a peacock.

In the end, I found three: a cock and two peahens. They were strolling along the edge of the grove, the male's tail trailing in quivering magnificence. And they were chatting.

"Oooh, how beautiful the sky is, and the sunlight. How sparkling the water!"

"My dear, how wonderful you look today! And our lord is glorious!"

"A marvellous sight!"

I realised, with a sinking heart, that they were, in fact, pea-brained. The male said nothing, only preened. I watched them for a while; they showed no sign of being aware of my presence. After a while I gave up and went in search of more peacocks, while the governess priestesses watched us indulgently. I found a second group, but they, too, were witless.

"You won't learn anything from them, you know." I looked up. A bulbul sat in a nearby tree, ruffling its feathers.

"How do you know I wanted to?"

"Oh, humans always admire peacocks. But they're idiots. All except two and you might meet those, you might not."

"Who are they?"

"You'll see," the bulbul said, and flew away, leaving me to stand and think.

We were gathered back inside well before dusk, and went early to bed.

On the next night, the nightjar came back. I was in the washroom, alone, and the window was open, revealing one bright star. The nightjar perched on the sill.

"Well? Have you discovered anything?"

"I have discovered that peacocks have no wits."

The nightjar did not laugh, but her pale eye brimmed with amusement.

"I could have told you that. It's something that everyone knows. Don't worry. You'll learn something eventually. I'll come back, every week."

And so the time wore on. I became more and more accustomed to the Temple of the Wife. I liked the peace and quiet, and found a deeper meaning in the prayers and invocations to which we listened. At last, when I had been resident for perhaps eight months, we were told that we were to enter the first stage of initiation.

We prepared for ten days, in which we ate only certain kinds of food: red and white. We spent hours with bowed heads before the statue of the Wife, listening for what she might say. She did not speak to me, but I felt a warmth in her presence. And then the night of initiation came.

We were taken to an antechamber and dressed in red. Our hands and faces were marked with sacred oil and we filed down, down, a long flight of stone steps into the heart of the rock on which the Temple stood. My face was veiled, but through it I saw a scarlet hued, flickering darkness. Below, we waited in a long line while the speaking priestesses chanted and we prayed.

Finally, my turn came. I was led into an inner chamber, which smelled strongly of smoke, and I heard a door close behind me. I waited. The smoke made my head swim. I could see a little through the veil, and there was a throne, but it was empty. Then, around the stone corner of the throne, strutted a peacock. It was at least twice the size of those in the gardens and its bright dark eye glittered with knowledge.

"You are one of the two," I said, without thinking. The bird pecked forwards.

"You can speak?"

"Yes."

"Wife! Come and listen!" A peahen, also large, came to join him. Her feathers, though less ostensibly magnificent, gleamed a soft sunset gold. "She can speak our language."

"I am from the House of the Moon," I said. "My name is Grania."

"Do you wish to remain here? It is a question asked of all initiates."

"Yes," I said, for I found that I did. I liked the silence, and the calm. I did not want to return to my mother's frustration and the politics of my sister's marriages, nor did I wish to be forced into marriage myself one day, as seemed possible, although it was hard to say who would have me. But this way, paradoxically, I could avoid that, by entering the service of the Wife. "Yes, I would like to stay. But there is one difficulty…"

"Tell me," the peacock said, and so, betraying, I did.

A day later, the nightjar returned.

"Have you discovered anything?" she asked, as usual.

But for the first time I spoke aloud to someone else, in my own language.

"I do not understand you," I said, and as I spoke, I felt the spell break and part of me fly away, into the darkness and towards the one bright star. The nightjar opened her beak and her rattling song fell onto the night air, but I could no longer understand it. She spread her wings with an angry cry and sailed out, leaving me standing in the window, bereft and yet content.

I never spoke to a bird again, and the peacock's empty chatter was just that, the sound of a bird's voice. I saw the peacock king and his wife, many times in the years to come, and although their gaze still seemed to brim with intelligence and, it seemed to me, compassion, I was never able to comprehend them. Nor did I speak again, and with this, I was happy. We make our own choices, and some of us do not need a voice.

# On Milk Hill

*I started writing these stories (they're set in the same world as the Fallow sisters novels) in lockdown. There's another one in this anthology, too. They take place around Avebury, one of my favourite British landscapes, in what's known in Comet Weather as 'White Horse Country.' The Wiltshire Downs are made of chalk, with the famous white horses of Uffington and Pewsey and others cut into them. This story isn't about those, but it's an ancient part of the country.*

I came to the village four times that year: on a wet green night in spring, a baking noonday in summer, on a golden afternoon in September and on an icy morning not far from the sight of Christmas. That last time, having finally taken retirement and sold my house in Bristol, I stayed.

The village I'd moved to is known for two things: an excellent pub, much frequented by cheerful bikers, and an immense interlinked stone circle. The pub is old and said to be haunted. The stones are older. They, too, are said to be haunted, or enchanted, or possessed, or channels of energy, or the centre of leys. Horror novels and at least one TV series have featured the stones, but, perhaps curiously, I have had very little to do with them. They are an element of my morning and evening walks with the dog, always on a lead, for the stones also provide convenient scratching posts for sheep and rabbits play around their bases early in the morning. But the stones appear inanimate to me: large, gnarled edifices of lichen-encrusted rock. Some of them have almost-faces, just as the lumps of flint that you pick up in the nearby fields have faces: a grimacing mouth, an eye. But despite the occasional feeling of being watched, as a stone loomed out of the chilly morning mist, the stones seemed to me to be sunk in their long dream, uninterested in myself or Monty the terrier.

To me, the most numinous place in the whole village was the big stand of beech on the curve of the road, as it approaches the little grid of houses. This was my lodestar in all weathers and I got to know the beeches well. Unlike the stones, they followed the transformations of the year; their stone-like trunks and branches bare in winter, then greening with bright spears which formed a dark summer shade and finally fell like pointed copper coins onto the sheep-cropped grass.

After my decision to remain, renting a small flint-fronted cottage on the edge of the village, I spent the next few months settling in. I got to know the local area: which pubs served a good Sunday lunch, which ones did not, where the local second-hand bookshops were (thank you, Marlborough), and which buses ran into Swindon and other local towns, to save me driving. I got to know the locals and because I am friendly and unthreatening (a middle aged woman in a bobble hat is feared by no one), and willing to join the occasional committee, I found myself made welcome. I even sometimes went to church: an old church, Anglo Saxon, with its curious serpent carved font.

As one does, I got to know a large number of people through dog walking. I knew the dogs' names before I knew the identities of their owners. I became known as Monty's Mum to an equally vague population. And walking Monty became one of my favourite pastimes: we went across the footpath to the inverted pudding basin of Silbury Hill, headed along the ridges which followed the curve of the stones, or out over the fields, cut with white slashes of chalk and studded with flints. But our favourite walk was to cut across one of the stone circles, along the field edge, up to the stand of beeches, and back again. From the cottage, it took perhaps half an hour.

On one particular occasion, since there were obviously no sheep in the ploughed field in which we walked, I let Monty off the lead. He scurried about the hedge, ignoring the last of the withered haws and the rags of leaves: he was more interested in the holes in the earth that betrayed the presence of rabbits. He did not, thankfully, head down any of them. Apart from the possibility of getting stuck, I could smell the musky, earthy scent of badger hanging around the winter air. It was bitter clear and close to dusk; the moon was already visible as a fat crescent in the east. Looking west, the beeches were silhouetted against the deep green sky. We headed towards them until my boots were crunching on last year's mast.

Something moved among the beech trunks and I called Monty sharply back, then clipped on his lead. Sheep don't always stay where they were supposed to and I'd caught a glimpse of white woolly back. Then it stood up. It wasn't a sheep, but a person.

The village is popular with contemporary pagans, usually at the quarter days of the year. It's not a path I follow myself but I'd learned a little bit about it, mainly from Druids in the Red Lion, out of sheer self-defence: the parking can become challenging at these times. Now, as far as I knew, we were between dates, but visitors still came, drawn by the romance of the stones. Sometimes people slept out among them although you'd be brave or foolhardy to do that in winter. But if you had a sheepskin cloak... Or perhaps they were just walking. They'd hidden, by now. I had evidently alarmed them.

"Sorry!" I called. "Didn't mean to startle you. The dog's fine with people."

There was no reply. I could sense the person lurking behind one of the beech trunks, and felt a moment of unease, as any woman does when on her own. I skirted the beeches, deciding to head for home. I did not like to look over my shoulder – it seemed a sign of weakness – but I couldn't stop myself. I was glad I did, because the person was not some man with dodgy intentions, but a girl. She was wrapped in the sheepskin, like a big woollen duvet, and her hair fell in strings around her face. I should not have been able, in this dim light, to see the colour of her eyes, but I *could* see them, and they were yellow, like a goat's eyes, like the last lemon light of the sun. She said something but I didn't understand it. It was hard to tell how old she was: her cheeks were hollow, as if she was missing teeth. She was clutching something and it moved, but I couldn't see what it was. A dog, a lamb? It was quite large, and squirming.

We stared at each other. Then she stepped behind a tree and did not come out again. With trepidation, I went back to the beech trees and looked. There was no one there. On the ground, when I examined it with the light on my phone, the beech mast lay undisturbed. My skin pricked. I tugged on Monty's lead and walked quickly home.

By the following morning, I had rationalised the whole episode. A traveller, one of the many van dwellers dotted throughout the English countryside, a response to the housing crisis and a wish to have at least the illusion of freedom. Probably she had been even younger than I'd thought, and nervous. As for the bundle – her dog, like Monty.

When I stepped outside the back door to let the dog out, I found the garden covered in hoar frost. There was a bite to the air and a faint veil of mist over the village. I made a cup of tea, drank it, put Monty on his lead and headed out across the fields. I told myself that I would not go near the beeches, but would follow the high bank of the ditch and the curve of the stone circle. I did this. I could see the beeches in the distance, looking innocent and picturesque in the mist, like a painting by Paul Nash. We crossed the road and into the flinty field, the ridges of the furrows knobbly with frost. My back was to the beeches now and I congratulated myself on finding a rational explanation. But then I saw the girl.

She was running across the field, surefooted as a hare, in fur boots that looked as though they had been stuffed with hay, although the furrows had slowed me, in my sensible hiking wear, down considerably. She was panting, however, and she still clutched the bundle. Then she caught her foot, nearly went down, recovered. Out of the mist behind her I saw a man, also running. He was bulky, wrapped in furs, and he threw a spear. Monty barked and the girl stumbled against me, making me stagger. But the spear whistled past and vanished and neither of us fell. The girl thrust the bundle into my arms and fled on, disappearing in the spear's path. The man gave a cry of rage, flung out his arms, and was gone. The image of the spearhead hung in my mind for a second, a bronze blade, bright as a beech leaf.

Monty was wagging his tail uncertainly. It had happened so fast, so dream-like, that I had not had time to be afraid, just startled and bewildered. I looked down at the bundle. A small goat's face peered out of the fleece in which it was wrapped, blinking.

"Well," I said, nonplussed. There was nothing spectral about the goat; it felt solid, indeed heavy. Feeling foolish, I carried it home and put it in a box by the fire. Then, since it was past nine by now, I shut Monty in the bedroom, just in case his ancient lupine ancestry decided to assert itself, and went to the local shop. This has a section for people with unusual diets, given that there are a lot of them round here, and bought a carton of goat's milk. I felt a bit smug about this: I had been presented with a problem, but I had found a sort of solution.

When I got back, Monty had not managed to escape from the bedroom and there was a sheepskin hump in the box by the fire. Gone to sleep, I thought. I looked. A human baby lay there, looking up, its yellow eyes bright and malign. I dropped the carton of goat's milk, which luckily did not break, and sank onto the sofa, shaking.

"Oh God," I said, aloud. The box was still. I forced myself to get up and look. The little goat again lay peacefully, eyes closed.

I had, on the way to the shop, thought about phoning one of the local farmers and asking if they wanted an extra kid. Now I was thinking more along the lines of calling social services. But what on earth would they do with a baby that was sometimes a goat and sometimes a human child? I'd never heard of such a thing. It also struck me that I might simply be cracking up. I didn't feel mad, but perhaps you don't?

When the goat woke up, it remained a goat, to my enormous relief. I got some of the milk down it, via a sippy cup that a friend with a small child had once left behind. It drank readily enough and went back to sleep. Random episode, imagining things, trick of the light, all went through my head as I chopped vegetables for my lunchtime soup. But in my heart I knew that the world had not lied to me, that I was not mad, that the child which had been entrusted into my care was animal and human both.

And a bit more than that. When I next went into the living room and looked in the box, a yellow eyed dappled bird was sitting there. It had downy, youthful feathers and a curved beak. It looked a bit like a curlew but I knew that curlews do not have long bills as chicks; those come later on. Milk was now out of the question. Mealworms? It stared at me out of those unnerving eyes, which seemed to me no more malign really than the eyes of a goat or a sheep.

Monty did not like being shut out of the living room, so I took the box and put it on the kitchen table. Now I was thinking more in lines of the RSPB. It was horribly tempting to just hand this over to someone and let them deal with it, but my conscience wouldn't let me. Was this why people left infants on doorsteps? Did this happen regularly and folk just didn't talk about it? I did not think this was the case. In fifty five years, one would surely have heard *something* about it.

Over the next twenty-four hours, the child continued to change, at random intervals. Sometimes it was a baby, sometimes goat or bird, but that seemed to be the limit of its transformations. I suppose I could have contacted the press, made biological history, become famous, but this was a ghastly prospect and I felt very strongly, without knowing why, that this ought to be kept absolutely secret. I felt a complicity with the girl – the child's mother? She had not looked old enough, but notions of maturity change throughout history. I also felt a responsibility to both of them, remembering the bright leaf of a bronze spear. And I was afraid that if I did tell someone, it might make the child stick in one shape and I'd just look like a lunatic.

The child absorbed milk, as baby or goat, but it did not seem to pass it at the other end, which I considered one of life's smaller mercies. Perhaps it needed all the energy it could get to change form? I didn't know how these things were supposed to work. I had no knowledge of magic: I'd never even read Harry Potter. I liked factual documentaries and non-fiction. I knew a lot about nature, but supernature was out of my wheelhouse.

Better start looking it up, then. I did a lot of Googling, but the closest mention I could find were references to changelings, and this didn't really seem to fit the bill. Witches were supposed to have been able to turn into hares and cats, which I did know about, but the baby/goat/curlew axis did not appear to be a thing. The girl and her pursuer were presumably Bronze Age folk, but the ancient tribes of Britain were just human beings like ourselves: evolution didn't work that quickly, as far as I was aware. Or did it? But we have not been animals, save for the very distant past, evolving from the shrew-like things nimble enough to escape the feet of the dinosaurs.

I continued to read up on all this, but got nowhere. I was also starting to feel trapped. An old friend was supposed to be coming down for a few days at the end of the week and I didn't know what the hell I'd tell him. *I have this baby now. No, of course it's not mine! A young woman on the run gave him to me. Sometimes it's a goat. What?*

I'd have to put Dean off and that would be awkward: he'd already left Scotland, where he lives, and was at someone's birthday party in Wales. I'd have to find some sort of excuse…

While I was debating all this, the weather grew colder. My walks with Monty shortened, but the countryside was so beautiful in its vestments of frost, and I was so nervous about the situation in the house, that I didn't like to cut out our walks altogether. Then, on the night of the third day, I woke to hear someone in the garden.

At first, I thought it was a fox: we get a lot of them around here and I've grown accustomed to that sudden vixen's scream. They say it sounds like a woman, but I've never thought that: it sounds like a fox, unique. Cat software running on dog hardware, someone once said to me about foxes. So when I heard the cry, my nerves, jangling me awake, said: *vixen.* I got out of bed and walked across the chilly room to the window. I sleep with the curtains open, liking to see the passage of the moon and constellations across the pane on clear nights. This night was very clear and the motion-sensitive security light had come on, illuminating the little fox standing in the middle of the lawn. Then no fox was there. The girl stood in the light, looking up at me.

My immediate feeling was one of relief: she had come for her baby. Thank God. I ran downstairs in my slippers, seized the box with the sleeping goat, and went outside. Hopefully, she wouldn't revert to fox and eat it… But she wasn't there. *Damn it,* I thought. I put the box on the garden table and looked around. The end of the garden edges one of the fields and I could see the fox, running away. Had she just come to see that her child was safe? But then the animal paused and turned, looking back. I got the message. *Follow me.*

Swearing under my breath, I went back into the house and found a Barbour and my hiking boots. My fleecy pyjamas would have to do and fortunately, since the house is so cold, I sleep in socks. The fox was still poised, waiting. I took the box and went after her.

She led me a quarter of a mile or so across the fields, often stopped and looking back to see if I was following. About halfway, she changed into a girl again. I pursued her through the avenues of standing stones, bare and sparkling with frost under the light of the moon, up over the cursus ditch and then I knew where she was heading: to the pudding basin-shaped hill, the man-made hill of Silbury, which stands just off the southern main road. It, too, was quite white: a dome like the moon rising out of the earth. I saw the girl, fox again, start to climb.

By now I was seriously out of breath. The box was heavy, the baby was human once more, and it took me some time to clamber up the slopes of the hill, which you are not supposed to do; the National Trust say it is too fragile. I didn't think I had a choice. I had thought it white with frost, but halfway up I looked down at the ground and saw that it was bare chalk: in my day, the hill is grassed over. The girl was standing at the summit, legs braced.

Breathlessly, I said, "I hope you're going to take him back!"

"Yes," she said. I did not think she was speaking English, somehow, but I could understand her. "Yes, I'm ready now."

"What about that man?"

"The warrior? Yes, he is still after me. But now we are ready for *him*. You have given me time."

"Why is he chasing you?"

"He is the new kind of man," she said. "The kind which stays the same." She turned her head and spat. Then she held out her hands. I put the box down, picked up the fleece-swaddled goat and gave it to her. She nodded once, perhaps in thanks, spun around and disappeared. In the east, the sun came up over the horizon in a burst of sudden gold, dazzling me. Beneath my feet, the chalk glowed the blue-white of milk, then gradually greened again, but it was still starred with frost. I picked up the box and walked slowly home in the growing light.

# Radioblack

*Years ago I started writing some short stories set in the Pale, which is the Western part of the UK after some unexplained catastrophe, in which people have reverted to a more or less nineteenth century way of life. This is set there, and involves another obsession which you'll also find in the fourth Fallow sisters novel,* Salt on the Midnight Fire: *the Shipping Forecast.*

I first found the device in a ruined cottage high in the Glen, overlooking the straits, on a dark day in November. I'd gone up there to look for bilberries. I knew about the cottage, of course, having lived on the southern shore all my life, in the huddle of houses that still hugged the shingle bank. There was a road, too, but this had long since broken up, soon after the placement of the Pale, when all traffic stopped. There were bits of old cars on the moor road still, but most of the metal had been hacked up long ago and used for other things. I had been into the cottage before, when I was a child, but it was filthy and the shelves were bare: anything of use had been ransacked.

Indeed, I had no intention of entering it that day, but I was trapped by the weather. When I set out it was fair, with puffed clouds drifting over the winter-grey of the straits, but when I got to the top of the Glen I could see a ragged lace of rain far out to sea and it wasn't long before it came further inland. I'd got my berries by then, picking fast, racing the rain. If it comes, I thought, I could duck into the shelter of the cottage: much of the roof had gone, but a section remained. There were no trees up here, only a scrubby stand of hawthorn beside the lean-to. Now, even early into the winter, its leaves had flown on the gales and the pulpy scarlet berries had been picked bare by the birds. When I straightened up, the first fat scalds of rain pattered onto my skirt and I hastened to the cottage, ducking under the sagging lintel. How old was this place? It must have dated since long before the Pale, perhaps one of those that had been abandoned in the clearances, even, then restored. Some incomer from the mainland, maybe, doing the place up, then having to flee in turn when the events that led to the Pale took place, many years ago. Or dying, although there was no sign of bones.

The rain was hammering on the remains of the roof now and beyond the small square of window the sky was livid black. Wrapped in woollens and oilskin, I did not feel warm, but found the worst of the November chill warded off. The cottage was dim and dirty. I poked about, trying to avoid the soot and dust that covered everything. In a far corner, half hidden under a fallen beam, there was a box. I dragged it out and forced it open. Inside I discovered a notebook, mainly blank but with a few jottings in a language that wasn't English or Gaelic, a bracelet made of round wooden beads, and the device.

I didn't know what it was. I thought it might be a kind of radio: it had knobs and a dial, and it wasn't unlike the village's single short wave radio, which was used to communicate – when it worked – with communities up and down the islands. They'd shown us how to operate it in school, in case of an emergency. The rain had now set in heavily. I picked up the radio and put it on the table, then dragged a dusty chair across the room and sat twiddling the dials. I was not expecting it to work and it did not. After a time I grew bored of pretending that I was listening to news from across the world, or speaking to friends far away, and I went back to the doorway to look out. The Glen was filled with murk and mist despite it not yet being late afternoon and the sky remaining light enough. I thought the rain was easing off a little, and I ought to collect my bag of bilberries and make a run for it before it grew worse again. But as I turned back to the empty cottage, the radio gave a hiss of static.

I stared at it. The thing couldn't possibly be working – it had batteries. I knew what those were and they would have run out long ago. There was a stain of greenish rust down the side of the place where they were installed. But the radio was hissing away and then it began to speak.

I did not understand what it said at first, but then it spoke names which I recognised: *Hebrides. South Utsire, Faroes*. They were the names of islands, the first being the chain in which I now stood. My island was Skye. The voice continued: English, speaking of rain and gale. The accent was odd, even through the static. Perhaps this was how English people spoke? Then the voice petered out and the radio fell silent.

I picked it up and wrapped it in my scarf. I put the notebook in my pocket; it would go into the village's communal resources as paper was so scarce. We had little need of it, I suppose, although there were still those of us who valued books. My mother, long dead now, had taught me to read and to worship the word, to speak properly. And I put the beads around my wrist. I thought that I would confess to the beads and even to the book, but not to the radio. That would be my secret. I was not even sure why, but I think I was afraid that I had imagined the voice, that madness had come to me on the west wind. I would put the radio in the box drawer beneath my bed, high in the eaves of my father's cottage, and tell no one.

When I got back, I did just that. The radio remained there for a week, my secret. I did not switch it on again: I was still half-convinced that I had been mistaken, that the static was the hissing on the wind, that the voice I had heard was the voice that sometimes comes in the deep silence of the wild places, when you've been listening to too little for too long. I went about my daily tasks with a renewed will, seeking to fill up the gaps in my life.

Perhaps if I'd had a lover, it would have been different. But there was only myself and my father in the cottage, and the older people of the village. The younger men – the few that there were – had gone south, seeking work or love or something else, and maybe they had found it, for they had not returned. Who knew if anything much was out there still, down the coast? The few travellers we met came from the north, a one-way journey, as though the north were a leaky sieve through which water poured, unable to go back up. My father had been north when he was young but now he was in his fifties and his mind was already going, as so often happened with the old folk these days – a legacy of the past. He could remember some things but not others and sometimes he altered stories I knew well, adding fanciful things, which I knew not to be true. He spoke of my mother, but often he could not recall her name.

So I spent my time in busyness, quietly, upon my own resources and the thought of the radio sat in the back of my mind, waiting.

Then came a bad day. It was not the first. The rain lashed against the coast, the fire went out with a hiss of water down the smoky chimney and my father chose that day to run away. He did this periodically, and this time it almost killed him. We searched for over an hour, up and down the only street and then out onto the high ridge of the cliffs. The turf was slippery from the wet and the seabirds wheeled and mewed, protesting against this invasion of their territory. If he had gone over, I thought numbly, we would have to wait till the body washed up, if it ever did. Sometimes the sea kept what she claimed. I grieved, as I so often did, for the man he had been: the strong man with the fair, clever mind, now rotten like old cheese. I was wordless with gratitude when Ben Overshore came panting up the cliff to tell us to call off the search, that he had been found in the drainage ditch at the far end of the village. He was soaked but living still. The men carried him back home, the women helped me build up the fire and he lay huddled before it all night, wrapped in sheepskin. I thought he would die but he did not.

He lay there all the next day, as the rain hammered on the roof. In the afternoon I left him and went upstairs and took the radio from its hiding place. I laid it on the woven cover of my bed. It had become the most interesting thing I owned, beyond even my books, and as I touched the dial, I did not expect it to work. Sure enough, it seemed dead. I left it there and went to the clothes chest, and behind me the device hummed like a bee and spoke.

*Forties, Cromarty, Forth, Tyne.*

The man who spoke sounded calm; a kind voice, I thought.

*Fisher. German Bight. Humber. Thames.*

The Thames was a river, running through the great city that had lain beyond the Pale, and Germany had been a place, or so I thought. I knew that Ben Overshore's family had an atlas, one of the few remaining in the village. I found a pencil and wrote down the names: it would help me to remember. The radio fell silent and the rain eased and I went back down the stairs to tend to my father. He was breathing, but asleep.

In the night, I woke. The radio was on again and the voice was speaking out, small and cold in the dark.

*Forth, Tyne. Fisher.*

The names rolled out; I believed they were all names now and in the morning I would go to the Overshore's house and look at the atlas. Through the window there was a single star, just above the horizon line of the sea, greensilver over the inky black. I watched until it passed beyond the window frame. There was a whole land out there, Eire, which I had never seen; islands to the north, the south, and I had been nowhere. The farthest I had been was the other side of the island. This was ordinary, few people had travelled, and those people were men. But I felt a sudden longing for that star. I got up from the bed and with my feet icy on the floorboards even in my rough socks, I craned my neck to seek it again: it had vanished behind incoming rain.

In the morning, the sky had cleared. My father ate a little porridge. I took the shore road, the old tarmac nearly gone now and half-buried beneath the shingle, and climbed the hill to the Overshore cottage. Ben was out fishing but his mother was there, and fetched the old book from the cupboard.

"I look at it sometimes," she told me. "But not for a while now." I sat down in her old chair by the smouldering fire and opened the book. I found some of the names in the list at the end of the atlas, which I think was only of these islands: the big mainland, most of which was now lost beyond the Pale, and my islands, and the north. But I found many of the names: they were the sea roads, or islands. They linked the land like a girdle, or a thrown net. I thanked Ben's mother and walked back down the hill to my own place and my father. The names were burning in my head like beacons. *Cromarty. Firth. North Utsire. South Utsire.*

When I reached the cottage, my father was staring into the fire. He was sitting up, with his back against the edge of the settle. He looked at me wonderingly when I came through the door and shut it behind me.

"Who are you?"

"I am your daughter. My name is Margaret." This had happened before.

"I don't remember." His voice was reedy and querulous and thin.

"I know. It's all right."

We had bread and cheese but he was finding it difficult to swallow, as though he kept forgetting that he had something in his mouth. I had to watch him, in case he choked. It was not a good sign. Later in the afternoon, as I washed the dishes, I could hear him speaking to someone who was not there: perhaps my mother, or his own. But then, I could not criticise that: I with my radio. Yet if the voice on the radio was not real, how had I found the names in the atlas, for they were real? I did not feel that I was going mad.

In the night, I heard my father calling out. I hastened downstairs, stumbling into the room. He was quiet by then and lay watching the glowing peat of the fire as it died. I built it back up, so it was warm for him, and sat waiting until the dawn's grey stain came up behind the cottage. He died as the sun was rising and so quietly that it was some minutes before I realised that I could no longer hear his breath. I had made tea with a frond of yarrow; it would be no good to him now. Then I sat with him until I was sure that the shadow had passed over his face. I went out into the day and down to the shore where the first of the boats were coming back in from the night fishing. There were exclamations, sorrow, but I knew everyone felt it to be for the best. I did so myself. The men carried him to the small church, and the one whose turn it was to be priest, old Nelson, spoke a few words over him, a prayer, before the bell was rung and we left him. The funeral would be in a day's time.

My father was buried without fuss on a cold morning, with the gulls wheeling and shrieking overhead. I walked through the churchyard – the old graves, not the new ones on the hillside, one of which was now my father's. I put a sprig of yarrow on the mound of earth and went down through the brambles to the reedy edge of the shore. I stood there for a long time, looking out to sea. Then I went back to the cottage. I packed a bag: the notebook, some clothes, and my mother's scarf, which I wrapped around the radio. Then I took the shore path out, heading south to the port, to follow the sea roads.

# The Teahouse

*This is a DI Chen story: the Singapore Three tales are one of my most successful series. I started writing them years ago after a visit to a friend in Hong Kong who had a houseboat on Deep Water Bay. I loved the city's teahouses and bars, but I didn't meet any demons in them. At least, I don't think so.*

You get used to a place, however horrible it might be. Zhu Irzh was accustomed to horrible places; he spent enough time in them, after all. And some of them he was fond of – he had no objection to the classy restaurants that he went to with Jhai, with their panoramic views and hushed atmosphere, but if he was honest, he really preferred the greasy, steamy eateries that thronged around the docks in the shadow of Paugeng corporation's skyscraper, where anonymity was regarded as paramount. Teahouses, noodle bars, dives that served alcohol of dubious provenance and legality. Rooms filled with steam that hid both the grime and the cockroaches. Some of them might have been there before the city itself, from their feeling of permanence. The demon often saw non-humans in these places, sometimes out of the corner of his eye, but not infrequently in plain sight. Small individuals, curiously squat, with burned red skin; an elongated person sidling out of a back door. Amid the noise and smoke and hiss of the kitchens, they went unnoticed, minding their own business.

They were from Hell, or other hells. Zhu Irzh did not greatly care, as long as they left him alone, but some vestigial professionalism required that he took note of each one, just in case. You never knew when one of those people might show up in the middle of a crime scene. Also, there was a certain nostalgia to it. He wouldn't have said he *missed* Hell, precisely, but he had spent a lot of time in it, and touching base like this, keeping tabs on other demons in the city, made him feel that he wasn't entirely severed from his origins.

When he found the teahouse down Sea Island Street, therefore, he felt right at home. He had been on a stakeout, but it was clear that the person under surveillance, who had gone into the warehouse entrance some while before, would not coming out again for a bit. It was close to dusk, with a warm rain starting to fall, when Sergeant Ma appeared to relieve Zhu Irzh.

"Good luck," the demon said. "I don't know what he's doing in there but it's been the same for the last few days – he goes in at two in the afternoon and doesn't usually come out again until midnight. Possibly an illegal gambling ring."

"He's new in town," Ma said. "But he came in from Macau with a reputation for drug running. Kept his nose clean here so far – mind you, he's not been here long."

"Opium dens are a bit passe these days. But you never know. Lao says there's a magical block on the building, too – it's heavily warded."

"Oh well," Ma said philosophically. "Nothing we can do except wait."

He took his seat in the car and Zhu Irzh ducked through the rain. It was a little early for a beer, and although demon physiology processed alcohol somewhat more efficiently than its human equivalent, he was finding it harder to bounce back these days. Must be getting older. And Jhai had said something about a party that night. Besides, he was cold. Cup of tea it was…

He moved quickly through the downpour, dodging along the narrow streets that wound between the warehouses. At this point in the summer, the air was like breathing in soup. Zhu Irzh was not overly familiar with this part of the docklands and he was relieved, therefore, to see a sign proclaiming the presence of a teahouse, flickering neon through the murk. He pushed the door open and paused.

Everyone was staring at him. Which would have been fine, but none of them were human. They were all manner of beings – he recognised two demons from the lower levels, a tusked and glaring gentleman, and two animal headed spirits. And a number of pallid people, with hungry, haunted eyes. A waitress appeared, outwardly human too, except for her pallor and the sharp teeth.

"What's the matter?" she snapped at the clientele. "Haven't you seen a customer before?" To Zhu Irzh she said, "Sorry. Come in out of the rain."

"I just wanted some tea," Zhu Irzh said.

"No problem. I'll bring you a pot. Ignore them."

Zhu Irzh smiled at the room and sat down. He might as well have been back in Hell, with everyone staring suspiciously at everyone else. When the helpful waitress returned, he said, "So how long have you been here? I don't know this area well, but I don't think I've seen this place before."

"Oh," she said. "Not very long, really."

"I hope you're here for a long time to come," the demon said politely. The woman looked disconcerted. "I don't know..."

The tea, however, was excellent. Zhu Irzh sipped it, listening to the rain beyond its steamed-up windows and covertly watching the clientele. The waitress and the kitchen staff, whom he glimpsed briefly, all looked oddly similar. Same family, probably.

He was half expecting something to happen, but no, all remained peaceful, if a little tense. Zhu Irzh drank his tea and stood. A sideways glance told him that the bowls before the clientele contained something that did not look like tea: something that was redder... Well, it was none of his business. He left, heading in the direction of Paugeng, where he found Jhai putting on a new frock and doing her hair.

Six hours later, he got a call from Ma.

"Sorry, Zhu Irzh. I know it's late and you're off duty, but Chen says you need to get down here. There's been an incident."

Which, when he got there, was one way of describing a bomb, the demon supposed.

The interior of the warehouse – if warehouse it had been – was gutted. It looked as though someone had taken a giant ice cream scoop and removed a 'u' shaped section from ceiling to floor, some seven storeys. The fires were now out, but he interior still glowed red and the rainy air was filled with a drift of smoke.

"So the suspect's definitely in there?" the demon asked.

Chen, standing by a patrol car, assented. "The fire team found his body." He indicated a covered form in front of the building. "We still don't know what he was doing."

"Do we know who he was?"

"Actually, yes. His wallet survived. He came into the city under a false name, which we knew him by, but he's actually a member of the Dao clan."

Zhu Irzh stared at him. "What? I'd no idea he was so important."

"Neither had we," Chen said. "If I'd realised he was associated with one of the city's premier gangs, I'd have taken him more seriously."

"I wonder what he did to get blown up?" the demon asked.

"Or if they were even targeting him alone," Chen replied. "We –"

"What's that?" Zhu Irzh said, sharply. He could see a dark shadow darting down one of the side streets, and calling something to Chen, he took off after it. But it was too wet to see properly, the rain descending in sheets, and the demon soon lost his quarry. This was the street in which the tea house stood: he could see its sign, now unlit, then it disappeared into the rain. He turned and trudged back to the scene of devastation.

"He's not in Hell," Chen said, a day later. "I checked with the Night Harbour. There's no record of this Ang Dao passing through."

"He can't be in Heaven, surely."

"No, not there either. So he's still here, somewhere. And he was a major player – the reason we haven't come across him before is that he's been living in Macau for the last thirty years. Old man Dao died ten days ago – he came back to claim his inheritance."

"Looks like someone disagreed."

"There are several brothers," Chen said. He held out his pad and showed Zhu Irzh a list of photographs: the demon could see, in the heavy featured faces, the lineaments of the suspect.

"All battling for the spoils," said Zhu Irzh.

"Yes. Dao left a criminal empire – Ang's been running one in Macau. I suppose he wanted to merge the two. But he'd have had to have got rid of his brothers first and it looks like one of them got to him before he could make that happen…Or someone did."

The demon was silent, remembering that fleeing shadow he had seen. More ghost than murderer, he'd have said, but he couldn't be sure. Something was nagging at him, a half-memory, nothing more. He let it be and resolved to think about it later.

And 'later' actually came up with the goods. Zhu Irzh woke, with a start. He could see from the clock that it was 3 a.m.: the edge of the blinds was still quite dark. Beside him, Jhai silently slept. He'd been dreaming – he was back in that odd little teahouse, with the waitress bustling about behind the counter. He'd been the only customer, apart from one other… Who had it been? The demon had known them, and yet not known them.

He went back to sleep, having made a note of the dream. Next day, he accompanied Chen around town, on various errands to do with the case, but when dusk fell, he asked for permission to go off on an enquiry of his own. Chen, having heard his account of the shadow, readily agreed.

Zhu Irzh hastened down the street. The air still smelled faintly of burning after the bombing; the rain had not yet dampened it down. He could not see the teahouse's neon sign through the renewed downpour. Squinting, he wondered for a moment if he had come to the wrong road – but no. It was just that the teahouse was no longer there.

The demon stood in the street, bewildered. He recognised the buildings which had been on either side – but now they were adjacent to one another. It was as though the city had shuffled itself together, bunching up and squeezing the teahouse out. How weird. Zhu Irzh walked methodically up and down the street, but there was no sign of the place. He went back to the precinct, and reported it to Chen.

Over the next ten days, the Dao clan broke ranks. An informer appeared, wanting protection and payment, both of which she received. In exchange, the police team learned that Ang's brother Cho had been behind the bombing, but Cho had fled to China. The other brothers were lying low; Chen put procedures in place with the mainland police, and moved on to other things.

The summer, too, wore on. The weather improved, growing a little cooler. Chen and the demon dealt with missing spirits, illegal demons, gambling rings, occult murders. The usual. Nothing untoward happened, and Zhu Irzh forgot all about the strange little teahouse. Towards the end of the summer, however, a string of deaths caused a stir in the area around Bharulay, some distance from the docks. Small people, minor runners and drug dealers. Initially, the police had worried that there was a serial killer on the loose, but the deaths were professional and apparently gang related. They still had to be investigated, though, which is why Zhu Irzh and Ma once more found themselves on a stakeout, in front of a hotel near the main railway station. It was a mild, pearly evening, with the light gradually fading behind the skyscrapers; a nice enough night to be out. The street was busy, filled with restaurants and cafes, an early evening crowd enjoying themselves at the end of the week. Zhu Irzh was just thinking how pleasant it was when a loud crack split the peace.

"That was a gunshot!" Ma said.

They bundled out of the car, to see a man running down the road, shoving passers-by out of his way. There were shouts. People threw themselves under tables and into the dubious shelter of the bars; a shot shattered the windscreen of Ma's car. And now Zhu Irzh could see the shooter: a figure in black, zigzagging expertly through the crowds. Ma had a weapon, but could not take aim without running the risk of hurting a bystander. The demon, however, had other options. He cast a spell, a sizzling spray of light that arced towards the gunman. It struck him, but too late: he'd already fired and the demon saw the fleeing man throw up his arms and lie still. There were screams. Ma was running towards the shooter: Zhu Irzh saw the fallen man's spirit rise up, one hand covering his mouth in horror, and then it bolted, flying a foot or so above the ground into the back streets of Bharulay.

"Keep hold of him," Zhu Irzh shouted to Ma, and went after the ghost.

In the back alleys, it was suddenly quiet. The sun had dropped, casting the buildings into shadow, though the air was still warm. He was at the back of the station, a long brick wall hiding the tracks and sheds from view. The ghost was moving along it, a heat shimmer against the wall. But the demon, somehow, was not surprised to see a neon sign flicker into view. The ghost paused, and then it was sucked into the building as if down a plughole. Zhu Irzh slowed to a halt in front of the teahouse. It looked just the same, the windows hidden by steam; only its location was different. He hesitated for a second, then pushed open the door.

The clientele was different, and yet the same types of individuals were there. They glanced uneasily at the demon. The waitress came up, still clad in her white garments.

"You came back," she said. "I remember you." She looked afraid, the demon realised.

"A man was shot," he said. "Not far away. His ghost came in here."

The waitess sighed. "Who are you? I can see you're from Hell, but – you'd better come in the back."

Zhu Irzh followed her into a small windowless office and accepted her offer of a chair.

"Would you like some tea? You might as well now you're here. It's perfectly all right – I'm not trying to trick you."

He'd drunk tea here before, Zhu Irzh remembered. He waited while a shy, pale girl in her teens brought in a pot. From the facial resemblance, she was the waitress' sister.

"You're with the police, aren't you?" the waitress said. "I've heard of you."

Zhu Irzh displayed his badge. "That's me."

"You might have heard of us," the waitress said. "But it was before your time. And we've tried to keep this establishment quiet." She went across to a cupboard and took down a photograph that had been resting on the top. "Here we are."

There were perhaps a dozen people, clearly one family. Grandmother and grandpa, an older woman, a middle aged couple, then younger members, including the waitress and her sister. All were standing proudly in front of a frontage, which bore the legend: SILVER STAR TEAHOUSE. Their clothes were old fashioned – not greatly so, but enough to mark them at a date of perhaps forty years ago.

"We are the Star family," the waitress said. "I am Yun. Our grandparents set up this teahouse, when they first came to this city. But there were problems – a family quarrel. A cousin of my father's felt he'd been cheated of his inheritance, when my grandfather died. There were arguments. One night, the cousin came to the teahouse and pushed rags doused in petrol through the door. The Silver Star burned down and we all died." She frowned. "I don't remember that bit. But after – we found we were in Heaven, but there were things left undone. My grandfather met us there – he spoke to the Emperor, the old one. They let us come back here, with the teahouse."

"To do what?" the demon asked.

"To feed hungry ghosts," Yun said. "When someone is killed by their family, like Dao, they become a hungry ghost and they prey on the living. But we can feed them, and save other lives. We have a deal with a blood merchant in Hell."

"You're like a soup kitchen," Zhu Irzh said. A faint smile appeared on Yun's spectral face.

"Yes. It is a public service."

"And the ghost I saw this evening?"

"I think you will find," Yun said, "that it has been a family matter."

She did not know where the teahouse would appear next. Its manifestation would be a clue, she told Zhu Irzh, to a family killing, either one that had happened, or one shortly to come. But he would always be welcome, she assured him, and he believed her. After all, the teahouse wasn't doing anything illegal, and it was a shelter, of a kind. He left soon after, pausing to give a covert glance at the rows of murdered faces, each one crouched over their bowl of blood.

# Saint Cold

*A Fallow sisters short story, starring Bee. This was written before* Blackthorn Winter, *where Bee finds another lost girl in difficult circumstances. But Bee's very capable. You'd want to be found by her. The story came from a discussion with my mother, Veronica, about this time of year: she follows a Victorian weather prediction system, compiled by a man named Buchan, and I can't remember whether this phenomenon features in that, but I've spoken to European friends who know about it.*

You think it's all red and roses, garlands and green. People dancing the maypole round and calling in the May. But there are years when the blossom is as cold as snow on the thorn and withering with frost; years when the ground rings out hard and the stars hang low.

This was one of those years.

I needed to speak to Dark about it, but I couldn't find him. This wasn't entirely surprising, given that he's dead, and has been for some time. Not that this seems to slow him down a great deal. I lingered in the orchard in any case after I'd called for him, watching the evening star as she hung over the apple trees, which were drifts of flowers now. There were clouds building up over the green hills and the distant estuary of the Severn: great anvil heads touched with pink fire as the sun sank down. May Day tomorrow, the old festival of Beltane, and the village was having a celebration, which would not be so much fun if it snowed or, more probably, poured. Still, we could always go to the pub.

I turned to go in and Dark was there. He wore, as he always wears, a black tunic and small ruff: he is Elizabethan, and would not, as a sailor and runaway, have worn such fine clothes in life. I can't blame him for wanting elegance in death. A pearl depended from one earlobe. He put a finger to his lips in Harpocratean mimickry.

"Hush? Why?"

He looked from side to side in exaggerated suspicion, then abandoned the pretence.

"Word is, someone's coming."

"Really? Who?" The apple blossom was faintly visible through his form, the overlay of ghost on orchard.

"I don't know. It's come down the grapevine – you know how it is. Whispers in the leaves. Someone's coming. Soon, but no *niceness.*" He used the word in its old form: exactitude, precision.

"Damn. No clues."

"No. Just *someone.*" Twilight shimmered through him. "I have to go." He bowed over my hand. "Tomorrow, then, my lady Beatrice." And was gone.

I walked back through the shadows to the house, with the air growing colder around me. May Eve or not, it would be a night for a fire in the hearth. But I remembered, as I walked, that this was one of those nights when the veil was thin: when the division between the living and the dead did not mean as much. Not that it ever did, round here. People think now that it's All Hallows that this happens and so it is, but in older times May Eve was the night when the dead come back. But Dark had seemed distracted, as though he had an eye on something behind him.

I had to take some paper plates down to the village hall, a just-in-case task. There are never enough plates, or cups. I piled them all into a plastic bag and set out: walking, since it wasn't far enough to justify taking the car. And it was bloody chilly, I thought, as I trudged down the lane, slick with recent rain and soon to turn to black ice. Not very spring-like. A shower of hawthorn blossom looked like snow in the hedgerow and its scent filled the air, like sweet cat's piss. When I reached the hall, it was still not yet dark. A window was lit in the hall, casting a cheerful glow out into the lane, and a yellow light lingered over the hills. Someone darted out from the side of the hall, making me jump.

"Scuse me. Could you spare a couple of quid? Just for a cup of tea."

I was used to this in the middle of Bristol, in the city, but not in the village. The day of the rural tramp is pretty much gone, went with Thatcher's policies in the eighties, so Mum told me. This was a girl, bundled up in a mess of clothes. Hard to tell what colour: the dusk rendered everything khaki. She held out a grubby hand. Her face was pinched under a mass of fawn dreadlocks. She probably wanted it for drugs or cigarettes, or a can of cider.

"Here," I said, and gave her 50p, which was all the change I had in my pocket.

"Cheers," she said, sounding surprised, and melted back into the shadows. I felt as though I'd imagined her. A New Age traveller kid, probably. I went into the relative warmth of the hall, deposited the plastic bag with a note where someone would see it, and made my way home to an early night.

According to the old folklore, you're supposed to get up on May morning and wash your face in the dew, thus rendering yourself even lovelier than before. I washed mine in the shower, some time after dawn, made a cup of tea and bundled up in a sweater and thick jacket, thinking of the traveller kid, and wondering where she'd spent the night. Maybe she had a van parked nearby. I took the dogs out straight away, their small woolly shapes bouncing down the lane like a lamb. It was freezing: never mind dew – there was a heavy ground frost on the fields, wilting the hawthorn. The dogs wriggled under a stile and ran over the glowing ground, the grass sparkling with the early sun. I didn't think there were sheep in that field but you never know – farmers move them around – so, cursing, I clambered over the stile and went after them.

"Oi, you horrible pair! Come here! What's this?" The last remark usually brought them running, for treats in pockets, but they did not respond. I could see them, though, and there were no sheep. They were down the far end of the field, nosing about under the hedge.

"Come *here!*"

Rabbits, I thought, or old bones. But I didn't want them eating somethingthey'd found: dogs can be poisoned that way. So I ran over the field, stumbling on tussocks, until I saw what they'd found. The girl.

She lay in a huddle, and in the sharp morning light I could see that her clothes were even rougher than I'd thought: they looked homespun, earth-coloured with the drab dyes you get from vegetable experimentation. Her hair was in elflocks, spread over the ground, and one outflung hand was clenched. Her cheeks were hollow: starvation or poor teeth. It was obvious she was dead. Her skin was almost translucent, sinking into the sunlight and cold.

"Shit," I said aloud. "Shit." The dogs were still sniffing. I dragged them off and snapped leads onto collars. I don't carry a mobile, usually, so it was a quick stumble back to the house and the landline. I felt curiously light, untied from time, and humbled in the presence of death. The police were helpful, would send someone right away. I went back out to the lane, leaving the dogs shut in. There was no sign of Dark in the orchard. But he's not an early riser.

I think I feared – hoped? – she might be gone, but she was still there, unmoving as a fallen statue. It was close to eight in the morning and the sun had started to draw up the cold into mist. I heard the siren before I saw the car, and then there was an ambulance with them. A nice policewoman asked me what I knew and I told her: they were quite thorough, but there was no evidence of foul play. They thought she had frozen to death. She seemed to have no identifying documents, no money, no phone. Eventually she was taken away, zipped up in a bag, and I went flatly back to the house.

I did not feel like May Day celebrating but talked myself into it. Towards eleven, I went back to the village hall where a small crowd was gathering. One of the local schools had organised a maypole: a strapping male member of staff manhandled it into place with the aid of some of the kids. It tottered alarmingly and I could see the whole thing falling over, but eventually they wrestled it into its ready-made hole in the concrete. Its ribbons, red, white and green, stirred in the icy wind. After a few false starts, the kids danced around it and got hopelessly entangled. Still, it was the thought that counted and it was entertaining. I noticed someone from the local paper taking a few shots and took a few myself, to send to my sisters. Most of the people present were locals – this wasn't a big commercial celebration. But a few were not known to me, tourists presumably, and at the far side of the crowd stood an old man dressed in a long grey robe. Revivalist Druidry is big around here, although I didn't recognise him. Bit cold for a robe, I thought, hope he had thermal underpants. He had one of those thin, clerical faces and something on a chain around his neck. Then someone moved in front of him and when I could see again, he was gone.

We all trooped into the village hall for cake and sandwiches. I did not see the old man again but when I got back home, I looked on the camera. No sign of him. Perhaps he had just been wandering about. But I did not like these sudden strangers; the dead girl, the old robed man. Not because this was a small rural village and I was insular and scared of strangers, not that, but because of what Dark had said, the previous day.

*Someone's coming.*

Not long after he'd told me that, I'd met a young woman who had frozen to death. I knew what I felt and it was guilt. I should have asked her where she was staying, if she had a place. Why was she even in the field, far from the village? If I'd been out last night, without shelter, I'd have found a barn – but perhaps she didn't want to risk it. A lot of street people have been assaulted in registered shelters, so maybe she was afraid. I couldn't blame her. I sat at the kitchen table with questions running through my mind and no answers. When dusk fell, I went in search of Dark.

But my ghost was not there. The orchard was empty of everything but owls. I called, but no one answered. Sternly telling myself that another early night was on the cards, I went inside, leaving the orchard to the owls and the rising fire of Jupiter above.

Next day, it was appreciably warmer and the hawthorn began to blossom along the orchard hedge. It felt almost like spring. I spent part of the morning talking to the police, but they still did not know who the young woman was. How sad, I thought, that no one seemed to have reported her missing. Days went by and there was no identification: she would have that old thing, a pauper's grave. I asked if there would be any kind of funeral. I ought to go, I thought. I might have been the last person to see her alive – and yet she had apparently spent, or lost, that 50p.

They said they would let me know.

I started looking. Some hundred and fifty people are found each year, and cannot be identified. She was in a big enough company, for a small nation. Devon and Cornwall, the next counties down from here, have the most, because bodies wash up and are damaged by sea water. Most have lost contact with their families, so are not reported missing, and most are not crime related: the girl had not been murdered. She had just died. She might not even be buried, but kept away in a morgue somewhere.

On ice, I thought. Just as she'd spent her last hours. I hoped it had been a gentle death; I looked up what it's like to freeze, as well. They say you just drift away and I hoped that was true.

I did the things I usually did, nothing exciting. A couple of days at the local library, and household things; talking to my sisters. I asked my friend Beth, when I saw her at the village hall, if she knew who the old man might have been but she looked puzzled and said she had seen no such person. Nor did she know the girl, but travellers had been around: a couple with a baby and a horse drawn wagon, old school road folk. She'd seen the woman yesterday, though: she was not the dead girl. I was drawing blanks all round and Dark had still not come back. But this happened sometimes; I did not take it personally, or as a sign.

Ten days after the May Day ceremonies, I woke to frost. It lay glittering in the branches of the apple trees and turned the world to white. That morning, I had to take some old clothes to the vicarage, for a jumble sale. Village life is essentially humdrum. The vicar, a tall, mild old man who could be nothing else but a cleric, and who had been a friend of my late grandfather, greeted me at the door and brought me in for tea. Of course he did: it's what they do.

"I'm not sorry to stop," I told him. "It's so cold out there! Not like May at all."

"Ah, but that's where you're wrong," the vicar said, with a faint air of triumph. "Often the way at this time of year. It's the Ice Saints, you see."

"The –?"

"Pancras, Servatius and Mamertius."

"I thought Pancras was a railway station."

"He gave his name to the station, but he is also an Ice Saint. They're supposed to bring a cold snap over their three feast days. An old story, drawn up no doubt to explain the chill that often comes in mid-May."

"Well," I said. "I didn't know that."

That evening, at dusk, I made my routine visit to the orchard. Dark was not there. A crescent moon hung low in the branches and Venus shone in the west. It would be a good night for star gazing. When I went back towards the house, I saw something moving in the hedge. Cat, or badger, I thought – but it was bigger than that. A person? I shouted "Who's there?" but there was no reply. I turned, to see Dark. The pearl in his ear shone in the light from the slim moon.

"You took your time," I said.

"I've been doing things."

"Someone came. A girl, who is dead. And an old man – I think. He might have been anyone."

"The girl is dead, but you have to save her," Dark said. He glanced over his shoulder. "Tonight, when Jupiter rises."

"*Save* her? How can I save her when she's dead?"

Things are obvious to Dark which aren't obvious to me. He said, patiently, "You have to save her so that she doesn't die again. She's stuck. Go to the lane when Jupiter rises."

So this is what I did.

I could feel the cold coming on, like a front of weather moving down the lane. Jupiter was over the hedgerow, framed in hawthorn blossom. As the light faded, I saw them. Three old men in grey robes. Their beards were like icicles; their eyes downcast. They carried a banner with a sign I did not know and the frost streamed out in its wake to cover the road. Behind them, something scuttled into the hedge. As they drew closer, I gathered my coat about me and stepped out.

"Excuse me." They looked astonished. I don't think they were used to being seen. "St Pancras, St Servatius and St Mamertius?"

"Yes?" They all raised their eyebrows. It was like talking to the vicar. "We are visible to you?" one of them asked.

"Yes. My family can see spirits." I peered past them. "Who is that?"

"Who is who?" They all turned and looked behind them. I could see something in the hedgerow.

"Come out!" I called. There was a rustling. The dead girl crept into the lane. Now that I'd adjusted to the presence of the saints, I could see that her garments were not a traveller's, not hippy homespun. They were Medieval. She came to my side and plucked at my sleeve. For a moment, I thought she was going to ask for money. She said, "I disobeyed my mother. The planting was too soon."

"You're supposed to wait until after the saints' days, to plant your seeds?"

"Yes. But the weather was so fine, I did not wait. And the cold caught me, unawares. I dropped in the field and died. Then I was snared in their wake. I have been ever since. May Day brings me to life; the cold kills me again."

"But, child," a saint said, greatly perturbed. "We did not know."

"No, you never looked." She was not accusatory. She had grown used to it, I thought.

I said, "You must set her free. She is a trapped soul."

"Of course."

The three saints joined hands. Their lips moved. I stepped back. The girl clung to my jacket. Gradually it began to grow warmer. The frost melted. The lane filled with the scent of hawthorn, summer-sweet without that sour undernote. Above, the great triangle of the spring stars, Altair, Deneb and blue Vega, wheeled overhead. The saints grew fainter as the warmth grew: removing themselves from the equation. And when they were no more than a shimmer on the air, the girl gave a cry and flung her arms wide and was gone into the golden. I stood alone in the lane, surrounded by the scent of the may.

I called the police next morning, but the reference number they had given me did not seem to have any information attached to it, and they were vague and a little bemused. The weather grew summer warm – unseasonal, but welcome, everyone said. I went into the church for a first time in a long while, and lit candles, three for the cold saints, and one for the spirit of a girl.

# Silence in the
# House of Moths

*Remember that alternative Constantinople? This is another story set in that world, and I wrote it for the anthology which commemorated Storm Constantine's untimely death. I wanted to refer back to the world of Dancing Day, the first story of mine that she ever published.*

The House of Birds is never silent; the House of Lions rings with the voices of priestesses, raised in the day-long chants. But the House of Moths is always quiet, filled as it is with the wings of ghosts. Here, children are sent away the day after their births in case they shatter the peace with their cries. When they return, years later once they are grown, they are muzzled for a time, until they learn.

I was one of those children. They did not have to muzzle me for long. Some stories tell of a child who returns to the place of her birth and finds it alien and strange, who does not fit in, who is not understood by those around her. This is not my story. I was an obedient child and grew up into a girl who did what she was told: not because I was cowed or frightened, or because I had no opinions of my own, but simply because my real life was inside my head and there I have always been free, no matter how many chores I had to do in the temple where I spent my early years, or how many hours spent in contemplation of the divine. In the hush of the temple room, where the long rows of girls knelt, bowed forwards with their heads resting on blocks of sacred cedar, the goddess with her lions frowning down upon us, I could do what I liked and go where I pleased. If the goddess knew, she did not punish me. I was certain that the priestesses did not: they held me up as an example to the others and considered me a model student. I think they would have liked to keep me and I would not have minded staying, there in Cybele's house, but the House of Moths required me back again, and so I went.

I was happy in the House of Moths, just as I had been happy in the temple. I had a role, as Second Sister. My eldest sibling, Tosay, ran the household and allotted tasks to me: embroidering clothes, at which I was good, and preparing food, to which I applied myself with diligence. I also found myself spending a lot of time in the garden, working alongside the ancient gardener, Menred, a woman who had been gardener there since before my own birth. My sister made it plain to me that there would be no chance of my having to marry and I greeted this pronouncement with relief.

Thus I was content and remained so until the arrival of Suleine.

For Suleine stole my silence.

During the first few days of her arrival, I was happy. Suleine was a distant cousin, the daughter of an aunt who had been sent to one of the Dark Sea towns, in marriage to one of the many petty kings who rule that region. I had seen a painting of the town, in the great hall of the House of Moths, depicting a sweep of snow-capped mountains racing down into the sea, with a tiny castellated town crouched between them. It looked precarious, as though the mountains were pausing for a moment, but would then rush on, carrying the town into the waves. I felt sorry for my aunt, and for Suleine. Then, a year after I had come back to the House of Moths, we had word that my aunt had died and her husband, deeming Suleine unsuitable for the marriage market, asked if she could come to us. My elder sister, hospitable and kind, said that she could.

The day of her arrival was hot, the garden steaming after an early morning rainstorm. Droplets fell from the long trumpets of the lillies and the birdsong was hushed, as if in awe.

"The Dark Sea towns are cold, at least in winter," my sister said. "Do you think she will find it too warm?"

"Perhaps if we close the shutters in her room?" I said. "And place a bowl of ice water in it, to cool the air? Even if you are used to the heat, that's never unpleasant."

"Aretrie, that's an excellent suggestion. Could you do those things, while I wait for her carriage?"

I ran down to the kitchen and found a block of ice in the ice store. I struck it with a hammer and it shattered into a hundred glittering fragments, diamonds on the stone flags. Scraping these up, I took a bowl upstairs, then found a jug and filled it. I was about to close the shutters, casting the black-panelled room into dimness, when movement caught my eye.

This room looked out over the city. I could see the dome of the Rose Temple, catching the hard noon light like a great pink pearl. The rooftops fell away, ochre, sand, tawny, fawn, with the occasional splash of rust red tiles, imported across the Inner Sea. From the bedroom, I could see down a side street to the Grand Avenue and down it, a curtained carriage was coming, drawn by two speckled deer. I could hear the patter of their hooves on the cobbles. For a moment, a face peeped out from the depths of the carriage, moon-round, moon-pale. Then the carriage was drawing up at the gates of the House of Moths. I ran downstairs to greet Suleine.

She was quiet and meek, a short girl, very stout, with her hair confined in a black spangled net, as woman wear it in the Dark Sea towns. A crystal droplet, reminding me of lilies and rain, hung quivering from it as she alighted from the carriage.

"How pretty," I said, nudging my sister.

"It's a sign she's unwed," said Tosay. "Once they're married, they put a garnet one on the net instead. And when they're widowed, one of jasper."

"Why jasper?" I asked, as the coachman carried Suleine's luggage up the steps.

"It's brown, like the earth into which a body is placed."

It seemed very logical. But Suleine's droplet was rainy-clear and it sparkled in the light as she smiled. She looked sweet, it seemed to me. Her smile was shy.

"Welcome," my sister said, and spoke the ritual words of greeting to someone who has never visited before. I echoed them, sounding small and hushed against the distant sounds from the Grand Avenue. Perhaps Suleine thought I was shy, too, for we smiled at one another and said no more. Then Tosay led her inside and the coachman carried her bags up the stairs. We left her alone to settle in, and told her that the noonday meal would be served when the waterclock struck.

"She seems modest and presentable," Tosay said, once we were out of earshot. "Frankly, I was fearing some little madam, all frills and finery and tossing her head. 'Unsuitable for wedlock' can take many forms."

"She gave me a good impression," I agreed.

Over the meal, that impression was secured. This was a speaking day. Suleine spoke when spoken to, proved informative and in fact quite interesting on the subject of the Dark Sea Towns, talked affectionately of her late mother, our aunt, and did not criticise her father, although she would have perhaps been justified in doing so.

"You will have a week to accustom yourself to the House of Moths," Tosay said. "You will find us quiet, even a little earnest. We have our weekly rites and rituals, in which you will be expected to take part, but our main celebratory cycle, dedicated to Cybele's shadow twin Cymere, is held in the winter. We thus have some months to prepare."

"I understand. I would like to familiarise myself with the rites, since I am to remain here. Besides, I am myself devout. At home we were dedicated to the service of Shtari, but I know a little of Cymere from my mother."

"Of course, she would have told you. But it is seemly that she did not worship one goddess in the household of another. I will give you a set of prayer books and texts."

Suleine thanked her and that was dinner over. She spent the afternoon in her room, but dined with us all in the great hall that evening. By the end of the week, it was as though she had always been with us. She was modest, kind, unassuming. Everyone in the household liked her. I was among them. I would not say that she and I became friends, for I valued my own company too much and we even had a conversation in which she told me she was the same.

"My father is overbearing. He told me what to think all the time, and so did my brothers. When my mother died, it grew worse. There was no peace, no peace at all."

I reached out and took her hand, in silence. We gripped each other's fingers for a moment, though some texts do not approve of affectionate touch. But I do not think we regretted it. There was no sensuality in this, only solidarity.

Tosay and I had decided that our next big project must be the sheets. We had many beds in the household, and the sheets were old, dating from my grandmother's day. We had turned them, back to back, and they were good Khemish cotton, but now they were wearing thin. So Tosay sent a servant to the market to make enquiries and at length new sheets were delivered: a big day for the household. Some were white, like snow, and some a pale ivory colour, like an old summer moon. We admired them as they lay draped across the dining room table.

"This is your job," Tosay told me.

"I know. I have ordered new silks. It only remains what manner of design you would prefer: leaves, perhaps, or coral fronds? The woods, or the seas?"

Tosay considered this and we agreed on a compromise, since I liked sea and she liked gardens, and the shadowy woods which fringed the city on the landward side. Half and half, and everyone could choose which set they preferred. The embroidering would take several weeks and I was looking forward to it. We had set up a table for me in the cool of the verandah, overlooking the gardens; I planned to begin early in the mornings, before the heat of the day took the house in its grip.

It was in undertaking tasks such as these that I could truly enjoy my silence. The cast of characters in my head took free rein: I journeyed across the Dark Sea to the steppelands beyond, or went south to Khem and its ancient ruins. I had a company of lovers, friends, beloved companions who had been with me since I was a young girl. I did not know if others had such an inner landscape: it would be childish to ask and would make me seem foolish. As with so many other things, I kept this to myself.

But on the second morning, when I had been sewing for no more than an hour, I found that my silence was no more. I looked up from the embroidery. The garden was loud with birdsong, the doves squabbling on the roof, the rush of swallows' wings in and out of the eaves, a peacock's harsh cry. The high walls and the magic which played about them usually kept out the noises of the city but now I could hear all of it: the cries of street vendors, the rumbling wheels of carts, voices raised in anger and argument.

How could anyone work in peace with all this racket going on?

I gritted my teeth and set my hands to the sewing and my mind to my latest adventure, in which I and the man I loved, who does not exist in this world, were setting sail to the Scarlet Isles to reclaim his heritage. But his face, usually so vivid to my inner eye, seemed curiously indistinct, and the sense of the ship, which on previous days had been so strong – the salt wash, the taste of the sea on my mind's tongue, the hiss of the sails and the screams of the gulls – were replaced by the sounds of the mundane world. I flung down my sewing and went back indoors.

During the afternoon siesta, I was, to my relief, able to recapture some of my inner realm. Yet something was not quite right. With some illnesses, one can lose a measure of taste and smell, and this is what had befallen my imagination now: it lacked savour and tang, images only, as if a transparent wall had been placed between my inner people and myself. I could not ask counsel of anyone; they would have thought me mad.

Instead, I went looking, though I did not know what I was looking for. I roamed the House of Moths, restless, seeking, all down its shadowy corridors, shuttered against the heat of the day. I found no answers until I came to the shrine room. Here I paused at the door for the ritual bow and this stopped me from barging in regardless of who else might be there. So I was able to see my cousin Suleine, crouched like a child before the altar and the smoky image of the goddess, her forehead touching the floor.

An altogether laudable thing to do, but all at once I knew who had stolen my inner quiet. I could feel it inside her, like one of the soap bubbles that small children make with a pot of water. It glistened and shimmered around her, and in it I could see forms. She, like I, was daydreaming. But she, unlike I, was free to do so.

I could not confront her. Did she know? Was there some limited capacity, some household store of dreams which, like sugar in a jar, could be used up if too many spoons dipped into it? I could not believe that this was a deliberate act, unless Suleine was more wicked than I thought her to be.

We were all silent at dinner that night: it was a day for unspeaking. This time, the silence weighed heavily upon me.

And that night, too, I lay sleepless. My inner worlds, a comfort to me in the small dark hours, were no longer available: I saw them as one sees a castle on a distant hill, a little shining image, and as inaccessible. Restless at dawn, I had reached the conclusion that perhaps Suleine needed this capacity more than I, that her difficult girlhood had rendered her more in need of the aid of dreams and that the goddess had taken my sugar to give to her in her greater requirement.

When the sun crept in, however, I felt that this was stupid. Thoughts were not sugar, or flour, or anything finite, but a vast realm: after all, the dreams of night were not subject to rationing. Were they?

That night would see the new moon, hence the unspeaking. I resolved to go to the shrine myself, when dusk fell and the call rang out across the city to welcome her. I would petition the goddess then.

In the meantime, there was the day to crawl through. We were relieved of ordinary duties, so I did not have my stitches to remind me of what I had lost, and had to devote the day to cleaning the house to see the new moon in. I met Suleine with our hair tied up in turbans and our hands carrying mops and brooms and buckets. We smiled at one another and were set to cleaning the hall, which we did peaceably. From her manner, her helpfulness and gentleness, I could not see her as some sorceress who had purloined my dreams; there had to be some other cause.

I thought it would be hard to wait for twilight but the day passed quickly enough. This was also a fasting day: the next meal would be served in the morning. This always made me light headed but perhaps that was not a bad thing – it brought one closer to the spirit world, the priestesses said. When the cleaning was done and the final day rite had been said, the shutters opened and the shrine room emptied, I crept back to it. The calls were sounding out and when I looked out of the windows, I saw the crescent moon low above the roofs and turrets, hanging like a rim of gleam in the evening sky. I spoke my prayer to her as much as to Cymere.

When I rose from the floor, I saw that Suleine had entered the shrine room. She came to me and took my hand, squeezing it. Her eyes were full of regret. She made a formal bow, to the goddess and then, strangely, to me, her hands clasped in the gesture of farewell. She put her finger to her lips but I did not know why, since this was an unspeaking day already. Then she sat down on the nearest bench, facing Cymere. I took a step back, uncomfortable and intending to go, but she put out a hand to stay me.

So stay I did, and watched as she gazed unblinking at the goddess. As it grew darker and the moon's curve grew brighter, so the light around Suleine began to grow, too, until she sat in a pool of pale fire. Squinting against it, I saw a black spot inside the glow, a square, opening suddenly like a window. Through it, I saw the Dark Sea coast, the snowy pine-clad hills running down to the sea. A young woman was standing on a headland, her fair hair in a golden net, a quiver of arrows on her back. She held a bow in one hand and she stretched the other out to Suleine. My cousin took it and the girl pulled her through the window and into the day. She glanced back once and raised her hand, as I raised mine. Then all the light in the room was sucked through the window, like oil down a funnel, and disappeared. Suleine was gone. A crystal droplet tinkled to the floor and lay still. I watched it for a moment, but it remained transparent. It did not darken to jasper.

In an emergency, we are allowed to speak. But it took an awful lot of explanation. I did not want to give away the secret of my dreams; I had not come across anything in the sacred texts which forbade them, but I intuitively knew that they would not be approved of. The priestesses placed a wafer on my tongue, which made it impossible for me to lie, but I told them only what I had seen and since it was the truth, it was accepted. Eventually Tosay and the priestesses decided that, since Suleine had been deemed unsuitable for marriage, that the virgin goddesses had claimed her for their own, that the girl I had seen was one of the Dark Coast deities, the Virgin Huntress, perhaps. There was a sensation for a week or two, and a series of letters to the Dark Sea coast, but Suleine's father had already written her off and although there might have been a question of honour all the same, the priestesses' counsel laid waste to any scandal.

Now, a month later, I sit and sew. My inner world has returned; perhaps the energy that Suleine needed to make her escape has now come back into balance. And with each stitch I take a step further into my own inner land, have adventures, choose love. I have returned, so far, yet sometimes I see my cousin, in a castle on a hill, tiny as a miniature. She is always laughing. Some day, perhaps, I shall go and visit her.

# Swallows

*I mark my year by the passage of birds – the wild swans in midwinter, then the lapwings, then the flocks which sometimes pass through Somerset for a few days like whimbrels, and then the swallows which herald summer. It's getting to be an anxious time now, as so many swallows don't return: they're either shot, or fall foul of bad weather, and their numbers are plummeting in the UK. This story provides an alternative explanation for that.*

I know summer is here when the flocks come home. I stand in the eaves of the high house that overlooks the harbour and I wait and I watch. I can sense their arrival, you see: early in the month when the sun begins to sink later and redder into the sea and the mornings are clear and fresh. When I wake, there's a humming in the wires of the world, electric across my skin, and I jump out of bed and run up the attic stairs to the window to see if they are here. I am usually a few days out; they are miles distant yet, still skimming over the storm-swept sea, diving down across the green islands, drawn by the magnet of home.

But this year, the world did not hum. My skin did not prickle with anticipation and even though the sun delayed its descent into the ocean a little more each day, they did not come back. And as summer wore on and the heat blanketed me when I stepped out of the cool house and ran down the road that followed the harbour, still they were not here.

I knew, then what I would have to do. I would have to go myself, and find them.

They said I was too young for magic. "They," the grownups, my aunts with whom I lived, my parents being long dead. The aunts expect a certain standard of behaviour, decency, rectitude. But these were unusual times, as I pleaded in the parlour, before a council of three. Part of the tapestry of the world was missing.

"And how do you propose to repair it?" Aunt Maria said, tapping her fan on the arm of her chair. A rhythmic beat, which I had to fight to ignore. She was up to something. "You don't know how to sew."

My embroidery skills were, at thirteen, quite skilled and I enjoyed it. This was not, however, what my aunt was talking about.

"I will have to learn at some point," I argued.

"This is true," Aunt Sefily, always the most sympathetic, said.

"But at sixteen. The proper age. Which you are not."

"No, but it's only three years. Do *you* intend to work magic, then, Aunt Maria? Do *you* plan to bring the flock home?"

Aunt Nettisa, speaking for the first time, murmured, "I have always thought of them rather as a shoal."

"That's immaterial, Tisy, and you know it."

Aunt Nettisa was silent. But she was thinking plenty, I could tell.

"And that is an end to it," Aunt Maria said. She shut her fan with a snap.

"Oh dear," Aunt Sefily said.

As Aunt Maria rose to sweep out of the room, I caught Nettisa's gaze behind Maria's back. It was dark and kind, but there was something calculating in it, too, something significant. When I came down the attic stairs that night, it was to find Aunt Nettisa standing at the bottom of them.

In her hand she held a key.

That night, I slipped from my bed, slipped down the stairs, slipped from the house. The summer night was singing, cicadas in the oleander. The huge flowers were wide open, drinking in the moonlight. And as the moon was full I did not need a lamp. I ran up the harbour road, following the line of the sea and the hill. At the summit I turned and looked back. The town seemed to hold the moon's light, for it shone, a crescent like the young moon herself, before her growth. The beach was a curve with the little waves ruffling its edge. The moon's path was a silver line to the horizon. Far out, I could see a ship, just the ghost of its furled sails.

Then I went on, over the summit of the hill and down to the long wall which marked the graveyard. In this, was set a big iron gate and I placed the key that Tisy had given me in the lock and heard it snick open. I went inside.

In my country, all graves are white. Marble and cold, bright when the sun is shining, or in the full splendour of the moon. Some – the grander monuments overlooking the sea – were carved with ships: the sea captains' graves, or those of sailors who had made their fortunes among the lands and islands beyond before coming home once more. But many were simpler: a small stone cross bearing a name and dates. Some had a posy of flowers laid before them, though I had seen at least one captain's grave that was decked with the green weed of the waves, still fat and wet before the sun shrivelled it. And all of them had a single scallop shell, white and rust, placed before them like the old pilgrims' markers. I made my way to the top of the slope, where the captains' graves marched along the brow of the cliff and, standing on the close-cropped turf, looked again out to sea.

It was almost sunlit. It was as though I slid into daylight as I had slid from the house. I saw the great ship riding the waves, her sails unfurled, heard the shouts of the crew. Down in the town, the long arm of the harbour was thronged with people. I could smell smoke and meat and hot cooking oil. Perhaps this would be tomorrow, high summer when the ships come in. Then it was gone and everything was quiet and moonlight.

I'd had a vision but no answer. I went across to the biggest, most ornate monument, where a marble ship sailed forever over a marble sea. Beneath, it bore a name, Captain Marten Harker, and the sides of the oblong block were carved with shells and fish and octopi, with coral and weed and waves.

I sat down with my back against it, hoping Captain Harker would not mind. I closed my eyes and tried to slide from my body. I had done this before but it wasn't easy. My flesh felt too heavy, weighing down my soul like an anchor. I had to latch onto the moonlight line, hitch a ride, let it pull me out to sea.

A tug. Then another, more insistent. And then I was out, sliding up through that pocket of flesh and blood and bone and over the wall and over the cliff. I soared down with the air sparkling all around me and just before I hit the dark and rising sea, I pulled out and arrowed forwards over the spray.

I had done this twice before, against my aunts' instructions. *It is too dangerous, you are not yet grown, you might not come back for there is harm out there, just waiting.*

I had tried to be a good girl and mind their warnings, but the moon shining in through my bedroom window had been too alluring, the pull too strong, and I had gone. At first I had floundered, flopping in air, then I had fallen, but the ground pushed me away like a magnet reversed and I had soared up, flying about the eaves. It had been twilight and the swallows had joined me, and the martens which nested all along the cliffs, and others, too. It was as though this first flight had opened my eyes and after that, I saw things that I was not meant to see, not yet.

In the morning I felt that it must surely be visible, some loss of innocence, but when I went down to breakfast, the aunts said nothing.

Next night, I did it all again.

This time, I rode out on the storm. I did not realise it was coming in: I met it, far out to sea where the white caps of the breakers seemed high enough to touch the stars. I could not feel the wind, being insubstantial, but I could hear its roar and I thought of my body, the vulnerable shell of flesh curled around Captain Harker's gravestone. But it was too late now to turn back and I knew what I had to do. I snatched at a strand of the storm, made of lightning and spray, black air and the boom of thunder. I wound it around myself and I tugged it behind me all the way to the nets.

I had not thought that there would be someone there, but of course, someone had to have set the trap.

When they sensed me, the souls began to twitch and twitter; they were not inert after all, just very tired and wan, and they responded to my silent cry. One of them, a little brighter than the rest, struggled against the edge of the net to greet me and for a second I had a glimpse of him as he had been in life: a sea captain, tall, with a powdered wig and gold braid on his jacket.

"Captain Harker!" I called and he still knew his name for his dim shape flared into sudden moonlight fire. "Captain Harker!" – and I passed the strand of storm through the net.

Then there was someone behind me. It was huge and dull red and it had horns of flame which gave it, briefly, the form of a bull. It struck my spirit a great blow, which sent me spinning. The world turned upside down. I felt winded, as though I had returned to my body and been struck by a thunderbolt. I fell wingless to the floor and could not get up. But Harker's spirit had passed on the strand of storm. I saw it flicker into blue lightning, the colour of seaspray and then the depths, and then indigo night. It flashed along the lines of the net, outlining them against the storm. The figure grasped at it but it was already dissolving.

I lay motionless upon a rock. I saw the flock rise, spiral, starling more than swallow but then each spirit shot away in a different direction, too tiny for the thing to grab, sparks in the darkness. The thing uttered a roar and it turned and stamped for me, making the wet rock quiver. I tried to shut my eyes but I could not; I had to see.

A bright-winged form shot out of the storm and it swept me up. There was a voice in my mind and it told me that it would take me home. Then everything faded.

I woke in a white bed. Everything was colourless, bleached by afternoon sunlight. Aunt Nettisa sat by my side, knitting. I did not think she had seen that I had woken until she said, without looking up, "We are all very cross with you, you know." But she did not sound cross.

"I'm sorry," I said. "I had to bring them home."

"You were found by the priest, in the churchyard. Sopping wet and freezing cold and quite unconscious."

"I'm sorry."

"He had a lot to say about it. So did we, and the story we spun him – you know, many think of us as quite respectable. We have a reputation to uphold."

"I'm sorry," I whispered again.

111

"You are to spend the next few days in bed and then you will be confined to the house for the rest of the month, with the mending. Perhaps then you will be too tired at night to go gallivanting about the spirit world – which is, as you may know by now, full of things you do not understand."

She set her knitting down with a clattering click. "I shall fetch you some milk and then you are to go to sleep."

I did so. But at twilight, I woke. The sky was golden blue as the sun went down, fading into dusk, and through the window I could see forms flitting and flickering about the eaves: the swallows, home at last.

# The Book Rustlers

*This story was inspired by the very brave real life book rustlers of Timbuktu, who saved many ancient books from destruction by Islamist fighters by hiding them, either in the desert or in their private homes. Timbuktu is a very old and sophisticated city, and its library contains thousands of volumes- a priceless heritage of Mali.*

The dust that day was red, a significant change from the previous month, and one that Sibiss took as an omen. It heralded a shift in things and Sibiss did not like shifts: they never brought anything good, and in this case, he thought, they were likely to mark the return of the Guenar. It had been a year, after all, and the township was just beginning to get back on its feet. High time for the rebels to sweep out of the deep desert and break everything into pieces again.

When darkness fell, Sibiss knew he'd been right. The gates closed when the first star shone out over the watchtower, as always, and to him the familiar sound had an ominous finality: the soft thud too much like the closing of some great cosmic door, not just the noise of the ancient gates. Living not far away, the sounds of the gates opening and closing marked his day and he tried to tell himself that he was imagining things. Across the street, two women stood in close conversation; the light cast the shadow of their skulls into high, pointed relief.

Sibiss shuffled back into the house. Its warm sandstone glow comforted him for a moment. The stove was still warm, containing a bowl of food from earlier in the day. Slowly, he ate the spicy tubers, pinched between first finger and thumb, thinking about the day: the red dust, the sound of the gate.

His left arm ached with the weight of the book. Curious, Sibiss thought, that the freight of words could be so heavy. He pushed back his loose sleeve and looked at his arm, fancying that he could see the

113

book beneath his red wrinkled skin. Nothing was visible, which was, of course, the whole point. He felt a satisfaction: the process had been difficult, and conducted in straightened circumstances, but rewarding nonetheless. He knew nothing about the book, save that it was very old. All books were. The younger people, having more stamina, carried more books; Sibiss only one, and he wondered sometimes what it was like to be a repository of multiple tomes: the words running along blood, sinew, bone, deep into the body beneath the skin, carving themselves into organs. They said it would kill you in the end, that weight of words, but then, so could so many things.

Sibiss put thoughts of the book aside. He could never shake the feeling that it was unwise to think too much about it, as if the thought might drift out onto the night air and be heard, rustling over the sands. That night, he did not cast aside his day robe, either, but wrapped himself more closely into it and took his position in the night chair. He wanted to be prepared, if anything happened.

And that night, the Guenar came back.

Sibiss had slept, a fact for which he was later grateful. He was woken by whistling: a huge sound which reverberated over the domed roofs of the township, like wind trapped in a drum. He knew it at once for what it was: the hollow standards that the Geunar rebels bore, travelling at speed. Next moment there was the boom and crump of explosives near the gates. He heard hisses of distress but he was already shuffling as quickly as he could for the nearest tunnel. It lay not far away, along the street in a wall that looked quite solid unless one knew the right code. A throng of young people rushed past him, sweeping him up. Two of them took his arms and lifted his old feet from the floor, hauling him with them into the tunnel. The door slammed shut behind them, leaving them in a sudden warm darkness. Sibiss wondered, as he always did, how many years ago these tunnels had been built, how long the doors would continue to function. Legend had it that the Guenar had first come four hundred years before; he did not know if this were true. Perhaps the information was contained in the book in his arm; perhaps not.

In times such as these, a person's greatest relationship was with their book. He could see it in the faces of the group he was now with: young people, and thus serious and sombre, prone to reflection. But

114

now their expressions were even more withdrawn as, seated on the benches of the first way station within the tunnel, they fled deep within themselves. Maybe they spoke to their books. Sibiss did not know. He focused on his own; again, it seemed to weigh his arm down, making him lopsided. Just a fancy, but he had to resist the temptation to lean sideways, against the weight of the words.

At last a young woman appeared. She wore the bell trousers and apron of an image-maker, and her hands were spattered with ink: she must have been working when interrupted by the invaders. She said, anxiously, "We think it's safe. At the other end, I mean. There are others in the tunnels. You can come through."

Sibiss wanted to ask: *how many?* And how many still remained behind in the town, but it was not the right moment and, besides, she might not know. He followed the group through the sandstone labyrinth, until the uphill trudge began and a faint breath of air began to sift down into the stuffiness of the tunnel. Soon they came out onto the hillside above the plain.

The town lay in darkness, but there were flares and flashes of red. Sibiss' hearing was no longer good, but he thought he could detect distant cries. A thin column of fire streamed out across the plain: the Guenar troops, behind the vanguard.

"It has happened before," the image maker said. Sibiss turned to see her standing beside him. People always said this, never said *it will never happen again.* Because they knew it would; the Guenar would always come back. How many books remained? Sibiss did not know this, either. The town was ancient, had once held thousands upon thousands of volumes. Now less, but many had been rescued all the same.

They were shown to caverns in the rocks: refugee holdings. Far within the mountains a fire was burning, flickering over the frightened faces that huddled around it. Sibiss did not want to engage. He was too exhausted. He found a warm spot in the back of the cave and claimed it. Soon, he slept.

In the night, someone came to him. He was wide awake, sitting upright. The flames had died down, leaving a carpet of wood ash. Around him, people slept; he heard no voices. But someone was standing in front of him. At first he thought she was the image maker, but her clothes were old fashioned: a binding in strips about her limbs and her cone-shaped skull. She said, "I have to tell you something."

"Who are you?" Sibiss asked.

"I don't remember my name. You need to release me. But not yet."

"Release you? How?"

"I am your book," the figure said. "This is what I have to tell you."

Skeins and chains of words, overlapping. They said that the elder peoples had been able to hold three conversations at once, speaking many words, that the structure of their mouths had been different. Sibiss did not know how they knew this: perhaps this knowledge, too, had come from a book. But what the book told him was no more than a babble, a flashflood torrent of words which he could not understand.

"Stop, stop," he whispered, but it seemed that the book did not hear, or did not wish to listen. At last it fell silent, the words dying away, and Sibiss felt empty and strange. The quiet breathing of the others was all around him, comforting, and as was his habit when wakeful at night, he retreated into the past. Memories of his childhood in the infant pits, happy among his siblings, and then, grown, living in the tall house in Ammerar with his mates. Tending the rustling garden and watching sunsets from the terrace. The visit to Holk, on the salt coast – a great adventure, crossing the Dry Sea and waking with blistered skin, then the sophistication of Holk itself, its many bridges and ancient courtyards, the sweet-sour perfume of the floating trees filling the night air. They had brought back books – actual scrolls for the library, in waxed canisters so that the killing air of the Dry Sea crossing did not crust or crumble the fragile parchment.

All the books came safely home, and he had read many of them, high in the cloistered rooms of the old house, over the succeeding years.

Then, change. His mates had died, within a five year span. He had sorrowed at the time but now was glad: they had been spared so much. The trade routes with Holk and the southern citadels had been severed; trouble in the north, with rebel armies like the Guenar conjured up out of the sands like white spirits. Landless, uncivilised, no one knew quite where they had come from this time, and their only aim seemed destruction. By this time Sibiss had passed the old house on to the descendants of his mates, and was living in the little house: he did not know what had befallen Ammerar in this latest incursion and now, in the red firelight, he thought that he would prefer not to know: let the house live in memory, its quiet rooms and peaceful garden intact.

In the morning, a single shaft of sunlight illuminated the cave and the group moved on, deeper into the mountains. They walked all day, following the tunnels, and eventually a great wash of light fell over them: they were outside.

Sibiss took a deep breath. The air was familiar, salty and hot. He had not thought to breathe it again. When he followed the others to the lip of rock that looked out across the flat lands, he recognised it at once. The tunnel had brought them to the edge of the Dry Sea; a pale, glittering world extending to the blue shimmer of the horizon. Despite his better judgement, his spirits rose: beyond lay Holk, and memory, and the past. The image maker turned to address the group, her face resolute.

"Those of us who wish to, may go south. Head for Holk and the citadels. We believe they are safer. If you do not wish to, we will understand."

Sibiss sank down onto a boulder. He could taste salt in his mouth; it reminded him of Holk. There was no guarantee of safety, but perhaps they would be better able to preserve the books, if the supply chain south was not too badly interrupted. It was years since he'd had word from the citadels. The old house in Ammerar rose up in his mind, preserved forever in memory. The Guenar would come back, with their whistling standards, their explosives. It would never end and one day he would not escape. He looked south at the glittering land and made his decision.

It would be dangerous, the image maker said. The Guenar were now occupied, but they left brigades in the Dry Sea, and these were unpredictable. They would need to cross by day, since the Guenar slept in the heat, but they could not be sure and this in itself was hazardous.

Sibiss could not deny that he was afraid. When he first made the crossing he had been much younger, and strong. Now, old, he thought that he might not survive it. But he did not want to return to what had been home, he thought of Holk and took courage, and besides, there was the book...

They set off just before dawn, heading down the slope in the pearly light. Sibiss hoped he would not hold everyone up: he had told the image maker that they were to take his book and leave him if this occurred. Her long face saddened, but she eventually agreed. In spite of the hard going, the blistered ground and burning air, he felt light and calm. He would focus on Holk, he told himself, for the Dry Sea was only a journey, a means to an end. He rebuilt it in his mind, squinting against the blinding light, remaking it from its highest tower down to the flat pans of paddy fields beyond its wall. And after that, the sea, that miracle.

Soon, he could almost see it. He walked towards it, one foot after the other. Nothing else was real. The group walked slowly, their shadows hunched and humped: all had stored water before setting out. Towards twilight, the group took refuge in a pinnacle of rock, taking care that it was not already inhabited, and ate tough dried tubers. Then they watched, saying nothing, as a scatter of lights flared up across the plain, too close. They slept with two watchers, but although Sibiss thought he heard distant shouts in the night, they survived until morning.

The next day was hard, and the day after that, harder yet. Sibiss was not yet short of water, but this long walk was wrecking his joints. He stumbled often and the young people, in concern, offered to carry him; he refused, feeling no pride, but only the worry that he would drag them down with him.

On the next dawn, the raiders finally came.

Perhaps they were late, heading for whatever huddle of rocks sheltered them in the morning's harsh light, or perhaps they had seen tracks and decided to spring. It didn't matter. They were bent on killing and maybe hyper from the plant stimulants that they took. They rode warbirds with beaks like stone and cold red eyes, whose clawed feet ploughed the salt pans into a churn of dust. The attenuated domes of the raiders' skulls, flattened into flapping crests after birth and pierced with charms, whipped like their banners. They screamed as they came, displaying filed teeth.

The group formed a tight circle, elders and young in the middle. Sibiss found himself at the centre, like a seed. As one, the group opened their mouths and emitted a shout, on a register high enough to panic the warbirds and send them scattering, but only for a few minutes. The plane became a swirl of dust, with flashes of red as the birds milled and their riders fought to control them.

"Let me out."

For a dizzying moment, Sibiss thought that he himself had spoken. Then he realised that it was the book. The group were drawing breath for another shout.

"Let me out!" The voice in his head was urgent.

"I don't –" But he could not ignore it and what did it matter? In a minute, he would die. He shoved his way to the front of the group, oblivious to their cries. The dust was still whirling up but in the cloud he saw the Guenar raiders, now massed in a spearhead formation. He opened his mouth, but the book was no longer speaking. Instead, he felt words boiling up under his skin, looked down to see them skeining into the air, layer upon layer. They fell into the salt and squirmed, worming towards the raiders. The leading Guenar gave a cry of rage. He urged his bird forwards, but the ground was splitting, breaking up. The warbird lurched a step, to be swallowed by the cracking salt. The words squirmed on.

Sibiss felt as empty as a hollow reed, as one of the whistling enemy standards. He barely heard the image maker's shout of triumph, as one by one the raiders vanished into the boiling salt. It was over in moments. Dimly, he saw her rush forwards, saw the book claim her, writhing up over her outstretched arms and into her skin.

"Sibiss?" He could not see the owner of the voice. Salt lay beneath him, but its scouring was a comfort. "Sibiss! I'll take the book back, to home. I'll let it out, upon the Guenar. We'll bring you back."

"No," he whispered, for there on the horizon was Holk, made out of memory, rising in a shine over the salt flats, and beyond that, finally in reach, was the sea.

# The Darker Half

*The narrator of the story is the father of Arthur Conan Doyle: he was a painter of fairy land and he died in an asylum. This is my take on his story, but some of it comes from an experience that my late partner Charles had in the Highlands one Hogmanay: he encountered a similar apparition in the middle of a friend's arboretum on the shores of Loch Tay, but in that case, it really was just a ram. Luckily.*

My son does not believe me when I tell him that I draw only what I see. Like my wife, he thinks that my illustrations are nothing more than whimsical fancy: the small, malformed things that lurk beneath blackberry leaves, eyes like old sloes, hair as soft as fur, clothes formed from the skins of mice and the carapaces of beetles, weapons made out of blackthorn spikes and hedgehogs' quills. My son Arthur, the doctor, believes that I am mad, and thus he has had me brought from Edinburgh to this grim grey place, to wait out my days amid the shrieks and cries of the insane. I say very little these days. I only watch. There is plenty to see.

The Other People, the Darker Half, seem to enjoy the asylum. It's a long way from where I first encountered them, that misty loch shore under Ben Lawers. When I first came across them, I did not realise what it was that I saw. Or perhaps I should say 'who'.

It was along the shores of Loch Tay, just where a burn tumbled down through mossy rocks to a shoreline grove of alders. It was spring, and the loch shore was muddy and littered with driftwood from where the winter winds had churned the water into a froth. The alders were just coming into leaf and I intended to do some sketches for a commissioned natural history. I had already made a drawing of the grove, with the great bald summit of Ben Lawers rising up behind it, but was not satisfied. I drove myself hard in those days, always striving to be a better artist than I was, my head filled with romantic fancies. I threw aside as much of my rigid upbringing as I was able, drank absinthe in London cafes, and imagined myself misunderstood.

The day was drawing on to a spring twilight: an icy green sky above the darkening hills. On the shore, only a few inches from my left boot, something moved. I frowned. It was very small. It moved again. I went down on one knee to examine it more closely, and saw that it was a mouse. It was struggling: something had snared it by a hind foot. I could not bear to see even the smallest creature in pain. Gently, I closed my gloved hand around it and lifted it up. The mouse twisted in my grasp, its jet eyes shiny with panic, trying to bite. Examining it more closely, I saw to my astonishment that it was wearing some kind of harness: a rough affair of braided grass, with a tiny fragment of bone between its jaws that served as a bit. As carefully as I could, I eased the contraption away from its body and put the harness in my pocket. Then I set the mouse down and it bolted into a clump of grass.

Back at the lodge where I was staying, I examined the harness more closely. It was a curious affair, very tightly woven out of strips of what appeared to be reeds. I could only think that one of the village children had made it in jest or sport, though it seemed cruel to me to snare a miserable little beast in such a manner. I put the harness back in my pocket and went downstairs. The landlady was at the foot of the stairs.

"Oh, Mr Doyle. I was not sure if you were back. Dinner is about to be served."

Thanking her, I sat down to tough venison and a better pudding, and forgot about the mouse.

After dinner, I found myself becoming restless. I pushed open the curtains of my room and saw that it was snowing, a light enough fall for Scotland, but one that soon covered the ground. The room felt stuffy and hot; suddenly, I longed for fresher air. I pulled on my overcoat and went out into the bitter night.

A path led from the lodge down to the loch, winding between clusters of rhododendrons, already bearing fat buds. Later, the place would be a sea of blossoms if the frost did not nip them first. I had a small lantern, but it was confusing, walking among the rustling, snow-heavy leaves. I took a wrong turning and came out to a dead end: a solid mass of shrubbery, laden with snow. The lantern-light sparked from it, turning the leaves to glass and diamond. I lifted the lantern, my artist's eye taking pleasure in the effect.

Suddenly a great head appeared, framed by leaves.

I gave a startled cry, then cursed myself for a fool. *Why, it is only a ram,* I thought. But it was not. The head was three times the size of a sheep's, the horns massive and black, ringed with silvery striations that glittered in the lantern light like the strange rocks they find along the Dorset coast. I had a sense of immense weight and great age. Its eyes were silver pools, without pupils. It smiled a human smile and said, "So, you are the one who is bridle-bound."

I would have turned and run, beset by images of the devil himself, but I was rooted to the spot, with awe as much as fear.

"Do you choose the bridle?" the thing said. "If so, you will gain much in return."

"The bridle?" I found my voice.

The thing gave a great sigh. I smelled grass and summer on its breath and the icicles rang in response. "The Darker Half are diminishing, growing small. They find it difficult to ensnare something as large as a man in these times. A mouse, a wren – the tiny things. But you yourself took the bridle up."

"You are not small," I said. It laughed in a voice like a bell.

"I am a god."

"A god?" Surely Satan himself, I thought, but the fear was evaporating like mist in the light of those silver eyes. "Then what is your name?"

"My kind do not use names. Only men are so arrogant as to name."

"And what of this 'bridle'?" But I already knew that it was the thing I had removed from the mouse.

"If you accept the bridle," the god said, "Many things will be yours. It is your choice. Wealth. A long life." Its smile widened.

It was my turn to laugh, though it sounded hollow. "I should like both of those things, so long as wealth does not come to me through the death of another, and as for long life, why, I should want it only if I remained of sound body." I had read enough folk tales to know that such bargains could be, in the end, literally the devil's work.

The god grinned at me. I saw blunt teeth, like those of a ram. "But what would you wish for most?"

I did not hesitate. "Talent. And fame because of it."

"For that, you would accept the bridle?"

"Yes," I said, filled with sudden bravado. The leaves of the rhododendrons, dark green and white, seemed to float and drift around me.

"Then you shall have it," the god said.

123

"And the price?"

"You will be their saviour."

Something writhed in the breast pocket of my coat, twisting like a worm. I felt a sharp pain just above my heart, a pang of anguish. I cried out. A hot wire entered my flesh. My chest constricted and I doubled over, certain that I was about to breathe my last. Next moment, it was gone, though there remained an unaccustomed tightness in my chest. My head reeling, I stood upright again.

The face still gazed out at me from the branches of the rhododendrons, but now it was nothing more than stone, sightless, smiling, encrusted with stiff, frosty moss. I reached out a wondering hand and touched the cold horns. Nothing happened. It was a statue, nothing more. It struck me then that I was frozen, chilled through to the bone. I hastened back to the warmth of the lodge.

I do not remember falling asleep, nor dreaming. When I awoke, it was to find the sun streaming in between the curtains. Outside, the snow was melting, gleaming in patches beneath the shadows of the shrubbery. I turned away.

Something was sitting in the grate. It was small and black and wizened, with limbs like twisted twigs. It raised a pointed face and hissed at me, displaying a thick red tongue. A flicker of fire showed behind its slitted eyes and then it sprang up into the chimney and was gone. I stared after it, mouth open. I barely believed what I had seen.

That morning, I went back down to the shrubbery to seek the statue of the god, but could not find it. I saw other things, however: a trio of creatures that at first I mistook for wrens, sitting hunched in the branches of a tree; a minute thing with a long snout and wrinkled breasts that scurried into a log pile.

Since that day, I have seen more of them than I can count or name. They never speak, and it occurs to me to wonder if they can, or if their voices are simply too small to be heard, like the high squeaking of a bat. Indeed, I have glimpsed them flittering among the leaves on summer evenings, catching insects on the wing. I have seen one who could be said to be beautiful: a maiden with a coil of pale hair and eyes the colour of forget-me-nots, open and staring as she hung limply from the mouth of a stoat. Often, they ride dragonflies, hurtling down to prick the skin with thorns or sharpened feathers.

I did not understand what the god had meant by saying that I would be their saviour. Always, I remembered his words: the Darker Half are diminishing. Once, so folklore tells us, they were the size of men. I did not like to think of this. But nor did I like to think of them growing ever smaller, too little to be seen. I imagined them creeping into open sores, infesting the ears and mouth, hiding among foodstuffs, being swallowed.

I became obsessed with the notion that, for some of their kind, this had already happened. I washed my hands over and over again, convinced that they were crawling over my skin. I insisted that the maids boil my clothes, not once, but many times. Marital relations ceased, for I could not bear the thought that something might be watching.

There was only one way to distract me from their constant presence. I took refuge in whisky. At first it was only the occasional glass, as this seemed to dull their appearance somewhat. But then, it took more, and still more, until a full bottle was barely sufficient to drown out the things I saw from the corner of my eye. I stopped working – at my art, and at the menial clerical work I was undertaking to keep the family together. For the god had lied: I had not achieved fame as an artist, and this was most bitter of all, that I had paid the price without the glory.

At last, I was dismissed from my clerical post and my son Arthur took me to task.

"This cannot go on, Father. Why are you doing this to yourself?"

And dazed from drink, anxiety and lack of sleep, I broke down and told him.

"And you say that these things – these fairies and goblins that appear in your illustrations, are real?" His face was filled with doubt. I could not blame him. Yet young Arthur was himself the owner of a powerful imagination, the writer of a number of stories that he had given me to read and which I greatly admired.

"Yes! Yes, they are real. I see them as clearly as I see you, sitting before me."

I could see a professional kindness creep across his face.

"Do you see any of them in this room, father, at this moment?"

"I do not."

"So they are not visible all the time, then?" He leaned forward, steepling his hands.

"They come and go," I did not want to tell him about the god. Arthur was an open-minded young man, yet there were things that a Christian

125

upbringing made it difficult to countenance, and it struck me that a horned god in a Highland shrubbery was one of them.

He was frowning. "When did this begin?"

"Many years ago."

"Was it when the nature of your illustrations first changed?"

I tried to smile. "You remember? You were very young."

"I remember very well." His own smile came with less effort. "I used to creep into your studio sometimes, late at night, and look at the drawings of the day. The flowers and fruit – the sketches of animals inspired my own interest in anatomy. I suppose they could be said to be responsible for my becoming a doctor. I don't think I've ever told you this. Then, one night, I went into your studio and the drawings had changed. I saw the strangest faces looking out at me." He grimaced. "I had nightmares for weeks. They infested my sleep."

It was an unfortunate turn of phrase. I reached out and clasped Arthur's hands.

"Arthur, I do not know what to say. They are everywhere. I see them everywhere. They horrify me. And yet my drawings of them have made me the illustrator that I am."

His voice was very gentle. He said, "Father, you cannot go on like this. Mother told me that you missed an appointment at the theatre last week because you were washing your hands and combing your hair, over and over again, and that it is by no means the first time this has occurred. And then there is the drinking. You are insensible every night now. I confess, I did not realise that things had come to such a pass. Mother tells me that it has grown worse over the last year, but being so far in the south as I have been, she did not wish to place an added burden upon me. I believe that there are those who can help you. Will you let us try?"

I thought of the nights I had spent staring into the shadows, the firefly things with human faces, swimming like eldritch spawn out of the darkness, the bat-winged children of a stone-eyed god. The thought of an institution alarmed me, but I found myself nodding. "But I do not believe that anything can be done," I said.

They put me in a place called Fordoun House, a refuge for alcoholics. Here, at first, I enjoyed some peace from the sights that so tormented me, despite the poor state of my health: the shakes and shivers. Even the visions that I sometimes underwent from lack of drink were better than the things I usually saw. I began to feel that there might be a little hope, after all.

But then things changed. The Darker Half came to find me, and they were different here. They were more akin to ghosts: shadowed forms lurking in corners, with gaunt faces and haunted eyes, like aged children. One night, I woke to find them standing around me in a ring, staring. Their musty odour filled the room.

I could bear it no longer. I flung myself from the bed and pushed my way through their leathery bodies. I struggled with the window catch, but it would not open. They were coming toward me like spiders. I hurled myself at the window and it burst outward. I found myself falling through cold air and when I hit the ground it knocked the breath from my lungs. I lay there, dazed, until the nursing staff rushed out and brought me back inside.

I was not seriously hurt, surprisingly enough, but I was shocked and incoherent. I begged the doctor not to leave me alone, not to put me back in that room, and when he seemed not to be listening to me, I put my hands around his throat to try to shake some sense into him.

After that, they took me from Fordoun, and put me in the Montrose Asylum. I remember little of the journey.

The asylum is a strange place. I have had many conversations with those who are truly mad, who believe themselves to be Mary Magdalene or our own good Queen. Many of them are women and, strangely, more accepting of the things that I tell them that I see. They nod and smile, half listening, and mumble about the Good Folk. I want to say that there is nothing good about them, but I know that this is only a placating term, to prevent the Darker Half from taking offence.

Often, when I have these conversations, I see the creatures themselves crouched close by, grinning up at me. The asylum seems to make them bolder than they ever were in my own home. They sidle close, tug at clothes and hair and beard so that I am constantly batting them away – a fruitless endeavour, since they move as swiftly as lizards. I speak to the doctor here once a week, but it avails me little. Arthur was wrong. The doctor does not believe me, even when I point out one of the creatures, sitting clear as daylight upon the windowsill, eyes fire-bright. He is a good, dour, Presbyterian and he tells me that the only answer is faith. But I cannot believe. I pray, but no one seems to be listening. I gain more solace from my fellow patients.

Most of all, I want to go home. I cannot shake the thought from my head that Arthur and Mary simply wished to be rid of me.

Nor can I rid myself of the god's promise: that I am to be the saviour of these creatures. The thought disgusts me and I cannot see how this will even come to pass, confined as I am. The last thing I want is to be their saviour. I cannot even save myself.

*

I have been writing what passes for this journal in secret and hiding my scribbled notes under the mattress. This week, one of the nurses saw what I was about and came to speak to me. She was a tall, raw-boned woman with a face rubbed red by the weather and knotted hands. I placed her somewhere in her fifties, but these Highland women age swiftly and it was possible that she was very much younger.

"Who are you?" she said.

"I am Charles Doyle. And yourself?"

"It is Anne McLeod. What are you writing?"

"A diary." I drew it protectively closer.

She laughed. "Don't worry yourself. I won't ask to see it."

I smiled in response. "It is not very interesting."

"Mr Doyle, might I ask why you are in here?"

I hesitated for a moment, but if I did not tell her, someone else would.

"I see the Good People," I said.

She put her head on one side and looked at me. "Made a bad bargain, did you? With one of the old ones?"

"You know of this kind of thing?"

"I shouldn't be telling you this, but I made a bargain of my own, you see. I used to speak with the herb-wives in the hills. I wanted to learn from them. But my father was a God-fearing old fool and would not let me. One day, I met someone out on the slopes: a woman. There was something not right about her, if you catch my meaning, she was too tall, too pale, and her eyes were like silver. She told me that if I listened to the plants themselves, they would tell me all that I needed to know."

I was listening intently by this time. "And the price?"

"I would give them my unborn children," Anne McLeod said. "It didn't seem much of a price: I had no use for men. And indeed, I have never married."

"So you have not paid?"

"Oh, I paid. Every month, I paid. The pain, the blood – more than other women, much more." I looked away, embarrassed. She went on, "Do you know how old I am?"

I shook my head.

"I'm twenty-four. When they started to murmur about witches, I left my village and came to find work here."

My surprise must have shown in my face, because she gave a small, grim smile. "I don't think I have long. But I've had knowledge, and I've been able to help others. The Darker Half are not all wicked in their gifts. What did they promise to you?"

I told her. And I also repeated the remark about myself becoming their saviour.

"But I do not understand how," I said.

Anne McLeod was frowning. "You already are," she said.

"What?"

"Do you not understand? You make them be seen. The Darker Half are dwindling because no one pays any attention to them any more. Folk dismiss them as fancies, or think themselves mad and refuse to see. But you have made them visible again, through those drawings of yours. You've lengthened their lives."

"So now that I have stopped drawing them..."

"They might start leaving you alone," the nurse said. Her gaze met mine and it was compassionate. "But I would not gamble on it."

I hoped, for a while. But she was right, and shortly after that, I was told by one of the other nurses that she had died in the night and her body had been taken from the asylum. The Dark Half did not seem to want to leave me be. I saw them everywhere, now, crawling over the walls and furniture like lice. I tried to crush them – how different from the tender care I had given that little mouse, so many years ago! – but they parted easily under my stamping foot or pounding hand. They seethed within the food that was put before me and at last I could stand it no longer. I kept to my bed, refused to eat, and turned my face to the wall.

The doctors tried a variety of measures, but I would not respond.

Arthur came to see me, to exhort and plead, on his own and Mary's behalf. I would not listen.

"If you die," he said, shaking me by the shoulder, "As you well might, what then?"

"Then I shall die," I whispered. "And be free of this." But he was my son and I loved him, so I added what comfort I could. "I will be free then, beyond the grave. I will watch over you."

He gave a grim laugh. "I'm not sure I believe in this new-fangled spiritualism."

"I promise," I said, though in truth I was barely in my right mind. I did not realise when he went away.

That night I woke, suddenly, in the small hours of the morning. All was dark and still. The crawling mass that had surrounded me for so long was gone. I looked up.

The god's face was looking down at me from the ceiling.

"Is it time?" I asked.

"It is."

"You did not give me what I asked for!" I cried. "What of the fame, the glory?"

"But you have had it," the god said, in its mild voice. "Why do you think all these creatures have come to look at you, for so long? You are renowned throughout the world of the Darker Half. By seeing them, by drawing them, you have saved them, just as the herb-wife told you."

"The herb-wife is dead," I said.

"The herb-wife is released, just as you shall be."

The room was opening up, the wall shimmering into nothing to reveal an open slope. I could see light out across the hill, soft and glowing as the moon on water.

"Come and see what you have helped to save," the god said, and I rose from the bed and walked out onto the hollow hills, where the women are beautiful beyond compare, and the men ride horses as swift and graceful as the wind. But even as I walked through the wild roses and the flowering may and the world of men faded behind me, I knew that I would not be content until I had kept my promise to my son.

# The Child on the Hill

*This is one of a series of short stories set in the world of Mondhile, which appears in the linked novels The Ghost Sister, Darkland and Bloodmind. It's a far-future world colonised by humans, who have changed significantly over time and who have forgotten their origins. Much of those changes are due to ancient terraforming technology. The 'forgotten origins' is an old SF trope, but one which I felt suited the stories set here. I suppose this is typical Science Fantasy, with tech that is seen as magic, and a people governed by superstitions. Their child-rearing practices are, by the way, somewhat different to our own!*

There was a cold wind blowing down from Snakeback when Eredruen went to find the child. He knew it was a mistake, and he had said as much to his sister, but she would not listen. That was the trouble. Taray had always been delicate, indulged, favoured, and he had been as guilty as anyone, but now he saw it as a critical error: a long, twisting weave which had its roots in the far past. Like watching someone at a loom, making a fault in the beginning and, though not failing to notice, deciding that it did not need to be corrected, would make an interesting part of the pattern. And then, years and wefts later, realising that the whole piece was flawed because of it and could not now be mended.

But if it could not be mended, they would have to wear the cloth as best they could, and so Eredruen rode out now, on a golden morning on the edge of winter, looking for Taray's daughter, his sister's child. The air bit, and Eredruen thought that the first snow would not be far behind. Taray had whimpered at the thought of her child out in the snows, no matter how many times Eredruen and others had pointed out that she had spent the previous thirteen unscathed. Or so it was felt. Both Taray and the satahrach had said that they would have known if the girl had died and Eredruen knew that his sister had gifts, could sense the small matters of the world even if she was not well enough to sit in council.

It was odd how things worked out. He had almost refused – had, in fact, done so, and for once the family had been in accord. Taray was – well, usually they were happy enough to go along with her demands; it made for a quieter life. But this was different, a wider matter, relating to human nature and not personal whim. He would not go to look for the child, they were agreed.

And then the stranger had come.

He was courteous, even apologetic. He did not like to bring troubles to someone's door. He stood in the main hall of Roskereth, twisting a braided scarf in his hands. He was not a warrior, but a man who makes bread, and they knew him from Ulleet, some *lai* down the coast.

"Good bread, too," Askithia said, kindly.

"Thank you. We use a special kind of grain, that's mixed with – well, you won't be interested in all that. I've come about a child."

His voice dropped on the final word and Eredruan saw everyone sit up a little straighter as a thread, which tasted of the future and fate, snaked into the room. Taray was not there, of course. She was upstairs in the turret room.

"A child?" the satahrach said.

"It – I'm afraid it attacked my brother. He was travelling, between Ulleet and Haupt. Through the hills. He was on foot. The girl set upon him, from a nest in the scrub near a ring of stones. He defended himself, of course. She slashed his arm and he knocked her out, but when he went back with a party from the town, she had gone."

"We do not believe that she is dead," the satahrach said.

"He did not hit her very hard. He was not aiming to kill, of course. You know how difficult it is in these matters. But he looked, and she had the caste mark of Roskereth on her shoulder. So we know she belongs to you."

The satahrach shifted uneasily in her chair. "She would. We have – that is, there is a daughter of this house in the world. She will return soon, if she is spared. We can pay a blood price –"

"No! That is not necessary," the man said. "I have not come here because of that. We want nothing from you, we are decent people, not ones who seek advantage here and there. We just wanted you to know."

And so they did, and so Eredruen was here.

It was, of course, a breach of taboo to go forth and find a child in normal circumstances. After all, who would want to? There was a natural degree of concern but it was not the way things worked. It was not the way things were done. When a child was old enough to walk, old enough to fight, you sent it out into the world to fend for itself until its return, when it would begin to change. But now, with the attack, Eredruen had an excuse to go forth on Taray's behalf and locate the girl, bring her back by force if necessary. Their primary duty was to their neighbours and although it was held to be an inauspicious start to one's life as a person, a conscious being, the satahrach had sanctioned it now and subdued Eredruen's uneasy conscience.

He rode higher, following the beast tracks into the foothills of the Otrade. Embar ai Elemnai, Snakeback, reared ahead, the flanks of its glaciers touched rose and gold in the fading sun. Soon, he would have to make camp, before the autumn twilight fell and left him on the hillside, exposed and vulnerable. He rode to the summit of a ridge and looked down: rocks reared up from the hill, turrets of grey stone encrusted with lichen. Best to investigate these, before the light died. He rode down to the outcrop of stones and dismounted. An initial exploration revealed nothing: the yellowed grass between the rocks bore neither footprints nor spoor. There were none of the characteristic odours of visen or other beasts. Reassured, Eredreun took food out of his pack and ate it; the bread reminded him of the man from Ulleet, and he smiled.

Night fell softly, fading out over the distant sea. The high peaks of the Otrade captured the last of the sun and then the stars pricked out, not quite at their full winter burn, but bright nonetheless. Eredreun amused himself by following the constellations, until the long day caught up with him and he slept.

He woke towards the small hours of the night. Something had disturbed him. The mount stirred, whickering. Eredreun kept his breathing even, and took care not to stir. Something was moving among the stones. Eredreun did not move. He waited until the thing was above him. He could hear it breathing – and his hand lashed out and caught it by the wrist. It shrieked and hissed, twisting in his grasp, but Eredreun did not let go. He wrenched its arms behind its back and forced to its knees.

It wore a tangle of moss and creeper and animal wool. It was wet, and this, Eredreun reflected, was probably why it did not stink, at least, not too much. He pulled the wool aside and saw the faded caste mark of Roskereth on its shoulder. Taray's daughter, a girl of his own house. The child whom he had come to find had found him.

She twisted in his grip. He looked down into silver eyes. The child whispered, "Who are you?"

Eredreun was so startled that he nearly dropped her.

"You can speak!"

"Of course."

"But –"

The child looked genuinely puzzled. "Why not?"

Cautiously, Eredreun let her go. "You haven't come home yet."

"I should like to go home," the child said, shyly sly. Eredruen found himself at something of a loss. He had never heard of such a thing before. Either a child died in the world, or it returned, passing over the moat of its house and receiving that lightning strike that conjured awareness and the dawning of understanding, like light breaking over the rim of the world.

"Well," he said, "That's where we'll go, then."

There was a flash of triumph in the child's face, swiftly concealed. Eredruen did not like it. The whole situation was strange. "You sleep," he added. "I'll keep watch."

The child smiled again. "There's no need. The visen don't often come down this far – they keep to the heights. I've been safe enough, haven't I?"

Eredruen had to concede this, but he did not trust the child and so he would, he thought, only pretend to sleep. The girl settled down some distance away, curled like an animal in a nest of rock. Eredruen waited, for perhaps half of an hour, and he was not surprised when, beneath the slits of his eyelids, he saw a shadow rise and slip into the rocks. After a moment's pause followed her.

It was not far from dawn, and the air was freezing. Above Snakeback, the stars were as thick as dust. Eredruen moved softly but the child was quick, darting in and out of the rocks. He followed, saw a yawn of dark appear amongst the stones and then the child was gone.

Eredruen waited again, for a moment. The child had moved with purpose: she knew where she was going. It occurred to him that this was some kind of trap; for a few seconds he balanced curiosity with wariness, and curiosity won. He headed after her, into the darkness.

It was a tunnel, cut into the rock. Eredruen's night vision took a moment to adjust after the brightness of the starlit world, but when it did so he could see that the walls of the passage were smooth, curving to the roof. The stone was like glass, and cool to the touch without a trace of damp. His footsteps seemed swallowed by the stone and he could not hear the child at all, so he proceeded with care. Then he took a step and it was like walking into a hive of bees. The tunnel hummed, burning and prickling across his skin, but it did not last. He took another step and it was gone. A moat, he realised, like the moats of energy which surrounded every house in the district, but it was not nearly as strong. It felt decayed, as though the power it had once contained was winding down. He looked back and he could see it in his mind's eye: a thin web of force, sparkling and glimmering, but erratic and patchy in places.

He went on and nearly fell into a room where the tunnel widened out. He moved back, hastily, but he had seen the child at the far side of the room, crouched against the wall with her back to the door. He could not see what she was doing. Her hands were pressed, pale stars, against the wall, which was rough and black in contrast to the rest of the stonework. As he watched, a faint network of silver light appeared across the roughness. A voice began to speak, in a language which Eredruen did not understand and yet which had resonances of his own – a word which meant water, and one for danger. The room was full of a whispering, whistling sound and Eredruen stepped back, but it was too late. He felt his senses begin to drown in a dark rising tide and then the room fell away, as if the walls were peeling down around him.

It was daylight. He was outside, looking out over Snakeback. The sun was high in the sky but he could not feel anything – neither the warmth nor the wind on his skin. And the familiar view seemed different – the small squat turret of Cernan Fortress was no longer on its customary hill, and the bridge that spanned the snaking expanse of the Watchwater had gone. Eredruen felt a shiver up his back: the fortress had been there on its hill for over a thousand years. Where had it gone?

Someone was walking up the hill towards him and he felt a familiar twinge of distaste and dislike. It had been growing ever since the crew had emerged and in the month of planetary orbit, very little had happened to abate it. Her face held a grimace of contempt, also familiar. He was bound to her, as his commanding officer, but he did not have to like it.

"This," she said, gesturing to the quiet river valley and the immense span of the mountains. "This is a land for peasants."

"They've sent exploratory teams in already after the initial – there's been a –"

"I know all that. Don't be stupid, LaHarje. There's nothing here for us."

"The mineral reports –"

"There's nothing *here*."

He knew what she meant. He looked down at his hands, at the ground, because otherwise he would have said something that he would have regretted, because she would have made him regret it. She wasn't interested in any wealth beneath the ground of this unknown world. She wanted people. People whom she could control, and there were none here. To her, this glorious world was empty. He looked out across the span of the river valley and for a moment he almost felt sorry for her.

"The equipment's set up," Shannar said, coming out from the entrance to the base and smoothing back a strand of red hair. They had an understanding, reflected in their colouring, he thought: both from Riechare, whereas Amitrie had been born and raised on-station. Perhaps that's why she sought to conquer people, not worlds. Shannar had, LaHarje realised, decided that the best tactic with Amitrie was simply to pretend she wasn't there, answering the questions her CO had put to her with the bare minimum of words and barely glancing in her direction.

"There's no point." Amitrie's voice was sharp.

"I think it's as functional as it's likely to be," Shannar said. Amitrie turned on her heel and strode away down the slope. Shannar and LaHarje looked after her.

"I've seen it before," LaHarje said. "The psychologists say it's a temporal thing. They can't cope with emergence from stasis."

"Oh no." Shannar spoke with conviction. "She was crazy before they put her under. She's not competent to command and I'm sending a message out to that effect. We pull out. We leave her here, if necessary – return to Hirnault's Hub and file her missing."

LaHarje was conscious of a growing sense of relief, combined with shame. It was not guilt over the idea of mutiny, but that he hadn't had the guts to make that decision himself.

"All right," he heard himself say. "Tell me what to do."

Through LaHarje's eyes, Eredruen, helpless, watched the clouds above the mountains speeding past, the sun going down in a blaze, the moons sailing up into the heavens and then he was once more standing on the hillside, looking down at Shannar's body. Her blue eyes were open, in anger and surprise. A great bloody gash stretched down her sternum, with the dissolving core of a boltgun blast singing the material of her uniform. LaHarje ran, zigzagging into the rocks and down towards the base. He thought he heard a shout behind him. Then he was down into the tunnel that led to the base, and activating the defences. He heard Amitrie curse, then her voice was abruptly cut off.

Eredruen saw what happened next through dual sight: his own, and LaHarje's. It was as though they were both stretched wide over time, with the river valley below outlined in a web of light. Eredruen could see the lines beneath the land, its veins and blood, converging on the nexus of the base and the technology that Shannar had installed.

Then it was as though everything was cut off. LaHarje stood in silence, a muffled quiet which enveloped him like a blanket. A huge calm descended upon him: he had a final glimpse of the landscape around and then it consumed him, Shannar's installation of pre-terrachanging tech interacting with the land itself and trapping his spirit within it. Dimly, he was aware that he was dead, but still present, and that the raging entity beside him was Amitrie, whose body lay just outside the base, a feast for the carrion. With relief and a vast sense of peace, LaHarje shut himself off from her, looking out towards the land and away.

Eredruen felt the presence of LaHarje, stirring as though insects walked inside his mind. He tried to move, but could not. His wrists were bound behind him in a tight knot, which would not give. Pretending to be unconscious, he opened his eyes a little. The child was standing on the other side of the chamber, feet braced against the floor. Her hands flickered over the rough stone of the wall, leaving lines of silver in their wake. Her movements were practised, and now Eredruen knew how it was that the child was conscious and aware. It wasn't Taray's daughter who stood before him, at least, not in spirit, but someone alien, adult, ruthless. A stealer of bodies and perhaps of souls. How was it that she could speak his language, though? He did not know, but perhaps she had done this before, skipping from form to form. Or perhaps she had learned it through the lines of the land themselves.

He closed his eyes again and tried to think strategically. Her advantage had been surprise. The trap had been sprung when he'd stepped over the moat of the fort. Amitrie had knowledge, but she was still in the body of a very young woman, and was therefore physically weaker than him. If he could get free…

"LaHarje?" he spoke inside his mind. He could sense LaHarje retreating, closing, drawing back inside a mental shell. Amitrie might want a new body but Eredruen had the distinct impression that LaHarje did not. "LaHarje!" The unfamiliar name was hard to pronounce, even silently in thought.

"Who are you?" The words were Mondhaith, his own dialect. Eredruen felt like a mirror, reflecting LaHarje back to himself.

"My name is Eredruen. You're in my mind."

There was the suggestion of a laugh. "No, you're in mine."

"I don't understand you."

"This fortress," LaHarje said. "This is my mind, this is who I am now."

"But you were a person." The fort must contain LaHarje's ghost, Eredruen thought. It happened, sometimes. A dead person became trapped by the land and could not break free into *eresthahan*, the world of the dead. And Amitrie, too: the same thing had happened to her but she was stronger, could possess others.

"I was a man, yes."

"Amitrie is your enemy?"

"Yes. And yet – several thousand years is a long time. People change."

This was not what Eredruen necessarily wanted to hear.

"And if she has not changed?"

"Then she must do as she sees fit."

"Look," Eredruen said. "I need your help."

"I am a voice, a breath, a sigh. How can I help you?"

"How do I send her back?"

"I don't know. And I am at peace, now. Leave me be."

The voice grew silent. "LaHarje?" Eredruen hissed, within, but the ghost was still.

Cursing silently, Eredruen decided that he was on his own. Typical spirit – showed you all manner of wonders, then vanished just as it showed promise of becoming useful. Well, he would shift for himself, then. He started to saw at the rope with a claw. It took a long time, and all the while, through slitted eyes, he watched the girl, busy at the wall. Eventually, barely giving his slumped form a second glance, she walked out and Eredruen was able to dispatch the bonds in earnest.

As he did so, he thought hard. He knew that he did not understand how this part of the spirit world worked: there were two ghosts, of people who had come here many years before, who had somehow died because of Amitrie's treachery and who had become trapped in the shell of the old fort. One – LaHarje – seemed content enough to remain where he was; Amitrie, the ruthless one, had stolen the body of Taray's daughter, but how was he to dislodge her and free the child? He did not possess the right kind of understanding, he decided. He was a hunter-warrior, not a satahrach. But there was a satahrach close enough at hand: back home at Roskereth. Back to the original plan, then: take the child home and instead of a normal returning, let the satahrach deal with her. To do that, Eredruen would have to free himself, and then overpower Amitrie. This should not be impossible. He was an adult and the possessing spirit was in the body of a child. He would not make the mistake of attempting this near the fort, and he remained wary of any magic that Amitrie might still have access to. He freed his wrists, flexed his hands, and stood.

Outside, it was light. Eredruen stepped warily over the moat, feeling a shiver of energy, but nothing more. Yet, to his surprise, he could see the moat – a shimmer of silver in the earth itself, as if the ground had become liquid. He scanned the land. There were other lines, radiating out from the fort, and no sign of Amitrie. He could see where she had gone, however. She had left clear traces – a footprint, a snapped blade of grass. Her trail led down into a grove of satinspine, its red leaves catching the morning light and glowing like fire. Eredruen followed, swiftly and silently.

The silver line that glimmered by her path led down into the trees, too, and now he could see that it was forming a pool of dim light. Whatever she had done within the confines of the fort had somehow made the energy lines of the land visible to him: something felt, but never seen. It was a form of magic that he had never experienced and he did not know what she was trying to do, but it could not, he thought, be anything good. He glided into the trees and now he could hear her up ahead. He doubted that the child herself would have made so much noise, but Amitrie did not seem to understand the first thing about subterfuge and this surprised him. Perhaps she had always relied on her ruthlessness and her magic. The red leaves shivered above him and he stopped, melting into the shadows of the trees. He could see Amitrie now. She was crouched on the other side of the energy pool, staring back up the path. And he realised why she had not bothered to conceal her passing: she knew he was there and was trying to lure him on. She must have realised that he could overpower her and was setting a trap, and perhaps she did not know that he could see the pool. Her gaze was intent on the path she had made. Eredruen smiled to himself. She was arrogant and that would benefit him… very well, then. He slipped around the back of the grove, moving as silently as he could and keeping Amitrie in sight. Her gaze did not waver: she was confident that he would follow. It was only when he came up behind her that, perhaps prompted by the senses of her borrowed body, she half turned and Eredruen struck her beneath the ear, a blow that stunned her. She fell across a tree stump; Eredruen put his hands around her throat until she was unconscious.

Then he lifted her up and carried her back to the fort. His mount was not far away. He found it dining on the body of some small creature it had killed and it glanced up mildly, as if wondering where he had got to. Eredruen loaded the child's body onto the mount's back and took its reins. He led it down through the hills into the morning light, leaving behind the quiet fort with its sleeping ghosts, and the crimson grove with its pool of silver light.

They reached Roskereth towards evening. Earlier, Amitrie had begun to stir and Eredruen had hit her again, gritting his teeth. He did not like to do this, but he could not risk Amitrie regaining consciousness. And even so close to return, it was a mistake to feel too much pity for a child: their fierceness remained, up until the moment they stepped over the moat. At that, Eredruen slowed, so that the mount nudged his shoulder with its long muzzle and displayed sharp teeth. It wanted its stable and its bucket. But Eredruen was not sure what would happen if the child was unconscious when she crossed the moat. He reminded himself that she was possessed – but what would happen? Would it kill her? Damage her in some way?

He had just decided to leave her strapped to the mount and to find the satahrach when the child once again began to stir. This time, Eredruen hesitated, since they were so close to the house and the moat. Amitrie muttered something in a harsh unknown tongue and this decided him. He slapped the neck of the mount and took it at a run down the slope that led to Roskereth. He glimpsed someone on the roof, raised a hand and shouted to open the gate. The moat was up, glittering blue in the eye of his mind. Eredruen plunged across it with the mount in tow and as he did so, Amitrie gave a terrible cry. Then they were across and Erdruen drew the mount to a snarling halt.

The child lay limp on the mount's back. Surrounded by a small crowd of concerned people, Eredruen decided that it would be easier to explain to the satahrach, who even now was bustling down the stairs. Since he didn't have much of a clue as to what had actually happened, he might as well let her explain it, he thought.

Later that evening, by the child's bedside, he watched with the satahrach and Taray as her daughter began to come round. His sister was white with worry, and at last the satahrach made her go to bed, leaving Eredruen free to ask the question he had been too cautious to utter.

"Is it Taray? She's so concerned for the child – it's not normal. Has it drawn the ghost to the girl?"

The satahrach's face was troubled. "I could not say. I have seen possession, of course, but not like this, and not for a number of years. It's a very strange case."

"I told you what I saw," Eredruen said. "It seemed to me that they were people from the stars, from very far away. I've never heard of such a thing."

"Nor have I. But spirits will take on all manner of lies and guises, being unchained from the moral world upon their death. Doubtless this is no more than that."

Eredruen, reassured, nodded, and at that point the girl opened her eyes. She stared uncomprehendingly at Eredruen; there was no sign of recognition.

"Do you understand what I am saying to you?" Eredruen asked, and the girl looked blank.

"Well," the satahrach said. "*That's* a good sign, at least."

In the days to come, Erdruen watched with a quiet satisfaction as the girl grew in confidence. By the third evening, she allowed them to wash her hair and her body and by the fourth, she had begun to use simple words. All was as it should be.

But on the fifth night, Erdruen stepped out onto the roof terrace, above the moat, for a breath of air. The year was growing on and the temperature had already significantly dropped. There was a bitterness to the air, tight on the tongue. He leaned over the balustrade and breathed in, and that was when he heard the voice.

It was coming up from the moat. It wheedled and sang, then grew angry.

"LaHarje?" it called. "Do you hear me, LaHarje? Do you hear?"

Amitrie. Her spirit had been snared in the fort, and now, it seemed, it was snared in the moat of Roskereth.

Well, he thought. This house is full of spirits, whispering. What is this but one more? And he stifled the flicker of fear as he turned from the voice and the darkening air, and went back inside.

# The Green World

*I have an abiding love of Shakespeare, some of which comes out in the Fallow sisters novels, and some of which inspired this short story. Some of my relatives live near Stratford, so the countryside around there, which inspired Shakespeare, also inspires me. I'm unlikely to be a household name, though!*

*Jules feels as though she's been running for days, weeks, months – but it's probably been no more than a couple of hours. Her lungs are bursting and filled with fire; her breath is coming in great sobs, coughed out of her throat. She knows she's got to stop but she's too scared, in case they're still after her, in case they find her.*

*But she doesn't know where she's going.*

It began in the club, just after midnight. She didn't know who he was, but he wouldn't leave her alone, kept pestering her to dance, to talk, bought her a drink she didn't want and then tried to guilt her over it. A tall, thin man, anywhere from twenty-five to forty, dressed in black. A thin face, too, and a lot of black hair. Good looking, if you liked Goths: not Jules' type. It wasn't the sort of club that normally attracted Goths; Jules couldn't work out what he was doing there, unless it was to perve onto girls who weren't interested. Eventually, when telling him to fuck off had had no effect, she called security and they told him to leave. Job done. Or so she'd thought.

She'd been careful leaving the club, of course. Tagged along with a big group who had been going in the same direction and there had been no sign of the bloke – except when she had turned, alone, down the short street that led to her flat. Then there he was, stepping out from behind a lamp post, like a shadow from the air, and another, and another – also tall, thin, black haired, as if he was copying himself, replicating out of lamplight and darkness. And that was when Jules ran.

She had a destination, originally: out into Broadmarket, where there would still be Saturday night crowds, police, help. The men were cutting her off from home: she ducked down a side street, trying to find somewhere that still had a light on, to hammer on the door, but when she tried, a thin man was there, sweeping his hair back from his forehead, a theatrical gesture, deliberate: *look at me.*

They were playing a game, she realised. If they could move like that, splitting, dividing, they could easily cut her off; she was being herded, corralled. The next road she took ended in the railway embankment: she saw this too late. One of them appeared in front of her, causing her to swerve, step on something that was not concrete, stumble suddenly into a tangle of loosestrife and rosebay willowherb, the steep scarp of the embankment. Then she was falling, rolling, her mind filled with the thought of the live rail – but when she landed, it was not onto a bed of metal.

Herbs. Crushed, green, growing. Their sharp pungency cleared her head and nothing was broken, not even bruised. She raised herself on her elbows, expecting to see her pursuers. No one was there. Above her head, huge fronded branches swayed in the breeze and the scented night was mild. There was a milky light everywhere, casting the leaves into silver: the moon was full and soaring. This wasn't the scrappy landscape of the railway siding – it was more like a wood, but there was nothing like this in the middle of the city, not even the parks. The trees were huge and mature; putting a hand on the soft ground, Jules found the sudden hardness of a pellet – an acorn. Even she, a city girl, knew that meant oaks. And she'd left the city at the start of winter, the trees had been bare, but here they were fully covered. Jules scrambled to her feet. In the bushes, something was rustling. A sail-winged moth drifted past her face and she flinched; someone laughed.

"Who's there?" But there was no reply. Jules started walking, aimlessly, trying to find a path. It was almost as though the place had been landscaped; she'd heard somewhere that ancient forest had been dense and impenetrable but this was more like parkland, with swathes of soft green grass between the trees and a frondy herb which smelled sweet-sharp. Soon, she came to a glimmering pond, with the moon's round reflected face swimming in it. Someone was sitting by it, on a tussock of grass. Slowly, and with caution, Jules walked around the pond. A man, but not one of her pursuers. He had a plume of fair hair, falling over one shoulder, a white fencing shirt, breeches. She could not see his face.

"Excuse me?"

There was no response. "Excuse me?" Jules said again, and this time, he looked up. He had no face, only a pallid oval, like a torn piece of paper. Briefly, melancholy features flickered across it and were gone.

"Oh my God," Jules said. She put a hand to her mouth, stumbling backwards. The figure raised a hand, held it there, palm out. She ran, again, back into the illusory shelter of the trees. But there was someone waiting for her there, too, by the great dark bulk of an oak.

"What the hell?"

A little girl, with roses in her hair, and a dress like filmy shadows. She was barefoot, unsmiling. The roses tumbled down her shoulders like small white moons.

"This is the Green World," the child said. "What are you doing here?"

Her voice was high and sweet but there was an odd resonance to it, almost a hum underneath the words. The thought flashed through Jules' mind that she was not human at all, but some kind of device.

"What's the Green World?"

"Where you stand. Where have you come from?"

"Birmingham."

"Is that in England?" The rose-crowned child frowned. "Yes, of course, it must be."

"Yes, it's in England."

"It has changed," the child said. "It was more like this, once."

"I think the city started as a village," Jules said. "Or a number of villages."

"We have few visitors now," the child told her. A light shone momentarily behind the girl's eyes, like the reflection of the moon, but that was behind her, visible through the oaks.

"I saw a man – men – in black. They chased me. And there's someone sitting by a pond. With no face."

145

"They are part of the Green World," the child said. "They adapt." She looked sharply to the left. "I have to go. She's calling me."

"Who?"

"She," the child said, her voice hushed, as though the word should be in capitals. She plucked a rose from her crown, thrust it into Jules' hand, turned and ran. Jules followed, but in a flicker, the child was gone. She looked up. The trees were all made of paper, cardboard cutouts, one dimensional. Jules blinked and the woodland was back. The rose lay cool in her palm. She could hear voices and she walked in the direction that the child had taken.

The voices seemed to be coming from all around her: sometimes very loud, and sometimes no more than a whisper. They made her shiver, as though they were running over her skin, raindrop cold. She could not see anyone and remembering the black-clad men made her start to breathe harder in panic. She told herself that they were not here, that she had not seen them, forcing the panic down. But the voices went on and as Jules walked, she began to feel that they were mocking her, that it was all a stage set-up designed to drive her mad. She shook her head but the paranoia continued. Something flickered across her vision, darting between the trees: she wondered whether it was the girl. At least the child had been able to speak, a semblance of human; she hoped it was not the man at the pond. The ground here was covered in a feathery herb, not grass, and fragrant. Jules plucked a stem of it and sniffed: its sharpness cleared her head. Here, the oaks were enormous, the biggest trees she had ever seen, and well-spaced. The sense of a stage set returned, for she felt suddenly small, dwindling in the light of the huge moon and the trees. She looked up. Someone was sitting in a tree, a figure dressed in rags that were like streamers of light.

"The child said a woman was here." The voice was light, and she could not tell if it was male or female.

"I – found my way in. Who are you? She said it was called the Green World."

"The Green World. Arden."

"Arden? What, you mean the forest of Arden? But that's nothing like this. It's all that remains of –" She stopped. All that remains of the forest that once covered this land, before the city came. "Shakespeare used it in a play," she added.

"We knew him. He came here, as did many more. When the world was thinner and the boundaries less. When people listened more."

"A Midsummer Night's Dream," Jules said. She'd quite liked English in school, but she'd only been to the theatre once. The thing in the tree laughed.

"He came to the court," it said. "He didn't understand it. He thought it was all real."

"What court? Isn't it real?" She felt like a parrot.

"Oh," the thing said. "You haven't seen it? Then let me show you."

The trees – trunks, branches, leaves – drew back in a sweep of motion, like curtains. Jules, gasping, saw a tableau open out before her. A woman lay on a chaise longue, surrounded by fronds of meadowsweet, skeins of wild rose, cow parsley. Like the man Jules had seen, she had no face above her trailing gown; she was a sketch only, a series of impressions. Forms and figures drifted about her in the long grass; they were easier to see out of the corner of the eye, where they approximated a semblance of human. Jules had an impression of colours, rainbow hues, trailing shapes of light. The scene was suddenly very large – she looked up into an umbra of meadowsweet, catching the light of the moon – and then tiny, a shoebox-sized court in the grass. Her senses spun, stabilised, and the woman on the chaise was standing before her. Her features solidified, like molten wax, into elongated beauty. She held out a hand and when Jules, reluctantly, took it, it felt akin to cool plastic. She did not speak, but led Jules into the trees. The trunks were rivalled by huge flowers; here, it was as though everything was the same size and Jules, for a second, found herself looking down on the crowns of the oaks. She had a vision of the whole forest tucked away into the corner of a city garden. Perhaps this was what had happened; it had not disappeared at all, but simply dwindled and slid, only to be unpacked again as a child's present is saved till Christmas. But had Jules herself unpacked it, or someone else. She pulled at the woman's hand.

"There were men – a man – after me. Do you know who he is?"

The woman spoke for the first time. "Of course." Her voice was like a bell. She changed, shifting into black and white; Jules' pursuer held her fingers tightly and Jules kicked out, connecting with a shin. The thing showed no sign of pain, or even that it had noticed. Jules wrenched her hand away and saw a streamer of light hanging in front of her face; she grabbed it and was pulled up, up into the branches of an oak. The thing she had seen earlier was sitting there, head cocked to one side like a crow.

"Perhaps I should have said. They are all one thing. I am the exception."

"What do you mean? The woman is the man?"

"The queen is the king and the king the queen. Here, the rules are different. Everything is the same material, written out of words and grass and flowers."

"But you are not the same. You are separate." She was trying to look down through the leaves, but she could not see the black clad man or, indeed, anyone. The ground seemed much too far away.

"I am myself and part of something else. I am from another place-and-story; I was brought here to move freely, to keep fluidity, to stop stagnation."

Jules was not sure that she understood, but the thing was, she thought, a free agent of sorts, and it had saved her. But from what, and was she even in danger here? At the club, the man had been intrusive, asking the same questions over and over: *why are you here? What do you want?* But if he was like a programme, or part of a machine, perhaps this was understandable. "What does he want? She? Whatever he is?"

"To change you."

"Into what?"

The thing gave its sidelong smile. "*I* don't know. You can only find out by being changed, can't you?"

She could not, she thought, sit here forever. "How do I get down?"

"Jump. I'll lend you wings." She felt a fluttering of light around her head, a band about her temples. She slipped from the branch and drifted down, a dustmote turning in the moon's cold light, to land in the untenanted grass.

"Where are you, then?" She looked around her, but there was no sign of the man or the woman – the queen, she thought, the queen of the court contains the king. Oberon and Titania are one and the same, and the forest, too. Made from words and woven starlight. She was no longer afraid, not even when the elder tree that sprang from the roots of the oak took form and stepped into air. It turned left then right; it was both man and woman.

"Go on, then," Jules said. "Make me change."

The figure held out a hand, the fingers long and pale, and the hand became a rapier. Jules felt the sting, the sharp unending pain, before she even saw it strike; as she fell, clasping her side, she saw the figure slide back into elder tree, but now the barren elder flowered, first creamy white, then red as her blood spilled onto the grass and coloured all she saw.

When she woke, white had replaced green. A hospital ward, where she was told that she had been the victim of assault. A mild concussion; no stab wounds. There was no blood on her clothes. She half expected, on sitting up, to find a single rose on the neatly turned sheet, or a sprig of elder or meadowsweet, but there was nothing. They kept her in for forty eight hours, to make sure, and then released her. Her handbag still contained her money, and her phone.

She went back to work a day later. Colours seemed brighter, but perhaps that had been the concussion. Looking out of the office window, she saw a small flowering tree: she had not noticed it before. Even though it was winter, this was a late blossoming one, the colour of mingled blood and moonlight. She went out that afternoon into a light cold rain and stood by it, scenting the air and the onset of dusk, the wind from the hills and the damp earth, the distant forest air.

149

# The Ontologist

*In recent years I've contributed stories to a couple of NewCon Press anthologies, including* Once Upon a ParSec, *a volume edited by my old friend and Milford Workshop co-conspirator David Gullen (a fantastic writer in his own right), and this one, written for an anthology edited by Ian Whates to mark the centenary of Arthur C. Clarke's birth. The remit was very specific here: the story had to be exactly 2001 words in length. I don't often draw explicitly on my academic background (implicitly is another matter), which was in Philosophy, but in the case of this story, I made an exception.*

Very far away, in both time and space, there is a tower. It is made of a pearlescent substance, which sometimes reminds people of shadows and sometimes of ice. It shimmers in the sun, but when moonlight strikes it, the tower hides itself, shyly, as if it has drawn a veil across its face.

At the summit of the tower sits an Ontologist.

He has been there for a long time, but he can't remember exactly when he first climbed the shell-spiral of stairs to the summit. Nor can he remember his family, although he knows he's got one: it's on record somewhere. He thinks it is probably in File A, Category 1, at the bottom of the tower. Below ground, in fact: Category 1 ("things which definitely exist") is enormous and the files require special storage.

Secretly, the Ontologist thinks Cat 1 is a bit boring. It's – well, it's stable. Though that's not saying much. Things which definitely exist can definitely be troublesome, after all. But they are a little dull. The Ontologist has always been much more interested in the other categories. He prefers Cat 1092-1199 (annotated), which is also huge – much bigger than Cat 1, in fact – and consists of things that

151

definitely do not exist. He keeps a careful eye on these in case something flickers into Cat 1 and needs to be reclassified.

But his favourite category is Cat 10. The Ontologist finds Cat 10 enchanting and he peruses it out of work hours, often over supper, or a brandy. He nurtures Cat 10 as though it was an infant in a pram. But he wouldn't like everything to fall into Cat 10: too much of a good thing would be boring and also, frankly, impossible.

The Ontologist doesn't have epistemological objections to *impossible* but he is wary of it.

The tower itself sits on a nexus point of two great highways: not the only highways in existence in the Ontologist's realm, but the largest. One of these – the broadest – is formed by scientific enquiry and this is a fast, bright road with some interesting byways. The second leads from magic to magic, and this is less brightly lit, more opaque, and filled with strange presences. The Ontologist can only see these from the corner of his eye and he has been obliged to put many of them into Cat 10. The second highway is frequently concealed by shadows. The Ontologist is not sure about those shadows. Something is waiting in them: he can smell it.

He bides his time and doesn't go poking things. Then, one afternoon, he sees a figure emerge from the shadows and progress down the darker highway. Soon it is at the base of the tower. The Ontologist sends a servant to open the door, in haste. You never know what you might find on the doorstep. But when it emerges at the top of the staircase, it turns out to be a young man, rather earnest and wearing a long grey robe.

"Forgive me. I have come to you with a problem. My elders have sent me."

"Where do you come from?" the Ontologist asks him. He gestures for him to sit down, clearing a pile of papers with a sweep of his hand. Hopefully nothing will flicker into existence because of this, or out of it.

"I'm from a place called Aight. We have something that we can neither name nor place. So I have come to you, because it is rumoured that you deal with such things."

"This is not rumour, but truth," the Ontologist tells him, kindly. "I am an Ontologist. In fact, it is fair to say that I am *the* Ontologist, as for reasons which I hope are obvious, it would be confusing to have more than one." Look at Wikipedia, the Ontologist nearly adds, but the young man won't have heard of it in this realm and it's only going to confuse him.

The young man looks a little puzzled. "I understand. You are the one who catalogues everything in existence everywhere, aren't you?"

"Yes. I have been doing it for a very long time." *Too long.* "I make lists, and I decide where to put things, conceptually."

The look of confusion has not diminished. "I suppose someone has to?"

"It's helpful. But much of the groundwork has already been done. My predecessor, for instance, did valuable work in relation to proper nouns."

The Ontologist is trying to clarify things, but he doesn't think he's succeeding. The young man twists his robe in his fingers and asks if he can move some books. The Ontologist doesn't think he has enough leg room, but this tower can get awfully muddly.

"Anyway," he says. "We'd like you to come and look at something."

"Oh!" The Ontologist very rarely leaves the tower these days. "I am rather fearfully busy, you see."

"I know. But my elders think it's important. I don't expect they'd bother you for nothing."

The Ontologist thinks he is probably right. And it might *be* important. He agrees to accompany the young man the following morning.

They set out, down the spiralling stairs of the tower and into the hazy day. Seen close to, the highway is not solid, but filled with the spark and rush of information. Buildings loom on either side, only to flicker away when looked at directly. The young man – his name is Ylden – and the Ontologist step on hidden stars, deep nodes of concepts, clustering together as if for protection. These will have been things that the Ontologist has categorised himself. When they reach the trees, they can see that these, too, are only partially solid: their Platonic essence, set long ago, partly obtruding into this world of appearance and partly into the worlds of the notional and material.

The Ontologist does not say this to Ylden because he is ashamed of it, but he does not really like the material world. Its grossness, its corporeality, offends him. This is unfair and, the Ontologist realises, purely a personal failing. He loves his work because of its neatness, its precision. The material plane is too prone to expansion. It is *untidy*. Category 1. Urgh.

They make their way through neat categories of grass to a clearing. Ylden's people live simply, in huts. This is not because they were unable to build more, the Ontologist understands, simply that they do not choose to do so. A person comes out holding a stack of something.

"The nouns got out of alignment again," they say. "I'm just going to tidy them up."

So much of the Ontologist's work here is aided by the people of this realm. He finds himself filled with gratitude and he expresses this to the person. They smile.

"Wait till you see the *thing*."

Ah, the *thing*. It's a while since the Ontologist has experienced the sensation of anticipation. He greets the elders and Ylden hands him over with what seems to be relief. Doubtless he is glad to be free of the responsibility but he has carried out his task well. There is always room for promising youngsters in this work and the Ontologist says so. He is pleased that Ylden accompanies them to the place where the *thing* resides.

The Ontologist is not sure what to expect and this is just as well, because when they come to the place, he really doesn't know what to say. He stares, instead.

"You see our problem," Ylden remarks.

The Ontologist does indeed. He has no idea what the thing in front of him might be. One becomes used to what things are, their basis. *This* – he cannot assess its quiddity. Its haeccity is not understandable to him. Its relatedness is utterly opaque and its monism, if it has one, is unclear. It does not appear to be dichotomous, and he couldn't begin to determine its hypokeimenon.

He turns round to face a number of sympathetic pairs of eyes.

"I think you'd better leave me with this for a bit," the Ontologist says. One by one, they file silently from the clearing.

"Now," he tells the *thing*. But even that isn't right: suggesting one entity/item/category. A single, and it isn't. For the sake of his notes, he shall continue with *thing*, though accompanied by a sense of all language letting him down (he'd love to describe for his notes what it looks like but, well, *that*).

He hitches up his robe and sits on a nearby obtrusion.

"Well!" he says out loud. "And what might you be?"

The *thing* seems anxious to be understood. The Ontologist doesn't think it is dangerous, although they have had issues with that before now. It shows him a number of relatables, but the problem is, he can't understand these, either. They are too abstract even for the Ontologist, who has long conversations with Galois groups on a regular basis. He sighs. He wishes he'd asked the elders for some tea, and a hat. Gradually, slowly, he begins to unpack the constructs which are being presented to him for evaluation. By the end of the afternoon, he thinks they might have a tiny branch starting point for a taxonomy. But he's exhausted. It is definitely a *ding an sich*, a thing-in-itself, unknowable, except that it *wants* him to know it, he thinks.

No use asking the *thing* if it will be here tomorrow. The Ontologist doesn't think temporal concepts are going to be useful and, in any case, *tomorrow* is a relative term here. He returns to the village and sends a message back to the tower, to say that they are to carry on in his absence, which might be considerable. The villagers are sympathetic. The Ontologist plays with the children while their parents prepare the evening meal. They play *topology* and it's nice and simple, then they eat and then he sleeps. Or tries to.

Next morning, they do it all over again.

The Ontologist must admit, however, that he is excited by this. It is the biggest challenge he has ever faced in his work and it seems right to him, if perhaps a little ominous, that this comes at a time when he is considering retirement. There are various options as to his successor, all worthy. These posts are very carefully chosen and there is no political jockeying. They are all so aware of the importance of doing the right thing. So he feels that whatever happens here, the process will go on.

The *thing* attempts to communicate with him in other ways: emotional, visual, and by changing him. This has happened before, although it's always disconcerting to suddenly find yourself another type of being: a unicorn, say, or a bucket. The subcategory known as 'gods' do it a lot and used to do it more, when the corporeal world had a little more leeway, a bit more fluidity than it does now. The taxonomy comes faster and this time he doesn't go to bed. And gradually, they come to an understanding and it is a dismaying one: there are too many things, all manner of concepts and processes and stuff, in the universe. The *thing* has come into being because of this. It is the last *thing* that can ever be in existence, summing everything up, which is why it's so complex. But in order for it to become fully realised, something else must allow it to take its place.

No, not something else. Someone. It is the perfect Cat 10: things which both do and do not exist, but its existence is predicated on a categorical space. He has come to the logical conclusion of his job, now, and the Ontologist would never kill, although he has often been obliged to note erasures, extinctions. He doesn't like doing it and he tends to shove them into Cat 10 if at all possible. He must annotate his thoughts, and, to make room, predicate himself out of –

existence.

# The White Herd

*This story was inspired by a handfasting that my partner Trevor and I carried out in the Yorkshire Dales, near Malton in the North Riding. The little town was lovely and there was a big stately home behind a wall at the edge of it (I overheard the barmaid telling someone about it – 'all shabby rugs and dog hair inside' she said) which I made a bit more Gothic than it probably is. And once we were up on the moors the curlews cried all afternoon long.*

The tower rises above everything. It is black, turreted, and ivy covered. Even when the day is bright and fine, the tower has its own darkness. But I do not mind. To me, the tower is safe, a haven, and the place from which I look out upon the world.

The world: an irony. I know what the world is – it is circumscribed by the globe that sits in my father's study, a sphere of blue and cream, circled by words in a looping italic hand. When I was little, I wondered if the countries of the world were actually written upon, an arc of letters vast as a viaduct, which I had also seen pictured upon the study wall. There is one near here, but I have never seen it. I imagined England bisected by its component letters, running north to south, my own county straddled by the vast curl of 'E.' The letter 'n' bestrides the Dales, 'g' blots out the industrial expanse of Birmingham, 'l' is a sliver that looms above the spires of Oxford.

You can see that I travel more within my head than in truth. I have never left this house or these grounds, except once, and, were it possible, would not care to do so. I can journey more within my own mind than by carriage; stepping through the doorways of a map or a book, travelling down the poetry lines or the notes of songs. My world is my father's library, the globe the outward expression of the volumes within. I picture it at night, sailing free of its tethering brass arm and soaring like the moon up into the shadows of the rafters. Perhaps it spins faster than the world around its invisible sun, speeding up the day, or perhaps it slows.

On the nights when I do not think about the globe, which tend to be when the real moon is full, I make my way to the window seat and sit beneath her light. These are the nights on which the white herd comes and I like to see them. They arrive at midnight, spilling out of the bracken which fringes the edges of the park, and which is itself bounded by a high wall. The moonlight washes over the land like water, illuminating the park and casting the distant hills into molten indigo. I sit for a long time, growing cold and stiff, twisting the length of my braid between my fingers, waiting for the herd to come. As they always do, ever since I was a child.

They might be deer, or not. They move swiftly, flickering. Sometimes I think I glimpse antlers on their long heads, or the curled horns of goats, or that there is nothing there but their white manes, tossing. I have gone down in the morning and looked for the prints of their hooves, their passage through the bracken, but there is never anything there; the grass is as velvet as ever and striped where the gardener has gone over it with a roller. Yet the herd are several dozen strong. It is hard to tell, too, how big they are: they often seem very small, the height of a coil of bracken, but I have seen them as the size of horses or oxen, too. They are always beautiful; deep chested, with long curving necks and long legs. Their tails are like the tail of a lion, a rope ending in a plume. They are surrounded by a shimmering light, which makes them hard to see, but which might only be the light of the moon.

They always run against the course of the sun, around the south of the house, passing from evening through noon to dawn, when they vanish, racing north, and I can no longer see them. I do not know whether they are confined to the park, or if they leap its high wall and run free over the reedy, curlew-haunted hills: I like to think that they do. I wonder sometimes if they have come from the sea. They look as if they are made of foam, or milkweed. They have that creamy, light-filled paleness.

Have I gone down to see them more closely? I have tried. Of course. My world may be small but it is still mine and I am fearless within it. I have stolen from my bedroom, left a pillow artfully arranged beneath the coverlet, tiptoed down the stairs as soundless as a mouse. I have crept through the shadows of the hall, past lifeless suits of armour, beneath the family crest which rears above the great front door. But that door, which creaks open easily in daylight – or on nights when the moon is not full – will not budge.

Are there, you ask, other doors? Of course there are: the French windows which open out along the orangery at the back of the house, letting in the pungent spice of the box hedges on summer noons. There is the small cramped door of the scullery, which lets out into the prosaic, necessary world of the vegetable patch. There is the door to the attics, which leads onto the roof: the high realm of slate and battlement from which it is possible to glimpse the roll and wave of the Dales above the beech tree tops.

But on moonlit nights, none of these doors open, either, and I've tried the windows. The house is as tightly sealed as drum or ship, impregnable. Maybe you're not meant to get too close to the herd: perhaps neither you nor they would benefit from being seen. But I could not say for certain. I watch them from the window, that length of distance which may be safe for both of us.

On the morning after their latest run, not long after dawn, I went out into the grounds. The front door opened easily, as if oiled. Beyond, the grass was laden with dew and the day smelled fresh, as if after rain. Everything sparkled. It was April, and the beech leaves were just beginning to unfurl. I stepped out onto the grass, looking closely. No hoofprints, nothing – and yet, just above the ground, there was a swirl of mist. I stared.

The mist was faintly silver and, although I have said that it was a swirl, it remained static, a sculpture in the air. I walked around it, but the swish and switch of my skirts did not disturb. As I turned the corner of the box hedge, I came across the undergardener, an ancient man named Hodge.

"Hodge, do you see that?"

"Yes, Miss Magdalena. Mist."

"But it's not moving."

"Depends on the air pressure, miss, so they say. And on the level of heat. It'll go once the sun's over the wall."

"Have you seen it before, then?"

"On many occasions, miss, especially from Easter onwards."

So that was that. Nothing to do with white beasts that run through the night. Except I knew that it was. Hodge was right, however: the mist vanished when the sun's warmth touched the grass, but later it returned. At dusk, when I once more went into the grounds, the mist was back. I let my fingers trail through it, and they glowed with a silver light for a moment afterwards. Then it was gone. I walked slowly through the grounds, watching the cold evening light slanting across the box hedges and the vivid grass. Soon, as the sun dipped, it became too chilly to remain outside without a wrap and I made my way back in to my supper.

Later that night, the glow returned. I was in my room. The moon had not yet risen, though the sky was clear. I had extinguished the lamp and the room was in shadow, but when I raised my hand, I could see that it shone, very faintly. I woke throughout the night, and the glow remained, but in the morning it had disappeared, banished by the light of the sun.

It was around this time that my father decided it was time to think about my marriage. I had always known that this was a possibility, and it had not until now much troubled me, since it seemed so remote. Now, however, it appeared closer and closer yet, with the force of an on-rushing steam train, all hissing air and roar. For it seemed that, unbeknownst to me, my father had put considerable preparation into the matter and had, after much thought and a series of interviews, selected a suitable husband.

When he told me, I remained seated, calm and smiling. I remember that I glanced down at my fan and its delicate ivory struts and crimson tassel looked, for a moment, like blood and bone. I blinked and the illusion passed. Inside, I was in turmoil. I did not wish to be married, I realised; I had too much to lose. The world of the house would be lost to me – perhaps not permanently, but I would become no more than a visitor. My husband's house would be my home, and who could say what, if anything, it might contain?

"Who is he?" I asked, demure, but what I was really thinking was: *what is the nature of his house?*

I could not have cared less about the man, save that he would take me from my home. By degrees I learned that he was of an old and honourable family, somewhat decayed, and that the manor they possessed was likely to pass from their hands in the not-too-distant future. This, of course, would not do.

To those readers who might think that it is wealth that concerns me, you are wrong. A cottage in the woods would do well, a hut, but only if there was beauty that surrounded it, and familiarity, and I could not see that there would be either with Jonathan X. More than this, however, was the intense nature of my relationship with my father's home; my father himself might be shadowy and unclear – I would be hard pressed to describe him to you, even living in the same house – but every detail of the house itself appeared within my mind's eye with crystalline clarity, as though painted by one of the Dutch masters. It was the prospect of this loss that clutched at my heart and made my breath catch in my throat.

I showed none of this to my father, who, shadow though he might be, still held the power. I don't remember what I said, but it seemed to satisfy him, for he patted my hair before I left the room and smiled at me vaguely.

I went upstairs and sat down in the window seat with a thump. Outside, pallid sunlight fell over the lawn, lengthening the shadows into emerald and black. I longed for dusk but everything was sharp and hard at this time of day and there was no softness anywhere. I closed my eyes and thought of the white herd, running. Far away, beyond the trees and the wall, the blue hills lay, and when I opened the window a fraction, letting in mild air, I heard the piercing curlew's cry. It was repeated, again and again, and I let it carry me through the hour until the sky deepened and the sun began to go down.

By midnight, I knew I could not go. But how to stop a process that the men had begun and which was already in train? My world did not extend so far; I had no idea what to do. But I did know that it was close to the full of the moon – a day or so. I knew I could wait. I could be the dutiful daughter for a day, and perhaps beyond. Weddings did not happen overnight, I knew. Usually.

And indeed it did not seem that my father was in a hurry to marry me away. I did not see him on the following day – he was out hunting with his cronies, and I saw them streaming across the park in their pink jackets, the horses' tails flying out behind them. I thought of the white herd, and clenched my fists in the pockets of my skirts.

That night, the moon rose full and I found myself determined. This time I did not try the door. I opened the window, and took a handful of the thick entwined stems of ivy. I was light, but I did not know if it would bear my weight: there was one way to find out. I hoisted my nightdress, belting it with the cord of my dressing gown, and swung out of the window. To my relief, the ivy held, although the leaves were slippery. I tried hard to grip the tough stems and, with concentration, my bare feet were soon enough touching the stone of the terrace.

Beneath my feet, it was cool, but not cold. I walked to the edge of the terrace; behind me, the house lay in darkness. I stole a look at my father's room but could not see the telltale glow of a lamp. Box, lavender and rosemary breathed fragrance into the night air and there was a small, mild breeze. I had rarely been outside at night – an open window did not count – and it was exhilarating. I took a deep breath and closed my eyes. When I opened them again, the moon was coming up over the tips of the beech trees, flooding the grounds with light. The house was silver. A flicker at the edge of my vision betrayed them: the herd was coming. As they rounded the corner of the house, I stepped out to meet them.

"Take me with you! Please! Take me, too."

And to my surprise, they did.

How to describe it now, that first time? I ran with them, across the velvet lawn and through the stones of the high wall, shimmering into moonlight as we approached; down the beech avenue and down the long meadows to the river. Over, and up the slope, and then up into the Dales. A moment of starlight, a flash, and it was day, with the sun bleaching the grass to straw and the cloudshadow racing across the hills. Once again I heard the curlew's cry and the lamenting peewit, floating to rest. I had never before been so far or so high. The land stretched out before us in great waves. I could not see my companions so clearly, but one by one I saw that they were fading, then winking out like stars. And I myself did not want to go – but then I was back on the terrace, huddled against the wall and wet with dew.

I managed to climb stiffly back up the ivy and, shivering, sought my bed. I fell asleep quickly and did not dream: when I woke, the morning sun lay in bright bars across the bed and there were footsteps in the passage. I felt drained and hollow, a reed with the pith sucked out, and I told the maid that I did not feel well.

And so our pattern began. I waxed and waned with the moon, and each time it was full, I ran with the white herd. I learned the mysteries of the herd: how they took turns to be the leader, and conferred different gifts, of water and air, of earth and flame. I learned who they were – girls like me, turned ghost, hiding their true forms even from we who were their companions (I am sometimes doe, sometimes other things). We seek escape, but we do not simply take from the world. We speak to the corn and make it grow, rich with poppies that are our unshed blood. We whisper to rivers, steady them in their courses, prevent flood. We bring down the moon, its essence, and link it to the land. We are old, but over the years we fade for the last time and are seen no more. In life, some of us are scullery maids and some of us live in the great houses of the Dales, but all of us are dreamers and sought a way to escape. We found it.

I have said that I waned. I grew frail around the full moon, stronger when the crescent was new. Doctors were called in, all with different opinions. None could cure me, for all of the opinions were wrong. My marriage was called off, for it was deemed too much of a risk to my health and I did not think my father wanted to waste a dowry, just in case. I was not confined to my room, not entirely, but I took to visiting the library at night, remaking my own small world when I was not roaming the land at the moon's height. So here I remain, locked within the walls of the house and grounds, and yet as free as the air in which the curlew cries, unbounded.

# The Winter Garden

*This is a story set in the world of my novels Winterstrike and Banner of Souls, and the novella, Phosphorus. It's a futuristic, science fantastical Mars, run by a not very nice matriarchy. I started writing this series while stuck in the airport at Venice, and the Martian cities owe quite a lot to this ancient Italian setting.*

In Winterstrike they call it Milk Month, when the ice that thickens across the surface of the canals turns to the blue-white shade of milk and the silence that falls across the snow-blanketed city is as heavy as a lid. It's followed by Glass Month, when the ice clears to a luminescent veil and you can see the fish hanging in suspended animation in the bottom of canals. After that, the ice breaks up and is gone, and Winterstrike enters its short spring.

But it was in Milk Month when I first became aware that something was wrong with my cousin Selia.

Our house is not the oldest in the city, but it is *one* of the oldest. There are nine of us who live here now: five aunt-mothers, and four of us girls – my sisters Enticy and Heralice, then Selia and myself. Enticy is the oldest, followed by myself, and little Heralice is only small. At the time of which I write, Selia was fourteen, shortly before her Marriage. They don't do Marriage now, so many years later, but at the time it was all the rage – seen as a patriotic duty, for each girl upon her fifteenth birthday to wed the city. The ceremonies were lavish and involved frocks and presents; I could not understand, therefore, why Selia seemed so reluctant.

"It'll be fun," I told her. "I had a whale of a time at mine. That green taffeta – the one I wore at the Heraldic Ball last month – that was one of the Marriage dresses, although in the end, if you remember, I wore the pale cream and tulle…"

"It's all very well for you, Stasietta. You're not –" she paused.

"Not what?"

"Never mind."

I thought she was just seeking attention. I wish, ironically, that I *had* paid more attention. We were, I remember, sitting in the Winter Garden at the top of the house. Like most mansions then and now, there was a long, glassed-in gallery running around the roof. I considered ours to be very superior: it looked out over Gloaming Canal and was filled with very expensive orchidia, brought up from the south. I suspect that my mother thought more highly of her precious orchidia than she did her children, and I could not completely blame her – they were certainly more beautiful and they didn't quarrel all the time, either. Heat blasted out from the potbellied stoves which stood at each corner of the winter garden and Selia and I sat in a pool of warmth. Selia, indeed, was rather rosy in the face and I suspect that I was, too.

"Stasietta? Have you ever – loved anyone?"

"Of course. All the time," I told her, airily, and felt very worldly and sophisticated, being all of three years older. My current crush was on Estily Hademar, an actress with the Opera, whom we had seen just before Ombre. I had a miniature of Hademar, whom I had never actually met, in a frame beside my bed and I felt in my inmost heart that we were destined to be together. I did not say this, however.

Selia said, "No, not *schoolgirl* stuff. I mean really in love."

"Of course." I didn't quite know what she meant by this, but I was determined not to say so. I paused. "Have *you?*"

"Of course not." Selia grew even rosier. "I'm much too young."

Perhaps it was this, I reflected in my worldly seventeen year old way, that was worrying her about the Marriage. Sometimes being grown up is frightening. "Don't worry," I said. "You'll be fine."

Next day was the beginning of Milk Month and we celebrated it by having iced milk at breakfast, in the special porcelain dishes. I fed little Heralice with a long spoon, although she was so excited that she spat most of it out down her bib. Selia watched, moodily. There were plans for a visit to the theatre that evening, although I planned to sneak off into the Opera, which was next door, instead, and confess my undying love to Estily. I knew at the depths of my mind that I would do no such thing, but the plotting was fun.

Late in the afternoon, dressed in our finery, we went skating down Gloaming Canal. It was the fashion to promenade then, and the whole family, all nine of us, skated out, Heralice held by the hand by an aunt-mother. I went arm in arm with my sister Enticy; Selia skated ahead. She was a good skater, always an athletic girl with a long, smooth stride. She described curves and circles around us as Enticy and I glided on.

We were not alone: the canal was filled with skaters and we saw many people we knew. The air was filled with greetings and teasing as we rounded the bend which led to the great Eastern canal, passing a huge dark red building which housed part of the city's Matriarchy. White bunting hung from its lower windows, looking like a lacy collar slung around some armoured animal's neck, and there was an occasional spark from its weir-wards.

"Don't go too far!" my mother cried as we shot round the bend and I knew she was worried about the time: we would need tea before we set out for the theatre and she hated a scramble and rush. Selia, in any case, ignored her. I saw my cousin darting far ahead, and then she was lost around a curve. "Come on," my mother said, tight-lipped. "We need to turn back."

"Selia can look after herself.," said my aunt Marnia, who was Selia's own mother. "She's a sensible girl." And sure enough, when we were halfway down Gloaming Canal, there was a hiss of skates and Selia was there, pink cheeked.

"Sorry. I got carried away."

"Well, never mind that now," my mother said. "Into the house with you and have your tea. We'll need to set off at six."

By the time we left the house again, it was dark and starting to snow. The lamps along the canal were huge, hazy globes, illuminating the falling white, and a hush had fallen over the city, even though it was busy with sleds and other road traffic. We saw a convoy of military vehicles, their great fat tyres carving ruts in the snow, rolling south to the conflict in Erduvon. My mother clicked her tongue when she saw them but no one said anything: you never knew who might be listening. The aunt-mothers had learned not to say too much in front of Heralice, who was too young to keep silent. When we reached the end of the road, we caught a public sled to the theatre, passing the remainder of the convoy as we shot up the sled lane. I saw Selia's gaze fall upon the last vehicle and her face had assumed a brooding, unfamiliar expression. Thinking she was worried about the war – all those young women, heading off to a conflict which we should not have been involved with in the first place – I squeezed her hand, but it did not seem to reassure her.

The performance was good, of its kind, but in those days of frequent war it featured a heavy dollop of propaganda and I did not find it nearly as engaging as the Opera. I longed for Estily Hademar, to see the small perfect oval of her face through my opera glasses instead of the heroine of this epic, who was dark and pouting. I found my own gaze wandering around the audience, noting a fair few members of the Matriarchy, some frequent visitors to the house. My aunt-mothers bowed and bobbed and smiled, nodding their heads as they were recognised. But I was glad when the performance ground to a halt, the cast, most of whom had met their end in the final act, had taken a bow and we were released into the atrium.

"Good, that's over," Selia said into my ear and I felt a sudden rush of fellow feeling.

"I didn't like it much, either."

She rolled her eyes. "It seems to me that whoever wrote that didn't know a thing about what war is really like."

She sounded so world-weary that it took me aback. After all, what did a fourteen year old girl from a sheltered family know about conflict, either? Yet for a moment, it had sounded as though she was speaking from experience. But then an aunt-mother came over with a tray of sorbet and I forgot all about the play and Selia's reaction.

Next day, we were once more sitting in the Winter Garden. Our governess had set us a ridiculous amount of work, in my opinion, given that it was a holiday, and Selia and I had elected to go through it in the garden. We sat by the hissing stove in a pool of lamplight as the snow fell beyond the windows. Our task was a historical account of the war in the Olympian foothills three hundred years before, and I was finding it hard to keep all the dates straight. Selia, despite being younger, had a more mathematical mind than I did.

"Selia," I said. "Was the Act of Reunion in 19,005 or 19,007?"

She did not immediately answer, so I looked up. I could see the iron curve of the stove through the side of Selia's head, an image so startling that I found myself gaping. Selia glanced up in turn and the illusion was abruptly dispelled.

"Neither. It was 19,006. What are you staring at?"

"Nothing." I had imagined it, I told myself: it was some optical illusion produced by the wavering heat from the stove, or some malfunction of the weir-wards – but my aunt-mothers rarely bothered with the wards during the day.

But the next day, I saw it again.

*

This time, we had come up with my mother to tend to the orchidia. This was a precise task, dependent upon species, temperature and type of soil, and my mother did not trust it to the house servants, ever since the death of a beloved floridium which a maid had over-watered. Selia and I were the only children who showed an interest in the flowers, although I must admit that in my case, at least, it was more with regard to ornamentation than botany. I liked going around with a watering can – it seemed ladylike – but I did not care for feeding the esplumoir plant that was my mother's pride and joy. A tall pitcher, mottled mauve and black like a bruise, it had razor sharp fringes above a dark acid pool within. It ate scraps of flesh and, occasionally, unwary wasps, which was the only reason for tolerating it, in my opinion.

Selia and my mother were bending over a tall white stand of harcrocii when I looked across and saw that I could see the flowers through Selia's gown, as though two images had become superimposed upon one another. I gasped. The illusion did not go away as Selia straightened up.

"What's wrong?"

"Selia, are you all right? I thought for a moment –"

"I'm fine," she said, too quickly, scowling. "Why wouldn't I be?"

My mother, absorbed in her orchidia, smiled vaguely at both of us and paid no further attention. But that night, when we were all supposed to have gone to bed, I slipped out to Selia's room.

There was a crack of light under the door. I knew that the walls, too, had chinks: this was after all an old house, which creaked and settled in the winter cold, and it was usually possible to see a little way into most rooms. I put my eye to the chink, therefore, and looked in to see Selia sitting on the edge of her bed with her face in her hands. She was crying, silently.

I did not know what to do. Living as we did, so claustrophobically, we guarded our privacy from one another and although I was fond of Selia, I did not think that she would respond well to interruptions, nor to being spied upon. So I went slowly back to my own bed, wondering.

Next morning, Selia was quiet and pale. We sat through our morning lessons, and in the afternoon we went back up to the Winter Garden to do our homework. I kept casting surreptitious glances at Selia, but this time she was quite solid. Halfway through a translation exercise, however, I looked up to ask her about another date and saw that she was no longer there.

I stared. How could my cousin have vanished entirely from one moment to another? Granted, I had been absorbed in a difficult passage: Old Martian is not an easy tongue to decipher.

"Selia?" I said. I got up and ran around the garden, but Selia was nowhere to be seen. I went back to my seat and picked up my book, intending to go downstairs, but at that moment the door to the garden opened and there was Selia.

She looked flustered and hot. She gaped at me like a fish.

"Selia? What happened? Where did you go?"

"Nowhere, I – I forgot my special pen," she said. "So I went downstairs. I didn't want to disturb you."

But her face flamed with guilt.

"Are you all right?" I asked, again."

"Yes, why wouldn't I be?" The colour was ebbing from her cheeks. She sat back down on the seat and picked up her book.

I did not like to spy or pry, but then again – that night, once more, I slid out into the passage and looked through the chink in Selia's wall.

Her room was filled with shadows. I could see a glimmer of light through the heavy drapes which covered the windows, from the canalside lamp beyond. And there was another light, too. It was coming from the bed. A firefly spark, it glowed green, then faded, then glowed again. As its illumination increased, I had a sudden image of Selia lying on her side on the bed: the green pulse was coming from her throat, and she was whispering. But I was too far away to hear what she said.

Next day, all was as before. I did not see Selia that afternoon, as my mother took me into the city to choose a new dress for a ball to be held in Glass Month. This was some big civic function and likely to be very boring, but as a daughter of the House of Merope I would be expected to attend. I didn't mind: dressing up for a ball was always fun. After making a purchase (crimson velvet with a fur-lined hood) we had hot chocolate in the Mulneria Rooms. As we were sitting there, a news broadcast came over the public screen: a disaster in Erduvon. A bomb blast had ripped through part of a relief convoy, with thirty women dead. There were pictures of overturned vehicles and bloodstained snow. My mother tutted, and the faces around us were grim.

When we arrived home, I found that Selia was not feeling well and had gone to bed. I went upstairs and this time I knocked on the door, but there was no reply. She remained in bed for two days, and when she came out again, after threats of calling a doctor, she was as pale as the milky ice that coated the canal. She did not speak and she did not join me to do our homework.

That night, I woke with a start. My heart was hammering in my chest but when I turned on the lamp, there was no one in the room. I pulled on a robe and went out into the passage. Selia's room was black and silent, but the door was ajar. I hesitated and then, from above, I heard the creak of the stairs.

I followed, in time to see the doors of the Winter Garden closing stealthily. I went up to the long landing and in.

Selia was standing at the far end of the garden. Her hands were on the sill and she was looking out across the lamplit expanse of the canal. I could see the hazy glow and the thin fingered branches of the bare weedwood trees through her body.

"Selia!"

She did not turn round. The glow of the lamp was sharper now, as she faded, and there was a dim green gleam at her throat. At the window, the weir-wards spat and crackled, but Selia was still fading. I ran down the length of the garden, my bare feet soundless on the tiles, dodging past the nodding heads of the orchidia. By the time I reached her, Selia was almost gone.

I don't know what I was trying to achieve. I reached out, grasping at her fading form, and my hands closed around the green glow at her throat. Something small and hard fell into my palm like a jade bead and Selia's form grew abruptly more solid. I heard her gasp. I snatched my hand away and took a step away.

"Give it back!" Selia cried. I ran back down the gallery, Selia racing after me, and then I slipped in a pool of water on the tiles. I did not quite fall, but I stopped and turned. "Give it back!"

I did not. Instead, I put out my hand and dropped the green light into the maw of my mother's flesh-eating esplumoir. The pitcher yawned briefly, then snapped shut. There was a brief emerald glow from within and then the light was gone. Selia gave a wail of anger and loss, and crumpled to the floor.

We did not tell my mother, or hers. I hoped the esplumoir plant would suffer no permanent damage. In the early hours of that morning, I pieced together Selia's tale.

A soldier. She was the elder sister of a friend of Selia's, one of the Matriarchy's military clans. Her name was Sone, and she and Selia had fallen in love. I thought that Sone should have known better than to encourage the emotions of a much younger, impressionable girl, but my remonstrations belonged with Sone herself and Sone was dead, killed in the bomb blast in Edruvon. The jade light was no more than a little communication device, which allowed the girls to talk to one another.

"When I spoke to her," Selia said, sobbing, "It was as though I was with her. I could see her. I was *there.*"

I agreed. I'd seen her go. There had to be more to it than simple communication: the device had come from one of the military's own blacklight labs, Selia told me, and it is my own view that when Sone died, her spirit had begun to take Selia with it forever, dissolving her flesh into the weir… but I don't know for certain.

Selia and I grew up into respectable young ladies, made good marriages, are now stout matrons. We never talk of what happened that night, but sometimes, when we are back at the family mansion for my elder sister Enticy's events, I see Selia's gaze go towards the stairs which lead up to the Winter Garden and I know that she remembers. But as I say, we do not speak of it. This is a house, and a city, filled with secrets. One more makes little difference.

# When We Go to the Island

*This story was inspired by my complete failure to go to the Isle of Wight, a place I could see from my old flat in Brighton, and which I'd always had a hankering to visit. We finally got there during Cowes Week in 2022. It was great fun but not very mysterious.*

I watched the little boat cross the sound, with the storm behind it. To the west, the sky was indigo black, with a bright silver line where it met the sea. The boat had a white sail and it was moving fast towards the island. I thought of a dove, thrown from my hands up into the clouds, hawk-struck, lightning-slain. Mevan came up beside me as I stood on the quay, behind the strong stone wall against which the winter waves crashed. But the sea was calm now, high June, with the white roses spilling down from the gardens of the port.

"It's getting close," Mevan said.

"Yes. I didn't see it set out."

"And thunder on the way. You can feel it on the wind."

I nodded. The thought of electricity tingled my skin. We watched until the boat neared the northern shore of the island and then it was gone. I ran to the telescope which stood on the quay and looked through it, as I had done many times before.

The town of the northern shore of the island was clearly visible, quiet in the sunlight. I could see the turret which stood above it on the hill, possibly part of a larger building, red tiled. I could see the tumble of houses which covered the hillside, all the way to the tall houses of the quayside. My favourite was a square place, cream fronted, with attic windows like raised eyebrows and stone pineapples on the columns of its gate. They meant, so my mother had told me once, that a sea captain lived there.

There was no sign of the little boat. I felt the first spatter of rain on my skin.

"We should go in," Mevan said.

The sea had changed to an angry green. Reluctantly, I pulled back from the telescope and swung it down so that the wind could not snatch it and damage it. We made it to the front door just before the squall hit, rain darkening the slate step and making the flowers of the fuschia dance. Before I slammed the door shut against the squall, I looked back. Across the sound, the northern shore lay in bright sunlight.

When the weather was too bad for us to go outside, and if we did not have lessons or chores, my favourite thing to do was to go up to the attic and look out. The attic occupied the whole roofspace of the house and there were windows fore and aft, as I liked to think of it. From the back window, I could see the town and the distant fold and flow of the downs: their slopes bare and ploughed in the winter, with the seagulls distantly visible as a white swirl when the weather drove them inland, but golden with corn in the summer, bleached in the light.

I liked this northern view, safe and changing only with the seasons, but my favourite thing to do was to look out of the sea windows. I pretended that the house was a ship – if I stood a little way back from the window and looked out, the front garden and road disappeared and it was as though there was nothing between myself and the sea. I daydreamed that we were going to the island, that the ship on which I stood was plunging through those green seas and soon we would reach the north shore.

In bed at night, I thought of what I would do if I reached it. I would run to that house with pineapples on the gates, run up the drive, which I pictured as long and fringed with rhododendrons, and then to that glimpse of house. They would know me there; it had a cream front door, or perhaps a very pale green, and it would be ajar. I would run in and there would be the hallway, dim and cool with a great cascade of roses in the vase on the dresser.

I knew that house intimately, every room except the Captain's room, which must remain mysterious, but which I imagined as being filled with the things from his travels: conch shells and cowries, the red spiked arms of coral, sinister statues of other people's gods, beautiful fabrics that, perhaps, some girl had given him.

My own father was dead, you see, so I made one up. I knew exactly where he lived.

I did not tell my mother about these dreams, and Mevan scorned them but only, I think, because she had dreams of her own about the island. If I did not tell my mother, though, I told her sister, my aunt Sholie, who had known my father and had not, I think, cared for him overmuch. She always gave the impression that she approved of my fancies: after all, we were not able go to the island, then or ever. One simply couldn't. That is why we have the saying, on the southern shore: *when we go to the island.*

*"Perhaps they'll get married, one day, those two."*

*"Yes – when we go to the island! I've never met a pair who disliked one another more."*

*"Maybe I'll have a gown of that new blue silk in the summer. Reminds me of a butterfly's wing."*

*"Yes, when we go to the island! At the prices Sebastian Vayne charges, not likely. But it is pretty, I'll grant you that."*

So my daydreams were safe and we all knew that. Sholie did not exactly encourage me, but she did not discourage me either and once, after a party when she had returned and was rather merry (more, I think, for the sake of it rather than any drink she had taken), she said something that led me to suspect she, like my sister, had dreams about the island of her own. She had never married – the war had taken care of that, taken too many young men – and perhaps in the sky blue house, or the rose pink, or the yellow one that I could see through the telescope, Sholie had a love of her own, a perfectly safe love. If she could never visit him, at least he would never leave her. Sometimes, I think now, that is enough.

I longed for it, knew I would never see it, basked in that knowledge because that made it safe. Then one day, the island came a little closer.

We have a regatta, every year. It's a big thing in these parts: everyone comes to it, from miles around. Part of the summer season, not just boat races, not just the white-winged yachts from all along the coast, the sailors in from the tall-masted ships which throng the harbour, but balls and dinner dances and gatherings and champagne. It's a high point of the year, something to throng to and talk about. Mevan and I always have new dresses, a little nautical, summery.

That year, the regatta was held a week later than usual, because of storms. There was a dramatic view from the attic: they were always over the sea, and at night sometimes I used to slip out of my bed and go upstairs to count the huge pink flashes of lightning, and see how far away the thunder rumbled. But at last the storms stopped and we woke to a clear blue sky and sunlight that felt tropically hot. The church bells rang that morning to tell us that the regatta would begin.

That year, too, Sholie's brother came home. His arrival was unexpected: we came downstairs to find him sitting in the parlour, perched uncomfortably on the edge of one of the embroidered chairs. He was a sailor, burned to the colour of teak by the sun, and with a gold piratical ring in one ear. But this was the only piratical thing about him, for Uncle Josiah, known to all save my aunt as Joss, was a devoutly religious man, pious to the point of mania, my aunt said fondly. She did not greatly object, however, for in the narrow brand of religion to which her brother belonged, all must be absteemers.

"A lovely cup of tea, Sholie," Joss was saying.

"Thank you, Josiah," my aunt said, primly. "Girls, see – your uncle has returned from his voyages. Will you be staying long?" Her voice was a little anxious. Fond of her brother though she might be, I did not think she really wanted a man in the house. There was a glint in his eye as he said,

"Don't worry, Sholie. Guests are like fish – they stink if they're on the slab for too long. I'll be heading down the Water at the end of next week, to take ship for the Spice Islands. In the meantime I shall pay my devotions to my master the Lord Jesus at the chapel, and to my mistress the sea in the form of the regatta. I saw James Turnabout as I walked up the harbour road, he says he will lend me the *Sorceress* – an ungodly name for a boat but a beautiful craft, I must admit – to take part in Friday's race. I thought the girls might like to come out with me one afternoon, too."

"I don't think –" my aunt began, but then she caught sight of our faces, filled with mute pleading. "Very well. As long as it is not a wet day and as long as they behave themselves."

"They're of a seafaring race, after all," Joss replied. "I'll take good care of them."

In the event, he did his best.

Sholie insisted that we wear light gowns, in case we fell in, and carried parasols in case we caught the sun. *Sorceress* was a small boat and rocked alarmingly against the dock, but the afternoon sea was millpond-calm.

"Have you sailed before?" my uncle asked.

"No," said Mevan.

"Once," I replied, feeling quite an old sea dog in comparison. "On a boat out of Dover, but only a little way." This had been with a distant cousin's family and the boat had been large and fully rigged. That, too, had been at a regatta.

"Very well. I don't expect you to know what to do, but I suggest you sit tight. Don't stand up suddenly and mind the boom – that's this one here."

"We'll be like mice," I said. He laughed.

"That should do the trick."

Expertly, he rowed us out of the harbour then hoisted the sail. It caught the breeze at once and billowed out; there were now little cats' paws of foam appearing. Uncle Joss took us out as far as a large red buoy: other boats were stationed there, several with other ladies in them. Their male relatives, too, had evidently been pressed into service for regatta-watching.

I took care to study the island from this new vantage point but it made me uneasy. Sometimes it seemed very distant, no more than a thin green line against the sky, and sometimes its towering white cliffs and the little harbour town looked close enough for me to reach out my hand and touch. There was a castle there: I could see it clearly, and a mansion whose green lawns ran down to the shore.

"Want to look through the telescope?" my uncle asked.

"Can I? Is it – allowed?" We don't talk about the island among ourselves, save for that one phrase and perhaps in relation to the weather. *The sky over the island's very black today – there must be a storm coming in.* That my uncle had verged on alluding to it made me uncomfortable and shy.

"Yes. But I don't know what you'll see."

This made me even more uneasy. Mevan said, "Do you think you should?"

I knew we shared the same thought but her disapproval spurred me on. If she didn't think I ought to do it, then I would. I took the little telescope and put it to my eye.

There were people walking along the shore, separated from the sand and shingle by a low wall. Above, more people sat at tables on a terrace, talking with animation: the telescope brought them so close to view that I could almost hear their laughter. Then one of them, a woman, looked directly at me, or so it seemed. She pointed. Unnerved, I snatched the telescope from my eye.

"What did you see?" Mevan asked.

"Just some houses. Do you want to look?" She shook her head.

We watched one of the races. The wooden boats were painted in different colours but all of them had orange red sails, the colour of the mace that my aunt ground in the kitchen for Christmas. They were small, and I thought that from the island they must look like the boats that children sailed on the village pond.

They crowded together, clustering as they darted around the buoy.

A westerly grew up, making me clutch my hat. I looked down the channel and saw black clouds billowing over the sea.

"There's weather brewing," I said to Joss, but he did not seem to hear me. One hand was on the tiller and the other clasped his pipe. Mevan was watching the boats. "Uncle Joss?"

The little boat gave a sudden plunge. I clasped the side but the sea was huge now, a great glassy wall towering over us. I did not have time to squeak. It was over us and I was in and falling. I saw the bottom of the boat above me, and then I was down into the greenblack dark.

When I came to, I was lying on my face on sand. I sat up, and found that I was quite dry, if a little salt stained. I looked around me. There was no one in sight and I felt grateful, embarrassed as if I had been caught sleeping. And I could see the castle, a little way along the shore. I was on the island.

I brushed the sand from my skirts and set off down the beach. It was a mirror image of the sands on the other side, scattered with shells and shingle. I tried to see over to the other side of the channel, but it was lost in cloud, and there was cloud, too, drifting low over the ridge of trees at the island's crown and hiding the red-tiled turret. A slipway led up onto the road and I climbed it, finding myself at the start of the village's main street. There were people here, not a crowd, but couples and families walking and strolling, just as we ourselves promenaded. I shrunk back against the wall and tried to remain unobtrusive but no one paid any attention to me and I was able to study them. Their clothes were colourful, bright as tropical birds, and some of the skirts were scandalously short, well above the knee. I had to look away. But everyone looked happy. There was a stiff breeze coming off the water now, dispelling the cloud.

I was intrigued by the little castle, but my first port of call was that house. I was drawn to it as if by a magnet. It was exactly where I expected it to be, the stone pineapples at the gates weathered by the salt air and the driveway overgrown. Just as I had done in my daydreams, I ran up the drive and found myself in front of the house. Its arched windows looked down at me in surprise and the front door stood ajar. What else could I do, but step inside?

The hall was just as I had imagined it. It smelled of polish and lavender, and there was a big bunch of roses arranged in a bowl, their pink and cream petals drooping a little. I could see a parlour with stiffly upholstered chairs but the other doors were closed. I went slowly up the stairs, gripping the bannister. The landing was wide, boards part covered by a pink and green oriental rug. At the front of the house was an open door: the Captain's room, I thought. Cautiously, I looked inside. Spires of crimson coral stood under great glass bells; a bookcase held leather nautical logs and all manner of curios. A big desk overlooked the channel, covered in maps. I studied the one on top, which had been spread out, but it showed a coastline that I did not know. I turned and saw a grinning human skull looking down at me from a high shelf; there were other things, too, a thing like a flail with a bone handle, and a statue of a god that I did not care to examine too closely. But there were some beautiful prints of flying sailing ships, too.

The room felt as though someone had only recently left it, a sensation of occupation. I thought I heard a step outside and my hand went to my mouth, but no one entered. I went to the door and looked out: the landing was empty. A second flight of stairs led upwards and I went up them, finding myself in a long attic room.

Dormer windows looked out across the channel. Hoping to see my own house, I ran to the nearest and looked out. The sea lay in bright sunshine. But all I could see was the island.

I blinked. There was the little castle, the long shoreline and the turret high on the hill.

"Do you want a closer look?" a voice said. I swung round. A man stood in the doorway, holding a small telescope like my uncle's. And like Joss, he had a sailor's air: he was an older man, with a grey beard, in a navy jacket with brass buttons.

"Who are you?" I whispered.

"Here," he said, holding out the telescope. "Take it."

I reached out and took it from his hand. Then I held it to my eye.

There was the house with the pineapples; the front door ajar. I raised the telescope and there I stood: framed in the attic window, in my red dress, but with no telescope in my hand. The girl who was me stared unblinkingly out. I nearly dropped the telescope as I snatched it from my eye.

"What is this place?" I asked.

"Why, this is the island."

"But what *is* the island? We see it every day, but I know no one who has been here."

"No. We have few visitors from the mainland. But they could come, if they really wanted to. As you did."

"What price have I paid, for coming here?" I was beginning to feel very afraid.

"No price at all. Not yet," the Captain said, and he took the telescope gently from my hand and put something hard and cold and small into it and closed my fingers. The attic room swam, light poured in, and I was underwater again in green drowning.

I woke in my own room, swaddled in blankets. I could hear rain smacking against the windows. Sholie was sitting by the bed.

"Oh! You're awake."

"What happened?" I murmured.

"You fell in," she said primly. "I am very cross with Josiah but your sister tells me that it was not his fault."

"The storm – the waves –"

"What? There was no storm. You stood up when you should not and toppled over the side when the boat rocked. Joss fished you out at once but the doctor thinks you hit your head."

"Oh."

"As long as you're alive, that's the main thing." I think she was too relieved to be cross. "I'll go downstairs now and bring you some broth. Do you think you could manage some?"

I spent the rest of the day in bed. Sholie had covered me in every blanket we possessed, so it seemed, and I grew too hot. I tossed and turned and then flipped the pillow over. Beneath it was a coin, very worn, but the image of a flying sailing ship was dimly visible. There was nothing on the other side.

I drank tea and broth, ate bread and butter, and finally Sholie felt that it was safe to leave me, going, she said, to collect Mevan from the neighbour's house. She was likely to remain a little while and take some tea, I knew, so when I heard the front door close, I flung the blankets aside and fled up the stairs to the attic.

The rain had drifted down the channel and away; a thin blue sky was visible. I looked across to the island. But the island was no longer there. Now, very small, our own village was visible, our house standing tall on the seafront. If I had a telescope, would I be able to see the tiny figure of myself at the attic window? But I knew it was not a dream, and I knew, too, that this would mark the end of my contentment with my life in this town on the shore. I did not know how I would achieve it, but I would travel. Dress as a boy and take ship? Not that, but with the Captain's talisman in my pocket I would find a way. I would find the coastline on that map. I would find the island again. And I would find the Captain, and ask him about mysteries.

# Ungiven

*Word of the day: "ungive" – to thaw, to melt (English regional, inc. Northants, Bedfordshire; carrying the suggestion that ice & snow are forms of gift or addition to a landscape, thaw their subtraction). Cf Flemish "ontgheven", to fail, & Dutch "ontgeven" to yield, desist. – from Robert MacFarlane's studies on words*

The weather's like childbirth. You go through it and then you forget and then it all comes round again and you think: oh, of course, *that's* what it's like.

The old people talk about a 'proper winter.' Like we had in the old days. They mean the third quarter of the twentieth century, up until the nineteen seventies. After that things started to change, but then they changed back again. And I think that people aren't thinking of the fifties, sixties, seventies at all, but the Victorians and all those Christmas cards of children in mufflers skating on ponds. Tiny, perfect icons of a world that never really existed. And all of that world is made of humps and hillocks of pure white, icing sugar snow. I'm sure that in a city like London, filled with coal fires, that wasn't the case for long.

A proper winter. I remember my school being closed, the excitement close to Christmas when you realised that the first fat flakes were starting to drift down from the leaden sky and you might actually get to go out in it, throw snowballs, build a snowman. Friends from abroad – New England, Sweden – laugh at me when I tell them this but we are in England, in the middle of the country, where nothing dramatic ever happens, weather-wise.

Until the ungive.

A proper winter gives everyone something to moan about. Well, we'd had a proper summer that year as well and everyone had moaned about that, too: the heat, not being able to sleep, wasps, no rain and the garden is all drying up and what if we have a hosepipe ban? Mind you, we haven't had this since '76, when, in fact, I do remember the family Triumph Herald breaking down in mid Wales, and we had to sit for six hours by the roadside under the scorching sun waiting for the overstretched RAC. See? I'm grumbling now myself. And we complained earlier in the year, too, when yet another Beast from the East swept in and quite suddenly we had snow in April, lots of it.

But we did not know what was coming. Late in August that year, God turned a dial and the year switched back to British Summertime Standard: grey skies, a bit of light drizzle and we were back to being pleased when the sun came out. It felt a little like autumn already, so when autumn came it was, well, normal. Mists, but not much mellow fruitfulness, because the snow in the spring followed by baking heat had seen to that. My neighbour said that his plums had amounted to nothing. *The Daily Express* started predicting apocalyptic levels of snow. Snowmageddon. Snownado. I'm sure there is someone employed by the Express, probably in a room in the basement, whose job it is to make up words of escalating awfulness to describe quite ordinary weather.

For once, however, the *Express* was right. The Wrath from the North, as the papers called it, swept in during the first week of December. People started talking about a white Christmas. I bought some Victorian retro Christmas cards, all crinolined ladies and Narnian lampposts. I couldn't help thinking, in fact, of *The Lion, The Witch and the Wardrobe*. Schools closed. I watched my kids playing in the garden, making a snow thing. They were quite specific about the noun. It had lots of legs and a head at each end. I suppose we all felt a bit nostalgic, watching them: just as we had played in the snow all those years ago, before mobiles and tablets and Wii. Rose coloured specs, said David. He'd been told off for watching too much television. Wouldn't that be square shaped eyes, I said, rather than rose coloured spectacles? We both laughed. School was closed for the rest of the week and eventually the educational authority gave up and merged it all into the Christmas holidays. By that time, we were all getting a bit fed up. The local Co-op was running short of bread: just-in-time deliveries meant supply chain issues. I had to drive into the Asda in Bedford instead and nearly skidded off the road. After that David said he'd do the driving and started talking about snow chains. Canadian relatives on Facebook thought we were hilarious.

We had a white Christmas after all, though getting a turkey was touch and go and I had to raid the freezer for some rather random meals. People had started talking about the war. David thought this was ridiculous and said so.

"After all, we're not being bombed."

"Yes, we are," replied our eldest, full of gloom. "By the weather."

By now, our children had pretty much disappeared into their various screens. The snow thing remained on the lawn, unmelted and faintly sinister. I did a lot of knitting, a lot of social media. But on New Year's Eve there was a bluer sky, a hint of sunshine. The BBC started talking about the weather breaking at last. There were an awful lot of articles about climate change. I looked up the latitude of Hudson Bay and read up on the Atlantic Conveyor and water wars. David and I woke up on New Year's Day with epic hangovers and told ourselves that we'd been celebrating our survival of Snowpocalypse. The snow thing started, very slowly, to collapse and patches of lawn began to appear. Bread came back into the Co-op in larger quantities and my neighbour met me in the car park.

"It's the ungive, you see."

"The what?"

He gave a familiar slight smirk: that *you're-not-from-round-here-are-you* look, even though we've lived in the village for twenty three years. Originally, I am from Gloucester, on the other side of the Midlands, and sometimes I might as well have a sign above my head saying so.

"The thaw. Old Bedfordshire word: *ungive*. It was given, and now it's going."

"Well," I said, "I won't be sorry to see it go."

He laughed. "No, I don't s'pose you will. My wife says the same. She's had enough of it. Twisted her ankle on the step yesterday. It's why I'm here doing the shopping."

I commiserated and then we drove to our respective homes. They'd cleared and salted the road by this time, but the countryside along the verges was still Christmas-card white. The bare branches of alder and willow sparkled in the thin sunlight. Now that the thaw had begun, and I could get out and about, I could once again appreciate the beauty of our 'proper winter'.

A day or so later and the snow thing was still present on our lawn, but – like the Loch Ness monster – only as a series of hummocks. It looked as though a large snow mole had been busy tunnelling beneath the grass. The shrubs lost their white hats and a large icicle under the guttering fell suddenly with a tinkling crash, causing me to jump and the cat to flee. A day after that and the snow thing was gone entirely. By then we were rather sorry to say goodbye to it, but we were pleased to have the thaw and we wondered if that was the end of the winter, or whether another Beast from the East would sweep in and put an end to any spring blossom.

Once the thaw was well and truly underway, I went outside one morning with a box of recycling and glancing at the lawn, I saw that where the snow thing had been were dark patches. Maybe the pressure of all that packed snow had caused the grass to erode? I went over and looked down. It wasn't earth. It looked shadowy. I squinted, wondering if it might be a trick of the light. Then I bent down and ran my hand over the grass. A faint black residue clung to my fingers once I'd straightened up, like ash, but it faded. Where I'd run my hand, a trail was left through the dying grass.

I didn't like this. It felt a bit creepy but I assumed it was something to do with the weight of the snow killing off the grass. If we had any more, I'd tell the kids to go and make a snow thing in one of the nearby fields instead.

The recycling men came and went and I took the boxes back in. The dark patch was still there on the lawn and it looked deeper, somehow. As I stacked the boxes by the back shed, I noticed something else. The edge of the guttering was fuzzy. Only a little, as though a cobweb had been laid across it, but when I ran my hand over it, there was nothing on my fingers and the fuzziness remained.

Must be going mad, I thought. But not seriously. You don't, do you? You find explanations and reasons and you move on. And no one else said anything.

Next day, the patch on the lawn and the fuzziness on the guttering were still there. I had to go shopping again, a weekly task, and I also had a dental appointment in Bedford, so I drove into town. It was a bright January day, blue sky, snow melting fast – only traces remained now, along the verges. I went to the dentist and the supermarket, had a coffee, drove home. By now it was quite late in the day, after four, and the light was starting to die: there was a low, winter sun, still bright. I put the shield down on the window, but the light was as strong as ever, flooding into the car, and then suddenly the world was full of light, bleached and pale, swallowing the skeletal trees and the road itself. I started to panic and I knew I ought to pull over, so I put the hazard lights on and took the car into a layby.

I think I got out. I should have felt the bite of cold on my skin but there was only a gentle warmth. I walked into glow, stumbling forwards, reaching out. I could see spines – what had once been branches – but my hand went straight through them. Eventually I must have wandered in a circle because I fell over the car. Wrenching the door open on the driver's side, I fell into it and put my head on the steering wheel. When I looked up again, the trees were back; a shaft of sunlight splintered the world and then a cloud passed over. Feeling shaky and weak, I managed to drive home.

Must be the menopause, I thought. I didn't actually think I was going mad although I started catastrophising a bit about things like brain tumours and had to have a stern word with myself. I made a doctor's appointment for the following week, with some difficulty, and similar with the optician. I checked the lawn and the guttering and to my dismay, the patches were still there and growing.

Next day, I woke up to bright sunshine. Good, I thought. It improved my mood immediately. It was about half past seven. David was already up and I thought I heard the kids' voices. I had a shower, wrapped myself in a dressing gown and went downstairs. Light was flooding in through the French doors of the dining room and I could feel at once that something was wrong. It was too bright. Like the roadside on the previous day, everything was leached of colour. And the walls looked brittle and thin as if the house had suddenly changed all to glass. David came in from the kitchen holding a mug and he had changed, too: he was attenuated, a stick figure surrounded by glow. I think he said something but then he was gone, swallowed by the light. I felt my knees begin to shake.

"David?" I said. "David, where are you?"

I made it across the room and through the French windows without opening them. There was a faint shattering sound and shards of light spun slowly to the floor. I stepped into the shine. I could see outlines of hedges and the car and I started walking: through what had been the gate and down the road.

I don't know for how long I walked. When I looked down at my hands, my body, they seemed insubstantial, wavering into shimmer. If I was becoming incorporeal, I did not want to know. I stared resolutely ahead. I wondered if I had died; if the world had gone away, or I myself. I thought of David and our kids and I tried to push the terror back.

I wish I could tell you how this happened, how I solved it. How I brought back the world; how it is that I am writing this now. But there is no neat resolution. My neighbour was not some old wizard, whom I encountered and pleaded with, who undertook some magic spell. I did not discover an ancient manuscript, with instructions for restoration, or figured out some scientific explanation with a *Eureka* moment which in a lightning-like flash allowed me to save the world.

All I did was walk, with the word my neighbour had spoken ringing in my head: ungive, ungive. The world is changing and we have effected the change, I believe, although the world changes all the time. I believe we have altered the climate, damaged it, damaged the structure of the world itself in some way so that when the thaw, the ungive, happened, it took more with it than just the ice and the snow. It took everything, because everything is on such a fragile knife-like edge. And I did nothing to make it give itself back, but give itself back, it did.

Slowly, by degrees, things began to solidify. I had come full circle again, and perhaps that was a part of it. Landmarks emerged as the glow faded, appearing like wrecks at the world's low tide. Cars and gateposts, a bicycle, dustbins. I've never been so glad to see someone's dirty old bin. By the time I reached my own front gate, it was dusk, a cold dry twilight with the evening star burning in the west. I hastened up the path, steeling myself for explanations. *Where have you been all day? Where did you go?* And with the star at my back I let myself into the house.

But there was no need. The family were all there in the kitchen, with a pizza in the oven and the BBC news on the box. They seemed to think I had been taking the recycling out. The news said nothing.

Naturally I wondered if I had imagined it. But I sat that night at the window, thinking about the ungive and if it would return, if next time it would be a permanent breakdown, with nothing given back. I looked out into the quiet dark, waiting for the shimmer and the glow, but nothing moved or changed, only the lamp of the evening star, travelling slow across the sky.

# West Wind

*West Wind comes from a trip we took to Tuscany with some of my great American writer friends. We rented a villa outside Florence with lemon trees and hoopoes in the garden, and had a wonderful time in the city itself, visiting guess what. I still feel that the Primavera is one of the great occult artistic works.*

I know when I'm being followed because the wind rises. It lifts my hair, strokes my face and I have to clap my hand on top of my hat to stop it from being torn from my head and flung into the waters of the Arno. It's a warm wind, for this is summer. The city is a furnace right now, but the wind is no relief. It's no weather for running or hiding – or chasing someone. But I know he's chasing me because I've seen him, twice now. Once on the Ponte Vecchio, and once near my lodgings. He ducks into a doorway when he sees me, the coward.

I've taken to locking the studio door, although I've never bothered until now: the main door was good enough and my landlady needs to get into the place to clean it. It's tiny: a little attic room looking out over the picture-postcard rooftops, all the way to the blue hills. If I squint sideways, I have a direct view of the Duomo. I want to draw it before I leave; a cliché, I know. But that's why I'm here, to study drawing. I'm so lucky. It was an eighteenth birthday present from my grandfather, this trip: a month in Florence. He was here years ago, and he's a famous artist now.

"Even if you don't follow in my footsteps, Bells, it won't be wasted. You'll learn something, I'm sure."

But I don't want to waste it. I've got to know a few people, other students, but I'm not really a party person. I took my Kindle with me and I'm catching up on books and spending the evenings quietly. I'm not looking for a romance – not since Jon and I split up before the summer. Everyone says I'm too sensible, but what's wrong with that?

Anyway, my landlady is teaching me to cook proper Florentine food. So with learning to cook and drawing and reading and walking and visiting all these amazing galleries, I'm too busy for a boyfriend and I'm certainly too busy for some creep who thinks he can follow me. Or maybe I'm just paranoid.

But then I see him again. This time, it's actually just outside the Duomo. It's a really hot day, as usual. The sky is a hard, brilliant blue: it looks as though you could knock on it and get an answering sound. And all the colours are in shades of burn – ochre, dull red, fawn. The Duomo is candy-coloured, really a most impressive building. I come back every week or so, to look at the Cathedral and I keep meaning to climb the dome, but it's so hot. It's when I'm coming out, on this occasion, that I see the man again.

He's tall and he's stupidly dressed for this weather, like a flasher in a long flappy raincoat and a slouch hat. I can't see his face but I can feel him watching me. I can run if I have to. I'm wearing espadrilles and I'm quite quick. I don't think I could fend him off – he looks large – but on the other hand there are a lot of people about and I can't see them letting someone just assault a young woman. I look around to see if there are any police; I can't see them but I don't suppose they're far away. Italy doesn't get much in the way of terror attacks but all of Europe's a bit jumpy when it comes to heavily populated tourist areas at the moment. Then he makes a gesture, as if he's throwing something. I glance down and when I look up again he's gone. But there is something on the ground. It's a little white flower on a stem. I reach down and pick it up. I don't know what it is – a crocus? It looks a bit like the windflowers that grow, earlier in the spring, in the woods at the back of our house. I don't want to take it, really, if some man is going around chucking flowers at people – he might read it as a sign that I'm interested. Or he might just be a weirdo. In the end, though, I do take it with me because it seems so unfair on the little flower, which is only slightly wilted, to let it be trampled into the dust. I know that's daft but I'm like that. I don't throw the alarm clock across the room in case I hurt its feelings. I know, I know... Anyway, I bring the flower back to the studio and put it in a shot glass of water, where it revives. Then I go downstairs and learn to make *papardelle*. Anna keeps saying we must try something called *lampredotto* but it's one of those cow's stomach type things and I don't think… Anyway, pasta's nice. I don't tell her about Stalker Bloke because I don't want her to worry about me. I'm not going out in the evenings and there are so many people around in the day that I don't think it's an issue. It's annoying, though.

When I go to sleep that night, I look at the flower. The streetlights must be shining in, because the little white petals almost glow, as if they have their own light. I smile when I see it and for a moment I'm grateful to the weird bloke, because he's given me the flower.

But in the morning, there's another one. Another flower.

This time, it's blue. Not the gentian blue of the Italian sky, but a soft misty colour like the wings of the downland butterflies back home. The petals are long and unfamiliar; I don't know what sort of flower it is. It must have blown in. I don't like the thought that my stalker has somehow been at the window, which is open. If there's another episode, though, I'm going to the police. But would they even take it seriously? God, they might think it was romantic or something.

But nothing happens after that for a couple of days. Then, midweek, it rains in Florence. The clouds gather over those shadowy hills and the next thing I know, big spots of wetness are dappling the russet tiles outside the attic window. The air suddenly smells so fresh that I know what I'll do: in the comparative coolness, I'll climb the dome of the Duomo. I pick up my bag. The two little flowers are still unwilted – 'fresh as a daisy', I think. I leave them in possession of the attic and go out, heading through the old winding streets to the Duomo.

Inside, it's cool and quiet, although there are actually quite a lot of people here. I find the entrance to the steps and go: up, up, up. Whenever I reach a window, I look out over the rooftops. The clouds are a ragged edge above the hills and it's still spotting with rain. And the wind's getting up, breathing in through the windows and drifting down the steps. I'm not the only one making the climb, but somehow, when I come out onto the wide ledge of the roof, I'm alone. The world smells metallic, that after-rain smell on sunwarmed tiles. But there's a drift of something else, a fragrance. I look down. A poppy lies at my feet in a bloody splash. Like the others, it's fresh. When I look up, the man is standing at the end of the ledge.

I ought to be frightened, but I'm not. I can't help wondering why the people who were behind me on the steps have not yet appeared. The man has dispensed with his coat and hat; he wears a red cloth around his head, and a long red robe, bunched at the waist so that his bare feet are visible. The skin of his arms, also bare, and his face are pale as marble, with dim blue veins. It's as though he's wearing a mask, the mask of a man, but under it is something completely different.

I say, "Who *are* you?" But I should have asked *what*.

The man smiles. It's not like a real smile, either. He holds out his hand and there's a rose in it; I didn't see that before. It's small and pink, a wild rose of the hedge. In Italian, he says, "For you."

There's a gust of wind and it dashes rain into my eyes. When I've stopped blinking, the man is gone. Over the edge? Oh Christ! I rush to it and look down. People are coming out onto the ledge now, behind me, chatting. There's nothing in the street below. The rose sits on the stonework; he has left it for me.

I take the poppy home, along with the rose, and put them in the shot glass. Then I sit down on the bed, thinking. I can't tell the police about this, or my landlady. It's not that I think everything's okay, because it isn't. What I do think is this: my stalker isn't human.

So what is he?

Next day, screwing up my courage, I go looking for him. The rain has stopped overnight, although it drenched the city and everything feels much fresher now. I wander all round the Duomo, have lunch in a café. Over coffee, I try to draw the man I saw, but it's hard to get a grip. Because that was not his true face, I hear my own voice tell me. He wears it. It's easier. And I've seen him somewhere before.

On the way back, I find another flower, a jonquil. It goes to join the collection. I've left the studio unlocked again, because I'm no longer afraid, and if my landlady has noticed the growing floral display, she hasn't said anything. Both the white flower and the blue are showing no signs of fading, although it's been several days now. I might have to ask her for the loan of a vase.

That night, I wake suddenly. The moon is full now and its pale light is pouring in through the window. It casts blue shadows over the floor but the flowers have kept their colour: the poppy, which should be changed by the moon, is still a deep red. They're almost like cartoon flowers, stark against the wall, and for the first time I wonder if they, too, might not be real.

Then a voice says, "Come with me."

"What?" I sit bolt upright in bed but there's no one there.

"Come."

I know it's his voice but I can't see him. I get out of bed and throw on a sundress and espadrilles, then, for the first time since I arrived here, I go out at night – the middle of the night, not evening. The streets are quiet in the moonlight and there's no one around. I'm not dreaming but it feels dreamlike all the same. I can see him ahead of me and he's walking quickly, almost gliding. He holds out a hand to me without looking back and I have to trot to keep up, not running exactly, but so as not to be left behind. As I pursue him, I realise where he's heading: to the old span of the Ponte Vecchio, over the river. During the day it's filled with tourists, of course, but at night it's probably empty. The breeze is getting up, although it's still warm.

He crosses the bridge but when I enter its roofed confines I can no longer see him. My footsteps echo in the enclosed space. I walk to the middle of the bridge, hoping he'll reappear. And then he does. His robe looks grey in the moonlight. He is holding out his hand.

There's a step behind me, too. When I turn, I see a woman. She's tall, rather dignified and beautiful, in a long dress. This time, I know who she is. I last saw her in a painting in the Uffizi, and her golden hair is crowned with flowers. I put my hand to my mouth. The scent of roses, summer-strong, fills the long room of the bridge.

She says, in Italian, but it's as though I hear her in English, "I have come to talk to you. He has a few words, but no more."

"Why not?"

"The wind has no need of words."

I look at him. He's evaporating, drifting upwards like smoke. The breeze stirs my hair.

"He's the west wind. In the picture. He's trying to grab a woman. A nymph."

193

"He's trying to show her the way."

There's something in my mouth, small and hard. I spit into my palm. Another wild rose, a bud, unfolding.

"He's offering you a job," the woman says. I bow my head.

"I'm just human. And I want to go home, eventually."

The woman – the goddess – laughs.

"It doesn't have to interfere with your other commitments," she says, sounding suddenly like the CEO of something, a businesswoman. Maybe she sort of is? "It's for later. We think ahead."

"When I – die?"

"You won't. You'll grow old, but you'll keep the power of the spring in you. When it's time, you'll know. Walk into the hills and you'll find him waiting. Walk west."

So I tell her yes. Together, we stroll for a short distance along the river. I want to ask her why he chose me, but she says before I put the question that the wind has his fancies and he can't explain it. Not enough words. Dawn's coming now, there's a line of light over the hills and she has to go, back to wherever she comes from. Her dress is the colour of wild roses and embroidered with flowers, but every so often one falls away to lie on the stone flags, made real. She fades with the light, yet grows brighter, and as the sun comes up over the roofs, she's gone.

I would like to draw her when I get back to the studio, but you see, she's been drawn already and I don't think I'm as good as that artist, not yet.

# The Wording

*Like most writers, I have a fascination with words, and the idea that you might have to venture out and find your own personal word has always struck me as a magical act, hence this coming-of-age story.*

Summer was ending when Helay went up to the heights of the Wordfell. She did not look back. She could feel the shadow of the fortress reaching behind her, pointing her way along the track, which in this dry weather was rutted and crumbling. It had been some time since any wheel had passed this way and the edges of the track were weedy and overgrown: Helay recited the names to herself as she strode along. *Rosestrife, mullein, oldease, fumitage.* Tangles of fading pink flowers and purple spikes, a splash of colour against the faded mountains and the dark trees. Above, the red sun rose in a bone-bleached sky. It was not too hot. Helay wore a leather jerkin over her shirt but her armpits remained dry. There was a breath of a chilly breeze, coming down from the peaks; she could smell snow. Summer, she knew, was not for long.

*When you find the word,* they had said, *you must be careful. Because it may not want to be known, and so you must carry it with care. Also, others may want to steal it from you.* Helay had laughed. "What if it's a little word? A bug, or a weed?" *But Annegren had not smiled. "You never know. Big things start with little things. You need to be careful."* And Helay had felt her own smile *freeze, and then fade.* "I'll be careful," she'd said, looking down at the tattooed band around her finger, that was her own Word, the name they had so recently given her, replacing the childhood nickname.

Time to be serious. She would take care, even if she knew these hills well, had travelled them with her mother and aunts, her father and uncles, each spring and summer until winter came and brought the roaring storms and the snows down upon Wordfell. Then it was time to light the lamps against the dark, close the thick curtains and shut out the night, and count each new word, inscribing them into the book.

And now, one or more of those words would belong to her, become her discovery. She felt an anticipatory pride, not unmixed with anxiety. But it was the task laid upon the Elter and all the other families, since the crossing, when words had fled from them in this new world, which was so like the old, and yet different.

They'd rounded a lot of them up in these last hundred years, but there were a lot of words, and not all of them were claimed. Helay had a net in her pocket and she thought she knew what to do. She had to climb, though. Words hid in the heights, and needed to be netted, so when she came to the fork in the old track, she turned left instead of right and started to climb, up through the ever-reds and the scent of resin, the fronded crimson bracken and the brambles beside the track.

How to hunt a word? She had learned young, along with all the other children. You have to smell it, first. Very light, upon the breeze. Then you taste it on your tongue. Finally, if you are very lucky, you might hear it. Wordsmith Annegren had been quite clear on this point.

"You won't hear it at first," she had said. "We don't know why. They are elusive."

"What does 'elusive' mean?" Helay's brother had asked.

"It means it twists and turns and runs very fast like a winter hare, so that you have to run after it and try not to fall off any cliffs."

Helay had never been sure when the Wordsmith was joking, and when she was not. They had practiced with words that were already known, of course, released into the wild. The children had run about, waving their nets, not knowing what to do.

"Oh, come now! Words are not butterflies! You don't catch them like that."

"Then how?" asked Helay's friend Marwys. "How do you catch them?"

"You wait. And then you listen. And then you strike."

Helay went on up into the woodland. The red and fawn foliage rustled as she passed, the stripes of colour making it hard to see. Perhaps she would glimpse a *hostera*, one of the gentle, deer-like creature whose name had only recently been discovered. She smiled to herself, thinking of the teachings she had received as a child.

*Words will run from you, as they have always run from us. You must be patient.*

*But how is it, then, that we can speak? If the words all ran away?* Helay had asked this just as every child had asked it, since the Crossing.

*The languages we brought with us remained. Those words are tame words, like pet creatures. The nouns, anyway. The verbs – the 'doing' words – and others, articles, adverbs, prepositions – the little words – they stayed, too. And words like 'mountain' and 'forest.' But it is the nouns for the new things we found here that we could not grasp. We tried to name them, but the names would not stick. We forgot them as soon as they were spoken and if they were written down, they would vanish from the page as though they had been written with rainwater. Hence the Wording, when we must go out and catch them. If 'catch' is indeed the right word. It's more as though they are shy, and come to us when they are ready to make friends.*

Helay wondered what her word would be. Her stomach tensed at the prospect of not finding a word at all: this had happened. And the young person was not drummed out of the settlement, not punished, and yet… There was something not quite right with those people, unclaimed by a word of the land, as though they too had not quite stuck, not quite taken. As though they, too, had been written in rainwater.

Helay hoped very much that she would not be one of those people.

She did not see a hostera, but she did see a number of the small red birds that were, as yet, unnamed. She stood very still, as they swooped like small scarlet arrows into the clouds of insects that frequented the damp places of the woodland. It would be too easy – but she hoped, even yet, that one of them might whisper its name in the ear of her mind.

No such luck. The birds were silent and then the flock comma'd off into the treetops. Helay sighed and walked on. During her trek into the heights on that first day, she saw many new things: plants and birds, insects and outcrops of crystal. Nothing spoke to her, but it was all fascinating. By the time she made camp, she felt that she had learned a great deal more about the land in which her people had made their home. She sat by the little fire, looking out over the great expanse of the distant plains as they fell into the twilight shadows. Roll upon roll of land, all the way to the unknown sea.

Over the last hundred years, people had set off into the plains, exploring. They knew that the sea was there, that this was one of two enormous continents: this much had been shown on the ship's scanners before the landing. In keeping with beliefs then, the ship had been cannibalised for parts: this was it, there would be no going home, if home even meant anything after such a long time. But her ancestors did make maps before they archived the viewing records and Helay, like all the other children, had studied the plans of Marek 5, or Worldhome, as it had now become. Since then, her ancestors had spread out across the mid-northern land, building the forts in the fells and farming the lower land, where the heights rumbled down to meet the plains.

It had been a while before they discovered the planet's etymological peculiarities, or perhaps humankind had somehow changed over the long crossing, some psychological or neurological shift which made this Wording process necessary. Or perhaps it was a cultural thing, as Helay had heard some of her teachers say: a kind of meme. She did not know. All that she hoped was that she would return with a Word.

For the next week, she ventured further into the heights. She could see winter waiting, poised to spring, up on the furthest slopes, and the air was cold. Helay did not mind this, warm in her fur jerkin. She washed in snowmelt and ate her way steadily through her rations and the edible fungus that grew on the moteleaf trunks. She had another three days before the moons aligned; then, tradition had it, she would have to return, Word or no Word. She saw only one person, far away down a slope, and thought perhaps that they were a herdsman or a Wordseeker like herself: other young people would have gone out into the land, too. She raised a hand in greeting but the person did not turn their head and soon they were gone out of sight.

That night, she spent the darkness at the mouth of a cave. The fire would keep any beasts away, but this part of the land was not known to be home to any of the big predators: those were found to the south, in the plains. It was very quiet, and Helay felt very alone, but when she eventually slept she dreamed that she had visitors.

She sat up. The fire had burned down to embers. Behind her, the cave was silent, but from the apron of scree before it she could hear rustling and whispers.

"Hello?" she said. The rustling stopped. Then there were people all around her. Helay could not see them clearly; it was as though they flickered in the dying light of the fire. She knew that they were very tall and carried three-pointed wands, like small tridents, or toasting forks. Helay's dreaming mind suppressed a giggle. She glimpsed long, narrow faces, with animal eyes. They did not seem very interested in her but just as she was starting to feel relieved, one of them bent and spoke. She could not tell if it was male or female, or perhaps those terms had no meaning here.

"Do not," the being said gently, "make our mistake."

Then they vanished, whisked away like smoke into the growing light of dawn, and Helay woke up. She lay, blinking, in the cocoon of her sleeping bag. Worldhome had been empty of sentient life. This was a tenet of settlement: you don't go where people are. Humans had finally learned that colonisation did not end well, and the initial scouts had been fanatical on the issue and therefore thorough. When her ancestors had arrived, initial investigations revealed no such life, which had been a relief. Had there been, the great ship would have been compelled to take off again – a procedure fraught with danger – or the inhabitants would have committed mass suicide. But there had been no one – or so they thought. Some fifty five years ago, an exploratory party had found a castle in the high fells. It had been very old, definitely (from its proportions) made by beings analogous to humans, although the doorways had been very high and thin. Other than the outer shell, however, and one room, nothing was left. An emergency council on the explorers' return had suggested a policy of watching and waiting, but in the intervening time nothing more had been discovered. All her life, Helay had been fascinated by this, had pored over the images of the castle, had gone to bed dreaming about being the one who made contact with those ancient peoples – even though it had been drummed into them all that this would be the end under the old Forchar religious law.

And now it seemed that she'd had the best of both worlds. They had come, but they had also gone.

She rose slowly and ate a small meal, then set off again. She was beginning to become concerned: last night, the moons had been drawing even closer and by the rules of the Wording, she was running out of time. There was talk of the tides of the land, of when the word currents turned, and astrologers had tied this into the movement of the moons. Trying to set aside her doubts, Helay climbed higher into the fells. Ahead, the huge ranges spilled across the world, their summits increasingly whitened with snow. The air nipped at her lungs, but the sun still warmed her face. Towards dusk, when that sun was boiling down into fire over the rim of the plains, Helay came out onto a plateau of rock and saw it.

She had never known where the ruined castle lay. The Elders had chosen not to make that knowledge freely available and their decision had been respected. Parents, Helay's among them, had not wanted to see their offspring sneaking off to try to find ancient alien life. So Helay had not known, when she set out, whether she might come across the castle – although she had wanted to.

It lay across the valley between this summit and the next ridge. She was looking down on it, and from this angle it could have been simply a spire of stone. But she had studied the images and she knew. She sank down onto a rock and stared at it for as long as it remained visible, until the sun disappeared and the striped bands of the land were swallowed by the dusk. Helay made camp among the stones and her anxiety about the Word was diminished by the sighting of the castle. But if she dreamed that night, no memory was left in the morning.

When the sun rose, she packed up and carried on. She was starting to feel desperate now: no Word had come to her, not even the smell of one. So when the attack came, Helay was thinking about this problem and nothing else.

She was young, about Helay's own age. She came snarling out from behind an outcrop and the first thing she did was knock Helay down. Helay was bowled over, rolling along the slope like a skittle, and perhaps this saved her life. She came to rest with her back against a wall of stone and she picked up a rock and threw it at the girl as hard as she could. It made her dodge and curse. She took in, so quickly that it startled her, that the other girl had dark hair and eyes, and the crest of the Burhali clan on his jerkin. From her age, she was a Wordseeker like herself.

"Stop!" Helay shouted. "What do you think you're doing?"

Spittle flecked the girl's face. Her eyes were unaware. The next stone she threw hit the girl in the leg and then the Word came to her: *etsubi*. The girl stopped, panting, and stared at her.

"*Etsubi*," she said.

It lodged in Helay's mind like a flung stone, and with it, walking out of the brightness, came a figure. It was tall and wrapped in a shawl like mist, and it said, "Etsubi."

"What does that mean?" the young woman stammered. Then she looked at Helay and her eyes widened. "Oh no! Are you all right?"

"Yes, I think so. Bruised."

"If you can speak it, then it can be bound," the figure said inside Helay's mind and as it did so, Helay saw understanding come into the girl's eyes, also. "Some words – they should never have been conceived."

And Helay, blinking, watched as the tall army poured out of the castle across the valley, roaring with rage. She watched as the ravines filled with bodies and blood. She watched the red carrion birds wheeling above the carnage, and the last few survivors stagger away, wailing with sorrow and remorse now that *etsubi* no longer possessed them. The sun came out from behind a cloud, the castle was again a ruin, and the alien was gone.

But the girl of the Burhali clan was still standing there, face filled with dismay. "What happened? I have my Word, but –"

"I'm so sorry," Helay said. She felt stiff all over and put her hand on the rock for support. "I hope your leg isn't badly hurt. But you attacked me."

"I – don't remember. I came up the side of the fell, as the sun was rising. I hadn't found my Word. I thought – But then there it was. It was waiting for me, it pounced, and then, nothing. Until that stone hit my leg."

"It is my Word, too," Helay said. "I've never heard of such a thing."

"My name is Isso. Isso ve Burhali."

"Helay ve Elter."

"There are stories in my clan of Words of war," Isso said, sombrely.

"I've not heard of such a thing. But – I cannot take this back to Wordfell."

"Nor I to Burhayze."

They stared at each other.

"We have bound it," Isso said. "But what if it breaks free?"

"What then?"

Helay and Isso made their way down from the heights, together. When they reached the road that led to Wordfell, they paused, and Helay looked up for a moment, at the lights of the settlement. When they reached the road that led to Burhayze, Isso did the same thing.

Then, without saying anything yet in mutual agreement, they walked on, along the track that led down to the plains, and the darkness, and the sea.

# Wrecktide

*The sea is a big source of inspiration for me, and ships. I've always been fascinated by the story of the Flying Dutchman.*

Ghost ships only ride on certain tides; you need to know the flow and the ebb. But it isn't the tide alone; when the Dutchman's ship is coming, there's a change in the light. You can see shadows of nothing over the surface of the sea and the gulls shy away from them. And his ship only comes in when the moon is dark. I had to learn when the Dutchman's boat was coming, you see. I had to get my daughter back.

Elise drowned when the *Salutation* went down, in a storm along the Cape. I knew when she died because she came to me, dripping saltwater, shuffling along the bare boards of my room. Her head hung low. She breathed a silver mist.

I struggled for breath and words, clutching the counterpane close to my throat. She looked up. There was something swimming behind her eyes. Her lips moved and the faintest whisper of sound emerged upon the air.

"I am dead, mother. But the Dutchman's ship has found me. He says I am beautiful." Perhaps, very slightly, she smiled. "Watch for the Dutchman's ship."

Then she was gone in a shimmer of light. A drop of water lay upon the floorboards and faded as I stared.

They say the Dutchman's ship takes sailors and so it does, for he needs a crew. Old spirits wear out, sifting down in a handful of dust. But there are more drowned men than one ship can hold, and it's known that the Dutchman is a ladies' man.

So I waited, for the dead tide, when the Dutchman's ships visits the relations of all the souls he has taken, when I would see Elise again.

I went down to the shore every day: how fortunate, I thought, that we lived by the sea. I had always loved it, even though a further ocean had taken my daughter. But this was a colder, northern coast, looking westwards towards the humps of islands and the granite cliffs. This had

203

always been a place of fishermen and wreckers, sailors and harbourmasters. Far down in the land, towards Cornwall's tip. And it is also a place of women who wait. I was not the only one who stood on the shore and stared out to sea. The only difference was that my dead would be coming back.

One morning, early in winter, I saw the signs I'd been looking for. The gulls, a white wheel, were keeping close to the cliff face. Dapples and ripples moved over the surface of the sea. The light seemed softer, as though a mist was coming in.

"This," one of the old men said to me as we passed on the harbour arm, "This is not a good day for fishing, Mistress Lambert." Our eyes met.

"Not a good day at all," I replied. I stood for a while, watching. There was a dark line along the horizon, a storm coming. Then I turned and went back to the cottage to make my preparations.

It is witchcraft, no doubt about it. And I had always said to Elise that I had no interest in my mother's ways, but now needs must. I took the feather of a gull, and wove it with the saltgrass that grew along the shore, and a strand of my daughter's hair, taken from a brush she would never use again. Then I anointed it with my tears, kept in a cup, and my own blood, pricked from my finger. I wove it into a little boat and at midnight, wrapped in a black cape, I took it down to the shore to wait.

There was no moon, but the stars were bright in the restless sky. A lamp at the harbourmaster's house allowed me to see, but hopefully not be seen. There was a black track, visible from the corner of my eye, at the base of the steps. They were slimy with weed, leading down into the water, and I took care as I went down them. I placed the boat with its cargo of blood and sadness in the sea, and waited.

Slowly, slowly, the boat began to grow. I watched as the shadow of it spread across the sea, but there was little light to cast that shadow. When I thought that it was sufficiently solid, I stepped into it. There was no rope to cast off, no anchor to weigh. The boat began to glide smoothly out of the harbour, and as we reached the open sea I saw that a ship was coming. It emerged out of the line of cloud at the horizon, dimly visible against the night. It was huge, a big brig, with billowing black sails and it came fast. I stood in the prow of my boat, which smelled of salt and blood, skimming over the churning water. I could scent storm on the wind, the coming lightning. I gave no command to my boat but let it go. The Dutchman's ship loomed over me. I could see the barnacles encrusted along its sides, the dark caulk of ancient wood. It should have been falling apart; its sails were in tatters. A pale face was looking over the side.

"Elise!" I cried. "Elise!"

"Mother?" The small figure ran along the deck. I saw a shadow and heard her pleading voice.

"Wait!" she called back. "Don't go – wait for me! He says he will let me go."

A rope ladder was thrown over the side and I saw her climb down. She looked the same as when I had last seen her: pallid and drenched, with sopping skirts. Soon she was in the boat.

"Oh! Let's go home," she said. She sank onto the seagrass weave as though her skirts had borne her down. Head bent, hands clasped in her lap, she did not look back.

But I did. I saw the Dutchman's ship turn on the dead tide and begin to move, sailing out into the darkness once more. And I thought, as I turned our boat for home, that I saw something else, a shadow, drifting over the water. I looked towards the shore, for the boat was beginning to tremble. By the time we reached the harbour arm, it was disintegrating. I jumped onto the step and helped Elise up. She was light, almost weightless, nothing like a sodden corpse. The boat sank into a few strands of seagrass, drifting on the tide in a slick like blood. Together we went back into the house and she made straight for the fire.

"Can you eat, or drink?"

"I don't think so." She was huddled around her wet skirts.

"At least let me find you some dry clothes. All your things are here. I've given nothing away."

She looked up. Her eyes, which had been a soft blue, were colourless. "I don't think it will make any difference."

It did not. Within minutes of her changing, her skirts were once again dripping with water, pooling on the hearth and fading into steam. She remained there all night, while I, exhausted, went to bed and a sleep filled with uneasy dreams.

You see, I had not thought it would really work. I had put all my attention into the spell, all my waking thoughts beyond those necessary for basic survival. My mother had said that intent makes magic, but now that the magic had worked, what then? Before her death, we had intended Elise to marry, like any other girl, but that was out of the question now.

She said that she could not get warm. She remained by the fire all the time, while I tried to go about my daily business. Thankfully I had no friends in the village: I had inherited this cottage from an aunt of great age, and all her friends were dead. Elise had died shortly after our arrival and there had been no time to exchange any other than the usual pleasantries with the locals. Now, I was thankful for that, since no one came to the house. Of course, we had gone to church. But Elise could not do so now.

A week went by. It was worrying, but there were better moments. We spent a lot of time reminiscing, about the time when my husband, and her father, had been alive, when she was small. Times in Bath and London, the social whirl of her younger womanhood – but she was not old now. She had died at twenty-two. She did not remember her death, only the coldness of the water and a taste of salt. She had woken on the Dutchman's ship. She felt always cold, but not heavy: lighter than when she had been alive, despite her dragging step. And the Dutchman had been kind enough, for she was one of them now.

I kept the house dim, because Elise said that the light hurt her eyes. The Dutchman's ship had sailed in darkness, or in storm. They seemed to pass from night to night, always avoiding the day, even in the tropics. And she did not remember seeing the moon, although the stars were bright and in configurations she did not recognise.

A night after Elise had come back, I saw the shadow. At first I thought it was one of the cats, but it was too dark, too still. It lay like a pool of oil behind a door and when I looked at it directly it faded into a trick of the light. But when I looked from the corner of my eye, the shadow was back, thick across the boards and faintly gleaming, and then it slid under the door and was gone.

How can I say I cared for my daughter, when there was no caring to be done? I did not feed her, or bring her tea. She needed no laundry, nothing but the fire, which we kept continually stoked. As well that it was winter. How I was to explain a roaring hearth in the summer months – well, we'd cross that bridge when we came to it.

I became more reclusive, spoke to fewer folk, and that briefly. One day, however, I had to take some letters to the post and the postmistress addressed me.

"Are you well, Mistress Lambert?"

"I am – well enough. Though it is true I have not been in the greatest of good health lately." It gave me a chance to make an excuse, I thought, for my lack of sociability. The postmistress shook her head sadly.

"Ah, you're not the only one. Something going around the village. A funny thing – not like a cough, or a cold. Perhaps this is what you've experienced? A languishing, among women."

"Why yes," I said, though it was not true. "It sounds like my own condition. A fatigue?"

"Yes, a listlessness, a languor. Poor Mrs Polvennon's Mary is almost dead with it, they say."

"Perhaps it is something from the sea. Or brought by a foreign ship?"

"Perhaps. They've had the doctor in to see her, but he's no use. They'll be having the priest next."

We shook our heads, she expressed her concern for me, which was kind, and I returned home deep in thought. Elise herself seemed no different, and I, despite what I had told the postmistress, was unaffected. But I did not like what I had heard. I decided to make further enquiries.

That night, I woke. It was past full moon, but not yet at the dark, and a rind of light shone through the uncurtained window. The shadow pooled below the sill. I had not yet raised my head and perhaps it did not realise that I was awake. As I watched, it uncoiled. It was like an eel: a long blunt body, swimming through air, with a blind head. Its mouth opened, displaying needle sharp teeth. It slithered above the boards, heading for the door and out.

I pulled on my cape and followed it down the stairs. I hoped no one would see me, in my nightdress and slippers beneath the heavy cape. The shadow slid along the harbour wall, keeping close to the stone. I watched as it crept down a garden path, and in under the window, flattening itself to gain entry. That house was the Polvennon's, I saw. I waited, cold and afraid, until it crept out again and returned; I hid behind the harbour wall until it had gone by. The night was very still, with a sparkling frost on the pavements. The shadow looked more solid, blacker. It oozed back into our cottage and did not come out again.

That evening, I closed the door of the sitting room and lit all the lamps, despite Elise's protest. I looked behind all the furniture, and then I told her.

For the first time since she had come home, she touched me. She reached out and grasped my wrist. Her hand felt frail, no more than wet bone.

"You have to take me back."

"Elise –"

"It came with me. They cling to the ship, they follow it. They are a kind of spirit, a demon from the deep sea. It's here because of me." Her face was filled with anguish. "You have to let me go. I am dead. Why should Mary die? I remember her in life – we spoke once at church. Only once, but she was kind."

At last I said I would sleep on it, but when I woke in the morning, I knew she was right.

"Only as far as the harbour arm," she whispered. "Only that far."

We had once more night. We spent it in conversation and that day, I tried to sleep. The dusk went down into the moon's dark and Elise and I set out for the shore. I did not look behind me. The harbour arm was slippery; Elise took me by the arm. I was surprised at her strength. Her face was set.

"Do you – do you mind?" I whispered once, and she replied, "What is there for me here?"

But at the end of the arm, she turned to me and said, "Pray for me. Pray for my soul to be free from the ship. Who knows, if you pray enough, we may see one another again."

"I promise," I said. Then she made me stand aside, waiting for the Dutchman's ship.

Its curse is this: it can never reach the shore, never make land. But it can send out a boat, and this it did, in answer to some unspoken call. In silence we watched it come in, from the great dark ship. When it reached the shore, rocking faintly on the tide, Elise turned and clasped my hand, and before I could speak she was down the steps and in the boat.

I watched her all the way, out past the harbour arm to the channel, and then to the deep sea where the Dutchman's ship was waiting. It was too far to see her climb back up the ladder, but I did see a thread of oily blackness, following the little boat as it sped, un-oared, towards the ship. It moved fast and sleek, quick as an eel.

I hoped Mary Polvennon would recover. I knew that I would not, from my own malady, but I knew what to do for them both. I went back along the hardbitten ground, to begin my prayers.

# The Man in
# the Glass Wig

*This is a Hermetic story. If you're into Kabbalism, the relevant sephiroth is Hod – the realm of Mercury. The lamp is a real one, and once belonged to Francis Dashwood, the creator of the Hellfire Club at West Wycombe.*

The man in the glass wig shakes his head when I show him the lamp, and the ringlets tinkle slightly, like tiny bells.

"It's not one of mine." He lowers his head carefully, and looks into the heart of the lamp as I hold it up. The lamp is a crystal globe and it catches the light and fire of the glassblowers' factory, the furnaces showering sparks onto the flagged floor. The lamp, which is the size of my own two hands, is bound with a serpent of bronze and held aloft, so the fancy goes, by a pair of silver wings. In reality, there is a delicate chain.

"I know it's not one of yours," I say. "This is older, I think."

The glassblower frowns. "Yet not so very old. I recognise the pattern – I have seen one such before, in the hallway of a gentleman's club in Piccadilly."

I laugh. "This, too, hung in a similar establishment once. But then it was bequeathed to me."

"Why bring it to me, sir? An elegant addition to your home, I should think, regardless of its provenance."

"Because," I tell him, "I've started to see the future in it."

This is what I do. I introduce people to one another. Mainly gentlemen, but sometimes ladies, too. Being the youngest son of a nobleman, I do not need to engage in common trade, but I have a facility, so they say, for charm, and for chatter. These things are shallow and yet – they have a use. I am like a bubble in a current of water, bobbing to and fro, sometimes upstream and sometimes down, and always circling around some weightier stone or fallen branch. I take note of what I see and hear, and I communicate it. I introduce this lord to that lord – and even though this city is large, it is small enough that many people do know one another. I know very many people, and many know one another through me.

"Why, Sir Flyte," said a young lady of my acquaintance some while ago, "Your name must be a true one! It is as though you have wings on your heels, so often do you flit and show!"

"My dear madam, I am a veritable Mercury," I told her. And it is true. As though I might indeed have wings, I bear messages across the capital. I try to do only good, though sometimes I fail – gossip is often irresistible, after all. But I try to help. I try.

I first saw the lamp in a private residence, the owner of which must remain nameless as he is high in the land and known to all. Thus I shall not say exactly where I first saw it, only that it was in London. It hung in the dim recesses of the hallway, illuminating the black and white tiles of the floor, and when he saw me staring at it, my host informed me that it should be mine.

"What! I cannot take such a lavish gift. Surely –"

"Surely, after what we have been discussing, it is merely appropriate."

"But –"

"I shall not tell you its gifts, its powers. You must discover those for yourself. I'm sure you're more than capable."

In the end, I had to agree and the lamp was brought to my house by his servants. I had it hung in the study, with a fancy of illuminating my work. But it was not long before the lamp began to misbehave.

It was night. I had been pursuing my correspondence, finishing some overdue letters, under the sputtering light of the lamp. The candle within it flashed crystal fire from the glass diamonds which hung beneath it, and when I turned to look at it, I was dazzled for a moment. I looked up, into the glass, and saw a city.

I favour myself that I am well travelled (London, the Continent) and yet I had never seen such a place. Its towers were higher than the dome of St Paul's Cathedral and there were paths and bridges of glass strung between them. Tiny slivers of metal, silver dragonflies, shot among the towers. And the city was bright: light fell, cascading, down the sides of towers and the glowing river. Above the tallest tower hung a great blue-white star.

All of this in miniature, in microcosm. I stared, fascinated; I had never experienced such a waking dream. It lasted for a few minutes and then the light began to become more diffuse, like a candle flame in a dark room, and eventually the little scene faded. I stared on, hoping, but there was no more. I turned quickly back to the desk and wrote my vision down, before I lost it.

I did not see it again for some weeks, but at last, one evening in the study, I glanced at the lamp and there was my city. It was a little further down river, I thought, but the curve looked very much like the Thames, and now I could actually see the dome of St Paul's itself. The towers encompassed the skyline but the steeples were visible, too. I watched until the vision, once more, faded.

I knew that London had never looked like this, certainly not now and not prior to the Great Fire, nearly a hundred years before. Therefore, I reasoned, this must either be some vision conjured from the whole cloth of my dreaming mind, or a glimpse of the future, and it seemed to me that the latter was more probable. A week later, it came once more, only a fragment, a shard of a view, gone seconds later.

When I looked at my notes, I found a pattern. All of these visions had occurred on a Wednesday. But what was special about Wednesday? I had no idea. I hurried around to my friend, the original holder of the lamp, and was informed that he had 'gone away'. Then I started to make enquiries of the glassblowers, and those who made lamps, and such like, and it was through this medium that I learned of the man in the glass wig.

The main house for glass blowing was down in Smithfield, and it was here that I came one sunny Tuesday morning in June, to enquire about the lamp. I had heard that this place was a great centre for the industry, with many forms of glass being produced, and ever of an enquiring mind, I thought to look about myself and learn something of the craft. It was indeed fascinating, although the blast from the furnaces made me bake and sweat in the early summer heat. There was colour everywhere – deep blue, flashing silver, royal crimson, and the sparks from the blowing shot forth in great arcs to die hissing on the cobbles. The air smelled of gunpowder and fire, overpowering the usual seasonal stench from the Thames. I picked my way between the glassblowers, marvelling, until I found the man I sought.

He had been recommended to me by an acquaintance as the person who knew all there was to know about glass and the art of it. His name was Erasmus Century.

"He has many foibles," my acquaintance told me. "You will find him amusing."

Indeed, I was not expecting the glass wig.

"Surely that is not of great comfort?" I ventured.

"Oh, no. It's desperately inconvenient. But it advertises my trade and one makes the most of what one can. I should like a glass shirt and britches next, but I fear these would be beyond the bounds of both possibility and decency."

In fact, he was wearing quite ordinary clothes with the exception of the wig. A kind, eager face, I thought, with a pointed nose and small chin. I explained about the lamp.

"I have not heard of such a phenomenon," he said. He gave me a curious glance, and I feared that he might consider me mad, but then he said, "Yet I have heard of others. With different glass. I knew a man once who could see the past through the square of a church window – such things are possible, I believe. Glass is strange."

"Do you think it traps an image in some way?"

"No, but I believe some kinds might operate as a window, perhaps when combined with other substances. Or even magic."

"I do not know if I believe in that," I said.

"Nor do I," he replied.

In the event, we agreed that I would bring the lamp to him, on the following Wednesday. The weather continued to be hot and I had my servant take the lamp down, wrap it carefully in paper, and have it conveyed to the glassblowers' quarter in my carriage. I was eager to see what the man in the glass wig would make of it.

To our mutual disappointment, I think, no vision was forthcoming. We studied the lamp at length, but although Mr Century could tell me that the lamp was not of English make, he could not determine where in fact it had come from. Reluctantly, we returned it to its packaging, and thence to my carriage. I returned home and it was when we were almost there, at the bottom of Lancaster Street, that the attack happened.

The carriage is an open one, and the day was, as I have said, warm. My servant was driving the gig and I was looking about me at the sights of the city, having made sure that the box containing the lamp was safely stowed beneath the seat. As we turned the corner, I saw a flash of dull yellow and the horse reared up, startled. My servant fought for control and as he did so, the gig swaying alarmingly, a man dressed in a long ochre robe reached over the lip of the carriage and tried to seize the box. I struck him a great blow with my cane and the villain fell back. The horse sprang forwards and when I looked back I saw another such man bending over his fallen comrade.

My servant and I were ruffled by the affair and had much to say about the matter, once the lamp was safely restored to its place in the study. My servant felt that the men were perhaps foreign, and I agreed, but what I did not tell him was that I had looked into the assailant's face: an ordinary enough countenance, quite pale skinned – but his eyes had been as golden-green as a cat's, with slitted pupils. I had never seen anyone like him before, and I did not know what he was. Perhaps I was indeed losing my mind.

I kept an eye on the lamp, and nothing untoward happened for the rest of that day. I consumed a lamb chop in my study along with some claret, and due to a lingering sense of unease about the safety of the lamp, I thought that I would sleep in the study, too, upon the couch, which was comfortable enough. I placed a length of chain across the window sill, which would rattle if anyone tried to raise the sash. And I made sure that the couch was out of sight of the door, which I wedged shut with a chair. I placed a sword beneath the length of the couch.

Let the villains try something, I thought, and they would find me waiting for them.

But the night was silent. I slipped into an uneasy doze, waking around midnight. I could hear the chimes of the hall clock, speaking away the hour. Moonlight shone through the crack in the curtains, illuminating the room with its soft light and casting flickering answers from the lamp, which was twisting slightly upon its chain. I watched it, dreaming, and gradually I became aware that someone was standing on the other side of the room.

I did not move. I knew where the sword was, and could reach it swiftly if I had to. The person stepped forwards and I could see a square of darkness behind him, as though a door had opened up in the wall. But I knew that no door was there. In the moonlight, his robe looked grey, but I saw a faint green fire from his eyes and knew him to be one of the men who had assaulted us earlier. He carried a long pole with a small hook at the end – an ideal instrument for detaching the lamp. As he reached up, I seized the sword, leaped from the couch and sprang at him.

He spun about to face me but he made no sound, only threw up his arms. There was a burst of fire from the lamp and the room dissolved. It was not like falling, more like stumbling over a step. I dropped the sword in surprise. Someone caught my arm and when I looked up again, we were no longer in my study.

The golden-eyed man was looking at me with compassion.

"I'm so sorry," he said. "An accident. We mean you no harm." He spoke English, but with an accent.

"Where is this?" I was standing in a hallway: black and white tiles upon the floor, and light panelled walls. Nearby were doors, with a curious symbol upon them: it was familiar, somehow, but I did not recognise it at once. Then there was a commotion upstairs and people were pouring down into the hall. Men, women – many were young, although when I met their eyes, their golden gaze was strangely old. The doors which bore the symbol were opening.

"Come!" my new friend said. "Join us and know."

Bewildered, I let the tide of yellow-robed people carry me through the doors. Beyond lay a room – I hesitate to describe it as a temple, but I now know that it was. A great lamp, like the grandfather of my own, hung above the tiled floor and inside it was a light like a captive star. It shone out across the room, filling it with a bright blue-whiteness. We sat on benches, and the man with golden eyes made an invocation: I cannot tell you what he said, for I could not understand it. It was Greek and yet not Greek, and he spoke much too quickly, the words racing away from his tongue. Gradually, the room began to fill with a presence.

It is hard for me to describe this, too, for it was like nothing I have ever known and also everything. It felt familiar, a person I had always known – a person I *was*. It spoke to me of many things and as I became aware that it was leaving, for an instant I saw it: a young man, with pale silvery skin and glowing eyes. I thought there were wings at his heels and his fair hair streamed out behind him as if caught in an invisible wind. He left me with many ideas: ways of talking to folk across great distances, of miraculous devices that showed marvels as if on a moving page, and vehicles that travelled through the air.

There was a hubbub of conversation around me and I blinked.

"You must go now," the man said. "For we are retiring, to discuss what we have been shown. But you may keep the lamp. We shall not trouble you again."

"But I should like to see you!" I protested.

"It is not always safe. This isn't your realm, although you may think it is. It's poisonous to humans if you stay too long. But you'll find a way."

He raised his hand and the temple began to fade, then darken. I was back in the study, with my sword at my feet and the lamp a brief fire-flash above me.

I did, in fact, find a way. The children of Mercury tend to do so, being curious and not easily deterred. It is a Wednesday evening as I write this and soon the man in the glass wig, and others, will be coming to my house, to light incense to the power that others know as a winged god, in the hope that we will be vouchsafed a vision of a future which we seek, now, to make happen.

# The Salt Star

*Another sea and follies story. If you read my fourth Fallow sisters novel, Salt on the Midnight Fire, you might recognise a few familiar elements.*

There's a window in the wall and from it, you can see the sea. The window is an arch onto nothing: step out through its glassless eye and you'll find yourself falling, all the way down through the salty air until the waves reach up to kiss you and you, drowning, see one last glimpse of the waveriding moon.

There's a window in the wall and if you, clutching at the stone sill for comfort, look through, all you will see are shells. Porcelain in the cliff, curled, coiled, gleaming.

There's a window in the wall and through it, everything is black, except the stars.

I have been running since the winter of 1753. Over two hundred years, from wall to wall. Sometimes I slow down; sometimes I sleep. But not often, because it is close behind me always and I must dodge and sometimes dive. I go deep, but it is used to deeper places yet. All the same, I have learned, and it must be done, for otherwise it will come for my family first, and then for the world.

Before Crabb died, he told me that it was a lunar thing, but I have come to doubt this. It does not feel like the moon: aerial, shining, pearly. It feels more as though it has come from the depths of some unknown ocean, very far away. It is part shadow and part bone and the snapping lens through which it feeds slides and glides over its dark sharkskin. It moves like water flows, sometimes swift and sometimes slow. I have watched it from the eaves of the places through which I run and it can ebb, a black tide. Perhaps it is, after all, moon-linked. But I am not an expert on marine life. I am just a girl who liked shells.

It was my cousin who first suggested a grotto. They were all the rage in our young days. The big houses had them, some secret and shell-encrusted at the heart of things and some standing at the centre of gardens, Neptune and Venus overlooking the fountains' gush and splash.

"We ought to make a grotto," my cousin said. She smiled at me in candlelight. "It's good for a girl to have such an interest. You said you were bored."

I liked the idea. I loved shells. My uncle, her father, was a ships' captain and brought all manner of things back from the far parts of the world. He had named his own daughter after a nymph: Thetis, a Nereid, a being of water. Their drawing room held spires and forests of coral under glass, like veins against the creamy wallpaper. In my cousin's bedroom there was a shelf of shells. We used to hold their spined bodies to our ears and listen to the distant wash of another sea. But the real sea was close enough: it lay at the foot of the white chalk cliff on which my uncle's house stood, and I heard it in the night. During storms it boomed and crashed and I used to fancy that the house shook, but it did not, not really.

My uncle was indulgent. Thetis was his favourite and her mother was long dead. She commandeered a small room containing a linen cupboard. It had a pointed window facing south, across the sea. Thetis tried to persuade me that you could see the French coast on clear days but I did not believe her: I never saw it. We stripped the paper down to plaster and one of the local men whitewashed it. Then we set to work.

Thetis had paid a number of local children to find shells on the seashore and, thus fuelled, they brought back baskets of mussels and cockles, limpets and periwinkles. They found whelks and slipper shells and wedge shells. We washed them all in a bathtub and glued them to the walls with gypsum glue. At first, we got out hand in by doing borders, but later we became ambitious and produced suns and stars and moons and spirals.

It took a long time, for we had our lessons as well. But after a year it was done and with candles in our hands we showed it to my uncle.

"Well," he said, "you've certainly produced a thing of wonder! A fine grotto indeed." And he brought some of his friends to see it, and then forgot it was there. Thetis, too, became interested in other things: her engagement being one of them. But I did not forget the grotto. I sat and sewed in there during the day, surrounded by the faint smell of fish, and listening to the sea. And little by little I became aware that the grotto led to another place.

Sometimes, when I could not sleep, I went into the grotto at night. I took a candle with me, to light my way along the passages of my uncle's large house, and I liked to step into the narrow oblong of the grotto and close the door. At the far end, where the arched window lay, I could see a girl with a flickering light, reflected in the glass with the sea visible through her dark figure, and maybe the moon. I used to hold my breath and see if the girl moved independently of me, a childish fancy. She never did. But one night I saw something else.

It was in summer, after a particularly hot spell which had us all flinging off the blankets at night. I thought the grotto might be cooler and that I could open the window. I went into it as usual with my candle, but after a moment I realised something was wrong: I could not see my reflection in the windowpane. It was as though the glass itself had vanished. I put the candle down onto the little sewing table and ran to the window.

Beyond, the world looked underwater. The air rippled in slow movements. Within it, I saw stars: huge gleaming shapes whose light snaked out like tentacles. Before I knew what I was doing, I had gathered up my nightdress, was onto the sill and over.

But I did not enter that underwater realm, except for a moment. A cool touch on my skin and then I was tumbling onto a stone floor. Gasping, I looked up to see a grotto like my own, but green, studded with strange shells and curtains of sea-coloured silk. It, too, had a window, which looked out into the starred place. I explored it for a time and found that it was a gallery, a circular walkway looking down from a rotunda. The shells glowed with a soft sea light from a bronze lantern, hanging in the middle. I gripped the rail and looked down.

"What are you doing here?"

The voice startled me so much that I almost fell. I spun around, conscious that I was in my night attire. But it was a woman who faced me, in a golden gown.

"Don't be afraid. I won't hurt you.

"Did you come from a grotto like this one?"

I nodded then found my own voice. "Yes. My cousin and I made it."

She smiled. She was a lot older than I.

"Do you know why?"

"No – we just liked the notion, I suppose."

"Ah. Then perhaps you are one of us. A sea-traveller. Moved to do strange things without knowing why."

"Is that bad?"

"Bad? No. Dangerous? Perhaps."

"Dangerous? How?"

"You'll have to talk to Crabb."

"Who is that?"

"You'll meet him, if you keep travelling. I don't know where he is. There is no map. Many of us have tried to make one, but the grottoes keep changing. Geography does not pertain to us. For example, we are currently in Devon, on the estuary of the Exe River. You won't see it if you look out of that window now, yet it will be there in the morning. And you? I can tell you are English."

"Yes. My name is Hester Fainright."

"And mine is Lucy Moreton."

"We live near Hastings."

"You will meet others, if you travel. Not all are English. Italians, French… others. We talk among ourselves, when we meet. But stepping through the windows locks the lips. You won't be able to tell your family a single thing." She smiled. "It will be like speaking a secret into a shell. Lost forever."

There was something strange about her, with her pale face and smooth black hair. I did not altogether like her smile, or her talk of danger.

"I should be getting back," I said. She did not try to stop me.

"If you can," she said, and smiled again.

I fled through the window and indeed, despite her warnings, I did find myself at home. Filled with relief, I crumpled onto the floor. I had not got lost after all and I wondered if Miss Moreton had spoken only to frighten me. A cruel trick, I thought, but later found that it was truth.

And also, I found Crabb.

What did the grotto represent to me? Escape. Adventure. As a girl of my day and class, I had few choices: quiet schooling at home, with sedate outings whenever one of my late aunt's friends remembered to take me, for my own parents were dead. Later, I knew, there would be talk of a suitable marriage: I would be farmed out like a prize cow, or more likely the runt. But this was still a way away and in the meantime I chose to make the most of things.

A sea-traveller, you say? I could be that. As my uncle himself was, the ship's captain. I had no ship. But now I had a sea.

The underwater place did not appear every night. At first I tried to predict it, noting when it occurred, the phases of the moon or times of night (it was never in the day). But Miss Moreton, whom I did not see again, to my considerable relief, had been right it seemed: we were subject neither to geography nor time. Sometimes the window looked out onto the Channel, storm or calm, and sometimes not. But my heart always lifted when I crept into the shell-lined room and saw the starry dark.

...The warmth of an Italian courtyard at night, the air soft and filled with the scent of jasmine. Caryatids line the square, holding the building up, marble faces blank and sweet. Somewhere there is a man who is singing and a girl's voice is raised in laughter...

...A sea cave: indigo shadow, with the boom of the waves beyond and a pentacle of shells on the white sand floor. There is never anyone here. I don't know if anyone else ever comes. It is my favourite place in the world...

...A stone tower, ancient, massive. The shells seem too delicate for such a place, too little. Here, I meet a little boy, who says that he has seen a room in a house on the South Coast and the shells are very pretty. I understand that my grotto, too, is a destination for other sea travellers...

And then I met Crabb.

It was a night in winter. Storms had bashed the coast all week. My uncle, who was at home, clicked his tongue and said that he feared for the ships. Thetis, who was at home still, was busy with her sewing: her trousseau, for she would be married in the spring. I had helped her all day but that night I ran down the passage to the grotto and shut the door softly behind me. To my relief, the starry dark was there and I deep-sea dived through, barely touching the sill.

This time, it was into blackness. I couldn't see a thing. I got to my feet and reached out, touching cold damp stone. I felt patterns within it, grooves and lines. I began to make my way forwards and then the wall simply stopped. I put my hand out, groping for a handhold, and touched something clammy, that moved. I screamed and jerked my hand back and a lamp flared up.

"Oh," a man said. "It's one of you." He had a face like the moon, a fringe of hair. His eyes were large and watery wan. He looked me up and down. "What's your name, then?"

I told him.

"Not come across you before. One of the new ones, are you?"

"Yes."

"Not been travelling long?"

"No."

He grunted. "There are some things you ought to know. Sit down."

I did so, on a rickety chair before a table covered in papers and parchment. The place stank. I could smell fish and dung and something else, something burnt. I tried to hold my breath.

"The first thing – this is not a grotto in your world. Not some pretty fancy filled with shells. This – we – are somewhere else. You might not visit me again." Here he grinned. "Or you might come here every time."

"I know we are not bound to geography. Or time."

"That's right. Hard to know, eh? So I need to tell you what I can, in case you don't come back. You'll think this is a game and it is. Beautiful places, caves and shells, delicate fantasies. But there's a passage to somewhere else and sometimes things come through."

I let out my breath, as slowly as I could. "What sort of things?"

He spread his hands. "I don't know. I've seen the moon."

For a moment, this made no sense. Then I said, "Do you mean you have been to the moon?"

"No. I would have died. There's no air. I've seen it, through a window like the one you came from. There are places out there."

He shuffled to a bookshelf and moved a book from the bottom to the top. I don't know why. Maybe he was just tidying up. "Worlds beyond this one. Tell me, why should lining a room with shells open up a gateway?"

"I don't know. Do you?"

"I've no idea. Why should it? I've spent years on this, trying to work it out. Perhaps it's in the patterns we make, like a code, like a key. It's not by design. I don't expect you sat down one day and thought 'Maybe if I get some pretty shells and paste them onto the walls, I'll be able to journey through time and space?' I'm wagering you didn't think that."

"No."

He asked me some questions then, about the grotto, and I answered as fully as I could and he wrote it down. "You can go when you like," he said. "Perhaps I'll see you again, perhaps not."

"Thank you, sir," I said, but I was quick to leave. Like Miss Moreton, he frightened me and I wondered if one day I, too, would have that effect on someone else. I didn't like to think so, but I already knew I could not leave the journeying alone. It had become my refuge and my passion. Then, one night, I found out what Crabb had meant.

I kept a diary, in a code. A tally of the grottoes I had visited. Some of them were famous; some – like our own – known only to family and friends, a fashionable addition to the house. I never returned to the eau-de-nil silken refuge on the estuary of the Exe. I often found myself in the Spanish courtyard, although I hid from the ladies and gentlemen who strolled about its precincts. I saw the stone tower once, though not the little boy. And there were other places: a cold cavern where the shells were broken and the floor was wet, a cupola in a foreign garden where faces peered from the walls and a shell boy rode a dolphin.

But one night I travelled to somewhere different.

It was not solid. I stepped through the window and it was as though I were floating, drifting down through dreaming water. I touched one of the tentacles of the stars and it stung, but only a little. I should have been afraid but was not; it felt as though my senses had been damped down, muted in some manner. At last my feet touched something hard and I tottered forwards into a chamber.

I knew at once that it was alive. It was a huge ball, covered in spines like a sea urchin, and encrusted in salt, or some crystalline substance that resembled it. Filaments trailed outwards and before I could step back, one of them touched my face. Immediately I knew:

…what it was to be old, not the last of your kind, but the container for all that was to come…

…to have seen the fleeting forms of life, like mine, and not to understand…

…and to be horribly afraid…

Of me.

I knew then that something was coming. I twitched away from the filament of the salt star and ran, fleeing down crystal corridors, running over glass floors above machinery which I did not understand, past walls which streamed with water. I heard something behind me and it did not stop. My lungs were bursting but there was a hole in the wall ahead and I threw myself through – I was in a garden, with a nymph of marble before me, and the thing was coming after. I turned and glimpsed it. Wet and black and the chopping lens swirled towards me, shooting out on a long dark neck. I dived again. Cloth of gold and gilded shells, the strong scent of roses. But it snapped and I fled on, through place after place, until at last I fell through the window of my own chamber. I did not think. I ran for the door and slammed it. And the thing did not follow.

Perhaps there were rules after all.

It was still there, though. Later, after I had collapsed, exhausted, in my bedroom into what passed for sleep, I crept back and looked through the keyhole. It was still night and I could see the starry dark at the end of the room. Over its shoulder.

In the daytime, it was not there. I even went into the room. I thought of dismantling the grotto, of telling my uncle, but it sounded too strange and how would I show him? By opening the door onto an ordinary linen chamber? – for the starry dark was not always in evidence. Or onto a horror from the nightmare deep? At night, it was sometimes there and sometimes not. And, little by little, I became aware that it was using its time when the gateway was open.

To escape.

I first noticed the crack one evening: a tiny line of shadow down the length of the door. Three days later, it had grown. I did not know what to do. I had stopped sleeping well, people were worried about me. Then a friend of my late aunt's, a Lady Styles, took me in charge. She said I needed rest and air, would take me to her country seat for a few days.

"And, my dear, I know this will interest you: we have a grotto!"

I did my best to feign enthusiasm.

It was indeed a beautiful house: it was set among beechwoods and at that time, in October, everything was golden and crimson, fire against the grey skies. Lady Styles showed me the shell grotto, deep in a cellar. I was polite, but I am sure she thought me very ungrateful, an indifferent girl. Within, I was not indifferent at all. That night, I went downstairs.

It had not followed me. But I knew what I must do. I could not run the risk of the thing getting out, into the house, into the world. I had to lead it away – though I could not think how – and if I had to, I would give myself to it. The thing made me feel sick, it was like an octopus or something from the deep deep sea, something unnatural. But in the grotto below Lady Styles' great house, I could see the stars and dark, reflected in the faint pool of water that filled a stone basin beneath a statue. I took a breath and plunged.

And so it was that I became quarry and hunted, through many different places. Some were human made, some, I think, not. After a long time, because the calendar became lost to me, I gained a breathing space in Crabb's hole. He was not in residence, but there were bones on the floor and strands of hair filamenting out from a human skull. I hid there for a while, trying to find a clue among his books, but although there were drawings and calculations, closely-written notes and maps, I did not find the thing which hunted me. I did find a drawing of the salt star, however, and a series of questions in a different handwriting. Perhaps someone else had been to the deep place, and told Crabb before – what?

Gradually, the grottoes decayed. I never returned to my uncle's house, nor to the gallery on the Exe. But familiar places were now growing old and the shells were falling from the walls. Moss grew in the dampness and the smell of age.

You will ask: how is it that I am alive, have not changed? How did I eat, drink, sustain myself? And the answer is that I did not. When I started to run, I needed none of these things. I flew through limbo and the thing came after. I only realised how long it had been when I found a newssheet, torn, on the floor of a grotto and before it sagged in the wet I read the date: 1950.

Such a long time. I let the paper fall to the floor. Thetis, my uncle – all would be dead. And we could die too, for Crabb had gone. It was then that I realised I had succeeded. I could let it snuff me out. My family were safe.

I stood there, waiting. At last the darkness swirled beyond the window and I felt its familiar presence. It surged through the gateway like a wave, to settle on the floor. It bunched into a great round cushion like a sea anemone, and then the long snapping mouth reached out.

"No," I said. But it did not bite. I saw the room stream by in a swirl of lights and then –

Then I was inside the salt star and understanding.

"Welcome home," said Lucy Moreton. We stood within the green silk gallery, but the walls shimmered and I saw the simulacrum.

"The original room is still there, I believe. But we are not in it."

"What are we?"

"I don't altogether know. We are projections, perhaps, into human flesh. Born and not born. It seeks only to know."

"I did not have to run so hard, then." I didn't have a body any more, but it felt as though I did. I sank to the floor.

"Yet, in running, you have woven a pattern that we may be able to comprehend. A map of the liminal spaces, the interstices of the world. A network of gateways. But now," she said, her face kindly at last, "You must rest."

And so I did, cradled within the mazy sea urchin body of the alien, dreaming of the starry dark and a girl, running.

# The Lily White Boys

*The Lily White Boys appear in the Fallow novels, but in a slightly different form. I regard Green Grow the Rushes O as a mystical song and enjoyed working with it here. The Hunting of the Wren is a custom of Pembrokeshire, where my father's family comes from and where many of my cousins still live.*

*I know when they're coming, the boys in green. I can always hear them from far away: the shouts and clatter, the hoofbeat thud of the horseskin drum. Their coming makes the branches rattle and a breeze stir up under the sill, makes the ewes in the field draw closer together as though a wolf's on the loose. The boys in green come onward and the wind rises, roaring through the beech trees and making the nests of the rookeries sway. Any port in a storm: I stay down here in the hawthorn hedge. The boys in green are coming for me.*

It's not always quiet in the library. We have a crèche, and the smaller children often howl, their mothers lost forever among the stacks. My days are marked out in coffee mornings, school holidays, the paper frieze that runs above the side of the crèche – eggs for Easter, then pumpkins, then snowflakes and holly. In spring, a watery light fills the library when it rains, the sun dappling through the big skylights. In summer, it's simply hot; the long days drawing out so that even when I leave the library at seven, the sun's still sparkling over the estuary. But when September comes and the children go back to school, when the days begin to darken, that's when I hear that first faint beat of the drum and I know that winter's on its way.

I watch myself sometimes, as a hawk watches, hovering high over the coloured hills. I see myself leave the library, which sits as a small, Victorian oblong in the vastness of the landscape, the Carmarthenshire scenery rolling on into the endless west. I am a little brown form, dressed in jeans or shapeless skirt, climbing into my tiny car and beetle-trundling inland for a short distance before climbing out again in front of my very ordinary seventies bungalow.

Nothing at all is exceptional about me, except for one thing. And perhaps, not even that.

This last year, the boys were late. I didn't hear the first drumbeat until late in September, when the golden days were glowing down and the library was quiet. A wash of rain was blowing up the estuary, turning the hills to shadow, and I was stacking returned books. I heard a single, deep beat, running up through the land. I stood, listening, but there was nothing more. *All right,* I thought to myself. *All right.* Then I continued putting the books back in their rightful places, methodically, one by one.

The drumbeat came twice more, then ceased at sunset. I drove home in the blowy autumn dusk, remembering. The boys in green had first come for me on my twelfth birthday and that had been the day when my mother had taken me aside and told me what we were: the single thing that made us, an ordinary South Welsh family, special. That we were the hunted.

I often read some of the books that we get in the library. Tales of vampires and werewolves. Dark fae and demons. Their covers are in shadowy shades, with brooding women glancing over their shoulders; a pout, a scowl. I enjoy them but I'm not their target audience, I don't think. The brooding women are feisty, noticeable. They say things that people don't want to hear: they are brave to the point of foolhardiness. I am not like this. I have to stay undercover, out of sight. I am prey, not predator; the green boys are the hunters and I must hide.

I've hidden for decades now. I hide in plain sight, throughout the year. Everyone knows me here, in this little town; they knew my parents, my grandparents. I pass unconsidered, part of the fabric and seamlessly woven in. But once a year, for one night, I am something else. For Christmas comes but once a year, and so do the nights that follow.

At home, that night, I stood in the kitchen and looked out across the rolling hills to the west, where a smear of crimson fire told the trail of the dying sun. It would be a cold night and I knew that it would be the first time this coming winter that I'd see the Hunter rising in the east. In fact, I went out and looked. It was too early for frosts but there was a sharpness in the air, a smell of decay, and indeed, just where a faint glow on the horizon showed the position of Swansea, I could see the glitter of Orion.

The Hunter first, then the Seven, and then the Nine Shiners. But between the Hunter and the Seven would come the boys in green.

Autumn suited me, all the same. I never feel bright enough for summer, when the tourists come and the young people for the surfing, a bit further west. Dressed in rave colours, neon and flash. I am brown and grey. No one really notices me. It's how I like it. Some of us are made for love and some of us for running. But autumn, with the drifts of mist along the coast and the fading leaves, the grey light out over the sea and the dankness in the hedgerows – that's my time, going down into the winter black and the prickle of the stars. I could feel their light on my skin that night, their cold sizzle. I raised my head to the Hunter and it could have been a challenge, but the call had gone out long before.

That night, I dreamed of the boys. There are always two of them, and they were made, or conjured, very long ago: I believe them to come from the time just after the ice retreated from this country, but I might be wrong. There were folk living in the caves to the east of here thirty-three thousand years before and it could be that the boys are older even than that. They wear fur hoods which sparkle with frost, and there are bones threaded through the edges. I've been close enough to see, but just once and that was nearly the end of me. In dream, though, I was just behind them, seeing through their eyes, tracking what they track. And the world was different – a saltmarsh plain where the sea is now, and the river threading through it in a post glacial maze. In this dream, they were hunting a wolf: a big beast the colour of clouds, running along through the groves of alder scrub and thorn. The boys exulted, voices raised in an ancient call, a language which hadn't existed for thousands of years and maybe never did in the lands of man. This is some other place, you see, a perpetual time, frozen in dream. One of the boys, slow motion, extended an arm and I could feel the slick shaft of a holly spear in my own hand, feel the weight and throw. The wolf went down in a tangle of limbs and blood, staining earth and snow; one eye flared golden as it died. The boys, as one, turned to me – then I woke.

The bedroom was warm. I'd turned the heating up that evening. Outside a gibbous moon hung in racing clouds. I watched its passage across the sky and did not sleep until its dim light died. In the morning, I went in to work and did not hear the drumbeat again until dusk.

The year wore slowly on. Drifts of beech leaves lay along the pavement by the church wall, and up the path to the library. We are in an old building, Victorian, which used to be a church hall until a more modern one was built with lottery funding, alongside a new sports pitch. I always hoped the church would give me some faint protection, but it never has. This thing – this hunt – is too old for it, I believe now, runs too deep. If they came for me in the day, if I ran into the church, they would corner me at the altar. I thought of my body falling, blood staining the cloth, while a younger god stared down in incomprehension.

So I kept to the library and my house, the path between, a few village meetings. (I know my run. It's all mapped out. There are trees along the path which I can draw upon, a spout which leads from a spring. Not much but enough to turn the path of the boys, throw them off my scent. And I have a twist of sinew and bone in the pouch round my neck, under my sensible librarian's polo neck, along with a small brown feather).

The drumbeat grew on the run-up to Christmas. Long ago, I invented a niece, with whom I go and stay. If anyone thought about it, which they never did, they would remember me walking to the station a day or so before Christmas Eve.

"Morning, Miss Grey!"

"Morning!" they'd remember me saying. But it wouldn't have been me, not really. Just a shadow on the air, with enough of a human feel about it to convince the onlooker. When the holiday came, I was in the house, windows bolted, curtains drawn. Salt water to cleanse the sills and doorstep; a drop of blood berry-red beneath the holly tree by the front door. I read a book on Christmas Eve, watched a film. Something light and forgettable, nothing to snag the attention of anything watching with strong emotion. I could feel the power growing outside in the land; all kinds of it. Power of church bells at the midnight ring, power of the cold and the night with the candle birth at the middle of it. That goes back beyond the Christian faith, the light in the heart of the dark of the year.

I said a prayer, but not to God. I prayed to the stars: the six proud walkers, then to the Seven, the April rainers, the nine bright shiners. I could feel them shimmer in my head as if I flew too high, too close to distant suns. But no more than that, not today. We trembled on the edge of Christmas and then it was midnight, time toppling over into the countdown. The Twelve Days had begun and the boys were on their way.

Boxing Day and the real hunt were out: I could see them from the dormer window of the attic, red coats streaming across the ploughed fields with the pack swarming around them. They're not supposed to hunt foxes these days – it's against the law. They do anyway and everyone knows it. Today, I wasn't sure if they had a quarry. I hoped not. Their intention is to hunt foxes, not women, but I think a few of them know. You can see it in men's eyes, that ancient ice. I watched them weave their way into the woods, the stand of oak and beech at the top of the hill, and then they were gone. Later, it would be stirrup cups and camaraderie in the village square, outside the pub in front of the Christmas visitors. No harm in that; I wouldn't be there. I made sure the curtains were closed and went down to make my preparations. A tallow candle, lit. Salt again on the sills and then I took a holly berry from the bowl above the fireplace, put it between my lips, swallowed painfully. They burn like fire when they go down your throat. After that I made sure the doors were locked. The drumbeat started at twilight as usual, and this time it was very loud.

And so I went down into the dark of the year, these lost days between Christmas and New Year, except it wasn't the New Year, not for me. I watched the town fireworks from the dormer window, with the lights turned out. They exploded in bursts of gold and green above the estuary, their reflections like sudden stars in the blackness of the water. I thought of the Seven, and hoped; sent a prayer up like a squib into the heavens. I didn't know if it would do any good.

The drumbeat went all through the night now, and lasted beyond dawn. Then we were into January and I knew I'd have to go out. The

231

Twelve Days were almost up and then at last I woke in the morning of the Twelfth Day itself. And I thought to myself, *here we go again.* I could feel the pull, you see, the tug to the land on the other side of the door.

My bones and skin are in an old tin box on the mantelpiece. My mother showed them to me, when the time came, handing them over. I didn't understand at first. I knew about the Hunt because we'd been told about it in school. They don't do it now. It was an old custom, and cruel. A nasty thing to hunt a little bird and I'd agreed, all the girls did, although I wondered about some of the boys. They'd have been the hunters, if times hadn't changed. But there was nothing to connect it to me and my ordinary suburban life until my mother took the box down and opened it up and I saw the matchstick-thin bone inside beneath the smooth of feathers. Like a tiny little cape, a fairy's cloak, dead-leaf colour.

*Put it on,* she'd said, and I thought she was crazy. I laughed in disbelief.

*What do you mean? It'll only just wrap round my thumb.*

*Put it on.*

And then my world changed.

Now, years on, I took the little pinch of feathers between finger and thumb. In my other hand, I took the bone from the box and placed it on my tongue. Then I tossed the feathers into the air.

*I am fluttering. The room expands. I fight for air, falling. My sight changes, my hands are gone, my legs thorn thin. Clothes, flesh, huge human bones, weighty as anvils – all gone. Then I rise, wings beating against the glass of the window and the window opens and I am out into the winter sun.*

I head for the hedge. I know how to hide. I have twenty-four hours on the run like a TV show, the sun's passage and back again. The hedge is hazel and haw, bare-branched at this end of the year but still thick. I am brown and grey, tiny as a mouse. The drumbeat shudders through the world and when I peek out, I see the iron cold of the land, the frost lying across the fields. The bungalow has disappeared and so has the town. Smoke rises from a single hut, perched on the hillside. Beyond, the hills are pale and mauve and blue against the sky. The cold's as sharp as a wolf's tooth. It won't be long now before the boys come and I'm glad because when they do, this will be over for another year, or over for all time. I don't have a daughter. I thought I'd end it but now I'm not so sure: maybe it will just pass on to another girl, heedless now with her smartphone and her mates and her Taylor Swift obsession, never thinking that beyond the world you can see there's this world, this ageless place. Above the river there's a hawk rising in widening spirals. It's not just the boys I'll need to watch out for. A flash of tawny red and there's a big dog fox making his way along the hedge, picking his way over the icy lee where the puddles have frozen. He can smell me. I can see the flicker in his eyes but I'm too small for him to make an effort. There are ravens calling over the oak wood.

The land shakes to the sound of the drum. I fly, fast as a cork from a champagne bottle, down to the rushes by the river, hiding in the reeds for an instant then out over the river. I glimpse them behind me, the two boys running silently up over the lip of the hill. And they see me: they shout. The sound of the drum fills the world. I'm into the oak wood now, the hazy quiet. They won't be long. I know this road. Sometimes we follow the river, sometimes we become lost in the endless twists of the wood, and sometimes we are out onto the beech ridge just below the high hill. There's no shelter for me there and I've learned to avoid it.

So this time it's the oak wood. I can feel the boys' footsteps moving across the loam. All I can hear is the drum because they themselves make no sound. No bramble is snagged, no branch disturbed. The boys move fast as mist. If I was to turn – as I once did – I would see them ghosting through the wood, cloud-quiet, the white skins that they wear, pierced with bones, fluttering behind them. But I can't afford the seconds it will cost me. I fly on, wings burning now, shooting through the still branches of the oaks and I can see the curve of the river below, smooth with a thin curd of ice.

*You could fight,* you might say. Like the girls on the covers of the novels in the library, no face, just a back and a hand with a weapon. But sometimes you can't fight back: like this, myself a bird, and the ancient hunters are sharp-toothed men with talons at the ends of their fingers, the lily-white boys whose presence is so old that it's forgotten, remembered only in a line in one of the oldest songs of all. The lily-white boys are coming for me, hunting down the wren.

At the edge of the woods they pause. I'm hurtling down the bank of earth towards the river but one throws a net. Made of sinew and dried grass, it hisses through the air and brings me in a tangle of feathers onto the ice; I hit it with a crack. The breath leaves my lungs but I whistle a word and the net blazes up. I have a handful of defences and the game is that each can only be used once. The boys give a shout of rage. I'm up again and flying and they chase me down the river, skating on the ice and gliding just above the water in the deep mid channel, where it's not frozen. We'll soon be at the shore and I've not been this way before: the land maps my own country, but not exactly. I can taste the salt in the air. Wrens don't sing, they chatter, but I have one song and it's for the Seven: it slows me down to sing it and the boys are close behind me but I sing it all the same. Then we're out with the silver light of the sea before us.

I hear the noise of a slingshot, a faint crack. The stone doesn't hit me directly but it catches the tip of a wing and tilts me over and over. I fall down through the air and as I turn I see the faces of the boys: skin turned to leather, stretched over bone. Their eyes are white. Their long nails reach out and they will rend but I have fallen, all the way through the cold air and a girl's hand reaches out and catches me. I am enclosed in her palm but just before her fingers close I see that her six sisters stand behind her. Their gowns are green and blue and their skin is silvery like the sealight. They are stars from the sky and sometimes they save me, until one day they might not.

"No, no," says the star. "You cannot have her this time, not this year, not this day."

I perch in her palm and through her fingers the boys turn and glide away, almost without pausing. The bones in their clothing rattle faintly but the beat of the drum has pounded down to nothing.

The sisters, the Seven, place me on a cradle of bark and carry me up from the shore, singing as they go. They will bring me back across the hedge to the human world, to my human form. But for the fleeting *now* I am the wren upon the bier and they are the star sisters of the winter sky and the lily white boys have gone into the light, until next year, when we will do it all over again.

# The Language of Fans

*This story came about from two sources: a visit to a local auction house in which I overheard an expert explaining a collection of old fans to a customer, who had found them in an attic. In addition, one of our nearest cities where I live is Bath, with its fascinating fashion museum. My partner, Trevor, is related to the Woods-Jones, the father and son architects who built much of Georgian Bath and who are said to have designed it on Druidic principles: the moon for the Crescent and the Sun for the Circus, with its huge stone acorns. It's one of my favourite cities.*

I do not dress myself. My maid helps me: first chemise, then shoes, stockings, corset, busk, panniers, petticoat and gown. I am laced, trussed, ribboned, capped and finally, when I have found my reticule, ready to leave the house.

But not quite.

The last thing is the fan.

I have many fans and it is a question of which I shall choose today, for I must be careful. This is a day of note, when I shall meet eleven friends, all women known to me, all women who have been close to me. My Zodiac, and I the sun around which they revolve, but then we all think this. All of us are suns with our attendant stars, each to the other.

And one of those stars is a traitor.

I am wearing black, all of it: gown, cap, cloak, for I am in mourning. I am a piece of night, walking as swiftly as my heels allow me out into the sunshine, sharp shadow against the butter-coloured stone. I step into my carriage and am borne away in a jolting rattle of wheels on the cobbles. The air smells of smoke and the wheels of the carriage crush the russet leaves which have fallen from the chestnuts along the great crescents. It won't be long before we have another frost. Below, visible from the window, the city lies in rows in its mist, grey-gold and dim.

I am twenty four-years old, soon to be married, and Eleanor is dead. I feel that I have lived my life twicefold, that it is much longer than it has been, now that she is gone. And I have all the years to wait before I too die, unless childbirth takes me, or a fever.

Or another woman, someone I now call friend.

You see, I don't know who it is. I know they killed Eleanor, my sister, but I don't know how. I think they want to kill again, but I don't know why. There's no reason for it, it makes no sense. I have turned things over and over in my mind, rolling like the carriage wheels, or like a mill in which the water of my thoughts spills endlessly away. I'm grateful when the carriage stops in front of Lady Memory's house and I clamber down into the chill of the afternoon.

Memory is not her real name. None of us will allow those in one another's company. Disguise in plain sight, just a group of girls and women like any other, hiding among other women who suspect nothing. I have brought the black and white fan, with the pattern of leaves: one of my favourites.

I am shown to the parlour. Nine of us are already there, and some others whom I do not know. The heavy velvet curtains keep out the worst of the cold and there is a fire hissing in the grate. Lady Memory steps forwards, smiling.

"Ah, Juliet, my dear. How lovely."

Her fan – indigo and silver to match her gown – flickers: *beware*.

I smile with relief. This means she trusts me; it would hurt if she thought me involved in the death of my own sister, but stranger things have happened.

I curtsey. "Thank you so much, Lady Memory." My own fan flutters in a quick message: *I shall take great care*. Then I greet my friends, my sisters-in-spirit. Some of them are my coven.

A month ago, we were thirteen. Now, there are twelve of us. We have a language, as all witches do, that is private between ourselves and which cannot be spoken. We converse in taps, flutters, flickers, in subtle movements of the eye. We never speak aloud of magic but we practice it: rarely together, all thirteen, but secretly, in twos or threes, or alone. Yet in silent accord each with the other, until now.

I sit next to Emily, who is small and pale and whose hair is brown, like sugar. Her gaze is downcast, and her fan hides half her face. *We are being watched.*

I touch the tip of the grey and white fan to my left eye. *Where?* Her pink feathered fan dips to her breast. *A stranger. To the right.*

I give a sidelong glance. An older woman, with a hard thin face like a man's. I've never seen her before. We fear it has been one of us, to do the killing, but what if it is not? Lady Memory introduces us, speaking gaily, as if without a care. The woman is named Lady Somerville and she has come here to Bath from York. She has flat grey eyes like a northern sea, but she forces a smile.

"Juliet Tempest-Stewart, you say? Delighted to meet you." But I can tell that she is not delighted at all.

Later, with Emily and Ruth, I converse in the library of Lady Memory. We are pretending to look at a book. Our fans flutter and flash. We do not know if we can trust each other and there is a lot we are leaving unsaid.

*The third.* Taptaptap. That means Eliza, who is one of us and yet, and yet... Something odd about Eliza, a coldness, like a veil between herself and the world. But Lady Memory herself, a distant cousin, has vouched for her. And to kill? Again, there is the question of why.

*Juliet. You must look further.* A fan to the eye, then spread out so that we can see the pretty Chinese pattern.

*Yes.*

At home, I wait until my mother sleeps. Eleanor's room has been locked, but left as it was, as if she might step through the door and run up the stairs and be home forevermore. I find the key and open the lock, entering the room with a sharp swift hurt, then forcing the pain away. I need to think clearly. I also need to be quick.

Eleanor's clothes remain in the wardrobe: we cannot bear to part with them and their silk rustles when I open the door. I know where Eleanor hid things, and this is one of those places. The chimney is another but I don't fancy putting my hand up there and getting it all sooty – hard to explain if I'm caught. I take up the loose board at the bottom of the wardrobe and here are some discoveries: a narrow box, made of tin, and a fan of ivory and bone, which I have never seen before. I take it out and sit with it in my lap, wondering. The fan stinks of magic; it runs like a nettle sting up my arms and makes the hairs prickle. When I open the box, it's empty except for a small black key.

The key is a curious thing. It, too, smells of magic but I can't think what it might open. The tines are delicate, some no more than a cat's whisker or the frond of a fern. It looks too slight, too frail, to open any lock that I know of. I take fan and key and leave my sister's room on slippered feet, shutting the door behind me. Then I take the fan to the window seat and sit with it on my lap, looking down at it with the autumn light behind me.

I don't like to touch it. Ivory is pure and pale, but the bone looks yellow and stained, like an old chop that a dog has left in the gutter. When I touch it, I feel dirty, and so I go to the chest of drawers and find an old silk scarf to wrap the fan in. That evening, pretending I have forgotten my shawl, I return to Lady Memory's house with the fan in a bag. I do not take the key and I am not certain why: there is something so strange about the key that I feel I should not speak of it, not yet. And I've learned to trust my instinct. The fan is unholy, but the key is forbidden.

Lady Memory studies the fan carefully, touching it only with her fingertips and wincing.

"You, too," I say. "I cannot bear to touch it."

"It is unclean," she replies. "Dark magic, but from where? It feels ancient."

It has not really occurred to me before to consider when fans were invented, but surely they have been in service for a very long time, though perhaps not in their current form. It gives me a curious feeling to think back upon the past. I blink.

"Do you know where Eleanor got it from?"

"I have no idea. I found it among her things. Mama cannot bear to part with them, quite yet." I blink again; the sight of my sister, sprawled across her bed, skin grey like a waxen doll, flickers across my mind.

"Entirely understandable." Lady Memory's beautiful face is downcast, suddenly a pattern of shadows: white skin, black hair, black eyes. She wraps the fan in its silk and hands it back to me. "Keep it safe. Tell no one."

I half expect her to ask me to leave it in her keeping, but she does not. "We must learn its language," she says.

"Its language?"

"Yes. It may not have occurred to you that this language – this *tongue* – in which we converse, which I taught to you when you were fourteen, my dear, is not altogether made by ourselves. Much of it comes from the fans."

"I didn't know that."

"The fans taught our grandmothers, and they taught us in turn. Does it not seem to you that the pretty thing you brought with you this afternoon has an awareness all of its own?"

Now that I thought about it, this seemed obvious. How many times had I raised my fan to my face, for it to flicker a message I had not intended? And always for the good. I trusted the black and white fan, I realised suddenly. It felt like a friend. But the bone thing I had found among Eleanor's possessions? I might, I thought, be a little more careful from now on what I said in its presence.

I carried the fan home, still wrapped in its silk, and placed it on top of the wardrobe. I did not want my maid to come across it suddenly. But when I climbed into bed I could feel its presence, as though I shared the room with another, and despite the lingering heat of the warming pan I still felt cold.

My dreams that night were uneasy: I was chasing Eleanor through a dark maze and, just as I thought I was catching up with her fleeing form, she dropped to all fours like an animal and scuttled upwards, climbing the black hedge of the maze with ease and disappearing. I woke with a ringing in my ears and a dry open mouth.

The first thing I noticed was that the sash window was ajar. I sat up in bed. The nightlight illuminated the room enough for me to see two things: one was that the bottom drawer of the chest was also slightly open, and that something was coming over the sill. It was long, yellow, and jointed. A probing finger, that inched its way onto the window sill. For a horrible moment, I feared that there might be a hand behind it, a body – but then I saw that it was complete in itself, perhaps a foot in length. The first few inches hung over the edge of the sill, questing in the air. It was blind, unnatural, disgusting. I leaped out of bed, seized the heavy Bible that sat on the nightstand, and brought it down upon the thing.

The finger shattered into four pieces, separate segments which twitched on the boards of the floor, rattling like knucklebones. I hammered them with the Bible until they stopped twitching, then scooped them up with the black and white fan and threw them out of the window. I ought, most probably, to have found a box and kept them, but the prospect that they might reassemble back into the finger was too much for me to bear.

As I slammed the sash shut and stepped back, I saw a white oval face beneath the beech trees that edged the square. The figure turned quickly and ran and I could not see who it might have been, but Lady Somerville's spare presence popped into my mind.

In the morning, I woke with the knowledge of what I must do, and I did not like it. If I wished to discover the truth behind the fan and the key, and I could not quite trust my friends, I needed to ask the one person who surely held this knowledge: Eleanor herself.

Speaking to the dead is a thing that any village wisewoman might profess to do, but with care, less she be accused of witchcraft. The hanging days were gone, but one still had one's reputation to think of, particularly with a wedding in the balance. Our social position would protect us to some extent, but not with a traitor in our midst, and I was feeling unsafe enough already. Thus this would have to be done on my own, telling no one. I spent the day bent over my embroidery and assisting my mother with her flowers, planning and plotting. When twilight came I pleaded a headache and went upstairs. But I did not go to my own room. Instead, I took refuge in Eleanor's, locking the door behind me. I took with me a candle, a bowl of water, and the black and white fan. It seemed to me that it whispered secrets all the way up the stairs. I also took the silk-wrapped bone fan from the drawer, along with the key.

Once in Eleanor's room, I lit the candle and placed the bowl on the dresser, well away from the window. I hung the bone fan at my waist. With the black and white fan, I drew a circle of conjuration around me – conjuration, not protection, for I needed to leave it open in order that my sister's spirit might enter. Besides, I thought, surely I would not need to be protected from Eleanor. Then I knelt before the flickering light reflected in the bowl and shut my eyes.

I drew a picture of my sister in my mind, clad in her shroud, beginning at the soles of her feet and sketching her figure up in layers. I have a strong imagination, and soon, in my mind's eye, Eleanor herself stood before me, gazing sorrowfully. The room seemed to sing and hum. The hairs on my arms prickled and my eyes stung with tears. When I opened them, I fully expected to see Eleanor there in the circle, but she was not. Instead, there was a small, dark door.

I stared at it. It was not solid, but shivered, like ink in water. A keyhole shone silver as though there was a light behind it. As I watched, the real door behind me rattled and I looked round to see the knob turning. I had locked it – but the door began to open. I snatched up the little key and thrust it at the keyhole. The dark door rushed past me in tatters of shadow. I had enough time to see that the wind of its opening blew the candle out and then the room was gone.

But only for a moment. I blinked and when I opened my eyes, the room was once more around me. It was shadowy, insubstantial. I got up and went to the window, but the sashes were no longer there: the room stood open to the night. I could see through the trees to the houses opposite and they shivered, as though seen through a fire. A woman was standing below, her face upturned.

"Eleanor?" I called down, but she did not answer.

The door to the room was also missing. I ran down the stairs and out through the hole where the front door used to be. Beyond, the night felt cool and damp, quite real. My sister – I was sure that it was Eleanor – was walking quickly across the grass. I ran after her, crying her name, but like Euridyce she did not halt or turn her head.

When Eleanor reached the middle of the Circus, she spun around and raised her hand. I felt the bone fan leap at my waist and tear free. It opened and flew into her waiting palm like a bird. The black and white fan sang in my mind and I snatched it from my belt. Eleanor whipped the bone fan around and I was struck by a great, hot pulse which lifted me off my feet and slammed me onto the grass. The breath went out of my lungs and I gasped, but the black and white fan was unfolded before my face and when the next pulse came, I felt it stop. Eleanor gave a cry. I peeked at her through the lattice of my fan. She threw the bone thing into the air and it fluttered away like a leaf. Eleanor began to spin like a top and then she too was gone. I was alone in the middle of the Circus. I reached down and found that my hand passed through the blades of grass; they had become ghostly, and the houses around me looked dead, their windows and doors blank, but their substance also insubstantial. When I looked back at our own house, I saw that there was a single light in the room that had been Eleanor's: my candle was still lit.

I did not return to the house. I decided to explore a little, though my heart was thumping against my ribs. I walked down through the Circus. I could see the tower of the Abbey, but it was quivering, and beyond it the lamps that were usually visible on the opposite hill were dark. I felt that the edge of this city was much closer than it should have been, and perhaps beyond it there was nothing, as though someone had sketched a pen and ink copy of the city of Bath and placed it in a basin, so that it was becoming blurred and faded. I turned and went back up the street, and in the garden at the top, where there were a few cyclamen, I saw that their white blooms were a soft grey, and they crumbled into dust as I watched.

I decided to go back to the house and see if I could find my way back to my own world. When I reached it, there was a figure standing on the step. It was Eleanor, and when she heard my footstep she turned. The shroud was the same, but her face was a featureless oval of yellow bone. In its lower half, where her mouth should be, a small black slit opened. The ivory fan was in her hand but it was larger now, and the struts of it looked like a hand, the knucklebones prominent. The sight of it sickened me and I brought the black and white fan up to protect my face. Something passed between them, like a spark. I found myself pressed against the iron railings, but their cold hardness gave way and I fell.

Someone grabbed my hand and pulled me up. Lady Somerville's fingers were like a manacle.

"Miss Tempest-Stewart! You shouldn't be here!"

"Where *is* this?"

"You can't stay here," she repeated. She glanced over her shoulder. She looked like a governess. The pale cords of muscle around her mouth were very prominent. "Your sister died to keep you from this. It's Death."

I looked at Eleanor. "That isn't my sister, is it?"

"No."

The figure was coming down the steps, the bone fan raised. It struck out, but I was faster. I whipped the black and white fan upwards and with all the power of my will. The figure staggered backwards, slashing down with the fan. A thin line of blood appeared on the back of my hand.

"Don't let it touch your blood!" Lady Somerville cried.

I put back my arm and I threw the black and white fan with as much force as I could. It sailed through the air, beneath the figure's raised arm, and struck it across the throat. The fan clattered to the floor and the figure fell apart, cascading into a mass of bony fragments. I seized Lady Somerville's hand and together we jumped over the mess and up the steps, then up the stairs to my sister's room.

Eleanor stood in the candlelight. She gazed at me sadly. The bone fan was in her hand and as we stared, she touched its edge to the flame. It went up like paper, fire running up her arm. Eleanor changed into smoke, drifting. Lady Somerville clasped my arm.

"We have to go."

The dark door was waiting to encompass us. Its tatters reached out, streaming past, and we found ourselves in my sister's room once more. The candle had burned down, moonlight lit the room.

Lady Somerville took the key from the silver lock and threw it back through the door as it faded away.

"Enough of that," she said.

"Who *are* you?"

"A witch, like you. Lady Memory asked me for help."

"I thought there was a traitor."

"So did we all, but there was no traitor, Juliet. Only a young witch who reached beyond her grasp, saw her mistake, and died to protect her sister."

"Was it you, coming into the room when I began?"

"Yes. I hoped to stop you. But it seems you can manage well enough without my help."

She smiled, for the first time.

"I suspected you," I said.

"It doesn't matter."

A day later, we sat sipping tea in Lady Memory's parlour. I held the black and white fan; Lady Somerville, a fan of blue, shot with moonlight silver. We were not talking, between ourselves. We did not need to.

# The Seamistress

*I sometimes chose themed stories for the short story subscriptions that I used to run, and this is one of them: a series featuring water witch Isis Dane. It's set in a rather loosely constructed alternative historical period, which I did not examine too closely!*

Thamesis-side. Isis stood in the shadow of the wharf, looking upriver. A gull wheeled over the surface of the water, white against its choppy brown-grey. A boat swung at anchor, caught on the tidal swell. It had been a week of gales, the equinoctial tides lashing the woods as Isis had ridden across country, up onto the high downs and then into the capital, following the river from its source. Now, the dying wind scoured London's streets and battered at the weathercocks, which rose insouciantly above the city.

Isis looked at the boat. It was a long craft, with a white sail. Azure pennants flew from its masts and a long blue eye decorated its prow; she could not see its name. Amongst the barges and rowing boats, the ship was exotic, a swan among sparrows. Isis wondered whom it belonged to, and what it was doing here, so far from home – for surely it originated in warmer seas than this. But the beautiful boat was really none of her concern; her affairs lay in the bridge that arched above her. She turned back to it, heading up the steps that led from the wharf.

The bridge was guarded by lions. Carved from hard black wood, they stood on either side of the gateway, which was closed at night. Between their snarling mouths lay the entrance to the bridge, which was lined with merchants' shops and houses, a hustling, bustling place during the day, the tall buildings tottering above the river. Walking along the bridge, Isis caught sudden glimpses of the Thamesis through the gaps in the dark-beamed, whitewashed houses, without which it would have seemed like a normal thoroughfare. But the bridge was rich: a prime attraction for those visiting the capital, with first pickings of the wares that came from all across Europe: silks, enamels, tapestries... Isis had enjoyed just looking, peering through the small glass panes, diamonds looking into a treasure chest. Now, heading towards the middle of the bridge, Isis tried not to be distracted by the goods around her; she was here for a reason.

The woman who had hired her was unusual in herself: a plump plain person of middle age, who had taken over her father's business upon his death.

"I was no more than fourteen," she told Isis. "But I'd grown up in it, you see – here in this house. It was all I knew and when the men said that a young lass was never the person to take over, I saw them off. I told them: you work for me or you don't work. That was forty years ago and here I still am, in this same house."

Her name was Phyllida Frank, and she dealt in silks, though she herself wore worsted in the colour of mist and dark. Isis liked her, her practical manner and her square, uncompromising face.

"Frank by name and Frank by nature!" she told Isis, with a smile. "Why would I wear all these fancy things? They're for the young and the wealthy, to make into fine gowns and good luck to 'em."

Then she told Isis about the problem.

"It comes at night. We set a watch, but saw nothing. In the morning, the consignment we set in the cellar was ruined. All spoilt, and sodden, as if it had been drenched in rain – but I sucked a bit of it, just to see, and it tasted of salt, like the ocean."

"How curious," Isis said.

"Just as you say. We thought, perhaps a freak wave like the one which runs up the Severn – you know it?"

Isis nodded. "I am from the Severn shore myself. I've often watched the Severn Bore."

"Anyway, I asked the Watch – but they witnessed nothing. And it would surely have been apparent – it would have to have been an enormous wave, to touch the bridge. You know that this bridge is built to withstand such forces, for sometimes the tidal surges can be fierce – and my cellar floor is, I would have said, water-tight."

"And there is no way that water can get in from above?"

"No. Nor is there any way into the cellar than the hatch above it. A man was set there all night – a trusted person, he has been with me since the first. But he saw nothing and then it happened again. It has cost me a great deal of money."

"A rival merchant, perhaps? Magic?"

"So I would have said, but although there are other silk dealers, we take care to carry different kinds, and I would have said we were friends.

Perhaps that is foolish. I do not know that magic is involved, and yet –"
She paused. "I am not a fanciful woman, but after that first time, in the
cellar, I would have said that there was a feeling almost of malevolence
within the place. As though it hated me. Perhaps I am just being stupid."

"It is often wise to listen to such intuitions," Isis said. "I think I'd
better take a look."

Later, she stood within the cellar, holding a lamp. A tidy place, and
also dry: Mistress Frank had taken care not to store any more goods in
here. But Isis could hear the slap and hiss of the river beneath, against
the enormous buttresses which supported the bridge: it did not seem
beyond the realm of probability that water might, on some rising swell,
creep up through any cracks in the boards. But enough to drench an
entire consignment of silks and leave the rest of the cellar dry? Isis
pursed her lips. Moreover, there was indeed an odd feeling in the cellar, a
fading hate which was almost palpable. Phyllida Frank was not the type
to be prone to embroidering facts, and now Isis could see what she
meant.

She went back up the hatch and reported her findings.

"Who brings your silks? Where do you get them from?"

"Various merchants. This one came on a ship called the *Aphrodite*: she
comes from Athens, though the silk is from further to the east, and
Georgiou – the captain – collected them in Venice."

"This *Aphrodite*. Does she have white sails, a blue eye on the prow?"

"Yes," Frank said, surprised. "She is still here, waiting for a
consignment of wool from the north – did you see her, then? I reported
the damage and the captain was most concerned: Georgiou is an old
friend, we have known one another for years, but he is no wiser than I.
Nothing like this has happened before. And there is no question but that
the silk was in good condition when it left the *Aphrodite*: I inspected it
myself."

"Well," Isis said. "We had best set a trap and see what manner of
catch we can land."

The boxes were empty, but the men moved them from the barge below
as though they were full, laden with the heavy bolts of silk. Phyllida
Frank ordered one to be opened, and silk placed on top to give the
impression of a box-full. Then she closed the lid, but only partly nailed it
down so that the silk could be seen. Meanwhile, Isis concealed herself in
the shadows of the cellar, and when Phyllida and the men retreated

through the hatch, locking it behind them, she drew a warding circle about herself for protection. Although they had left a dim lamp in the opposite corner, there was something about the dark cellar, the locked hatch, that was claustrophobic, so Isis found herself projecting her senses downwards instead, to where the river flowed fast and freely. She listened, gradually lulled by the familiar sound of running water. She imagined the river widening out into the estuary, then the wider sea…

For an hour or more, nothing happened. Isis grew stiff and bored, and was beginning to think that nothing would happen, when she noticed a gleam of light on the floor of the cellar. She frowned. The light spread – a puddle forming on the floor, growing, sending out a tendril of moisture across the boards. It was coming up through a crack in the floorboards – but the bridge was fifty feet or more above the river and she could hear nothing to indicate that the tide had changed… She shifted position very slightly, reaching for the blade at her hip. She could feel its hatred, now, a black shadow creeping across the chamber: but what was it?

Then the moisture began to slide upwards into the air, forming a column – Isis grasped the blade, rose to her feet and stepped forwards.

Immediately the thing changed, rearing up from a few inches to the height of a man. It was made of water, glimmering in the lamplight, and it stank of the sea. Isis had a flickering impression of an oval face at the top of the column, filled with inwardly pointing lamprey teeth – and then the warding circle flared up into bright fire and the thing was gone in a gush of fluid, down through the floorboards. Isis raced up the ladder to the hatch and flung it open, then ran through the house, past the surprised Phyllida, to the back balcony, which overlooked the river. She could see a sliver of moon, riding high through the clouds, and a swirl of silver in the racing water below. Frank's rowboat stood below, at anchor. Without pausing to explain, Isis threw down the rope ladder and dropped into the boat; it rocked under her sudden weight. She cast off, rowing after the silver streak, like mercury staining the surface of the water. The rush of riverwater coming through the buttresses carried her along, so that she had to fight briefly for control of the oars, but it brought her closer to the streak of silver and for this, she was grateful.

The thing was heading for the *Aphrodite*. She did not see it climb the sides of the Grecian boat, but docked hastily against the boat where a ladder reached to the deck. Securing the rowing boat, she went up the side and on board.

It was not yet very late. Isis found the captain poring over some charts in his cabin: a thickset middle aged man with a curling black beard.

"Sorry to disturb you!" Isis said. He started, nearly spilling a glass of wine which stood upon the table.

"Who in hell are you?" She could not blame him for being surprised. The accent was foreign; his eyes snapping and dark.

"My name is Isis Dane. Are you Captain Georgiou? I'm working for Phyllida Frank." Hastily, she explained.

"I do not doubt what you say, but I don't know what you think you see." He rose, staring at her. "You can search the ship, if you want."

"Thank you. Will you help me?"

"Of course. But if you have used Mistress Frank's name as excuse –"

"I am in good faith," Isis told him.

There was no sign of anything untoward aboard the *Aphrodite*. The crew were asleep in their bunks, or in a couple of cases, engrossed in dice. The hold was still and quiet. Isis and the Captain went back on deck.

"You see," he told her, spreading his hands. "There is nothing here."

Isis followed him around the mast, to where steps led down into the ship once more. "What's that?"

The figure of a girl stood beside the doorway, carved into the frame. She was made of wood, her hair curling, her eyes the same elongated, kohled gaze of the ship's prow. She had the face of a beautiful hawk. She wore a long tunic, but her feet were bare. The Captain laughed. "Pretty little thing, isn't she? I find her in a market in Tyre, last year, but this ship is too small for a figurehead, so we make her into the door guardian."

Isis glanced at the deck and then she pushed the captain, shoving him to one side. Georgiou shouted and lunged at her, but Isis dodged him. She spoke a spell and cast it, all at once, just as the carved wooden girl dissolved into the spitting lamprey-faced thing. The captain cried out. The lamprey's mouth curved down towards her, an eel-like arc, but Isis' blade struck the thing in the midsection, magic singing along the metal, and the lamprey-figure dissolved in a great splash of salt water, streaked with mercury silver. The deck was suddenly awash and then, just as quickly, it was dry again. Isis and the Captain stood, wet-footed and horrified, beneath the moon.

"What was it?" Georgiou whispered. Isis looked at him.

"I have an idea. Can I ask a delicate question? What exactly is the nature of your friendship with Madam Frank?"

249

*

"A sea nymph?" Phyllida Frank said, open mouthed.

"Enchanted into wood by some spell," Isis explained. "She favoured her rescuer, the good captain here. But then all the beautiful silks that the *Aphrodite* carried went to you, Mistress Frank, and she saw it as paying court to you, and so she became jealous. The lamprey-faced thing is her real nature – I have never seen one before, but I have heard of them. The beautiful girl is the guise, the lure."

"There can't be so many around these days," Georgiou said. "I've heard of nymphs, of course, but I always thought them to be a dream."

"More like a nightmare."

"And how did you know that was what she was, if you have never seen one?"

"As we came onto the deck, I saw that it was dry," Isis told him, "but there was a small pool of water around the girl's feet. She came out at night, when no one could see her, but jealousy made her careless. You'll need to make sure that she is really gone, and I suggest consulting your own mages."

"I'll do that," Georgiou said, "Just before I sell the ship." He looked at Phyllida Frank. "I'm no longer young, Mistress Dane, and I think I'll be staying here. I've had enough of the sea."

"After all, they say she's a jealous mistress," Isis said.

# About the Author

Liz Williams is a science fiction and fantasy writer living in Glastonbury, England, where she is co-director of a witchcraft supply business. She has been published by Bantam Spectra (US) and Tor Macmillan (UK), also Night Shade Press, and appears regularly in *Asimov's* and other magazines. Her work has been shortlisted for the Philip K Dick Award on several occasions, as well as the Arthur C. Clarke and BSFA Awards. Her latest novel is *Salt on the Midnight Fire* (NewCon Press, 2023), the final volume in the Fallow Sisters quartet. She has been involved with the Milford SF Writers' Workshop for twenty years, and also teaches creative writing at a local college for Further Education.

### *Also by Liz Williams from NewCon Press:*
A Glass of Shadow (2011)
Diary of a Witchcraft Shop (2011) *with Trevor Jones*
Diary of a Witchcraft Shop 2 (2013) *with Trevor Jones*
The Light Warden (2015)
Phosphorus (2018)
*The Fallow Sisters:*
Comet Weather (2020)
Blackthorn Winter (2021)
Embertide (2022)
Salt on the Midnight Fire (2023)

# ALSO FROM NEWCON PRESS

### Polestars 3: The Glasshouse – Emma Coleman

Contemporary tales of rural horror and dark fantasies steeped in folklore from one of genre fiction's best kept secrets. A young divorcee relocates to a quaint rural hamlet but is mystified by the hostility of her neighbours…A man discovers an item in a junkshop that puts him in fear of his life… An impresario dispenses justice while performing as a magician…

### Polestars 4: Our Savage Heart – Justina Robson

The first collection in twelve years from one of the UK's most respected and inventive writers of science fiction and fantasy. A dozen short stories and novelettes, 100,000 words of high quality fiction. A collection that gathers together the author's finest stories from the past decade.

### Polestars 5: Elephants in Bloom – Cécile Cristofari

Debut collection from a French author who has been making a name for herself with regular contributions to *Interzone* and elsewhere. Providing a fresh perspective on things, Cécile's fiction reflects her love of the natural world and concern for its future. Contains her finest previously published stories and a number of brand new tales that appear for the first time.

### Polestars 6: Drive or Be Driven – Aliya Whiteley

The much anticipated new collection from a critically acclaimed author who has been shortlisted for multiple awards and is writing at the top of her powers.

"There are no misfires here; readers will think they've hit the standout story of the collection, only to turn the page and find another contender. It's a marvel." *– Publishers Weekly*

### Polestars 8: Human Resources – Fiona Moore

Fiona Moore is a Canadian-born academic, writer and critic living in London. Her work has been shortlisted for BSFA Awards and a World Fantasy Award. Her short fiction has appeared in *Clarkesworld*, *Asimov's*, *Interzone* and elsewhere, and has been selected for four consecutive editions of *Best of British SF*.

"A collection of intelligent, thoughtful, disturbing but ultimately optimistic speculative stories" *– Oghenechovwe Donald Ekpeki*